Sea Heiress

Susan Ambers

Contents

Chapter 1

I fidgeted relentlessly in the layers-upon-layers of white tulle and chiffon entrapping my body. The tight corset of the dress pressed into my ribcage and I sighed, letting myself go limp; defeated.

I really didn't want to get married.

I could hear people shuffling around through the doors separating me from the grand palace throne room, where everyone in the kingdom expected me to walk down the aisle to my imminent doom after being forced into this engagement in the first place.

I allowed a servant to finish pinning up my long locks of dark hair before the doors burst open, and I spun around.

Goridian sent me a chilling grin, his eyes trailing over me from the tip of my head to the bottom of my gargantuan, death-trap wedding dress.

"My bride," he growled, walking his enormous frame toward me. Goridian was unusually tall and muscular, veins protruding from his obnoxiously-sized biceps; poking through the fabric of his black-and-blue suit.

His dark eyes continued tracing over me. He reached forward and took one of my hands. I gulped down a shudder.

"After today, all will be well in the Kingdom," he drawled. "I'll have Triton's territory, and his little plaything. You know, I see how he whispers things into your ears. He knows you're smart...and I know it too." His voice was sickening, like the purring of a catfish. I shivered.

"Not only are you smart," he continued, walking around me in circles. "But you're alarmingly beautiful. How couldn't I marry you?"

I didn't speak, for if I did, I knew all the built up rage I had for this man would accidentally boil over, and I couldn't let that happen. I wanted to rip Goridian's face off, and unfortunately, one does not simply rip someone's face off without drawing attention to one's self. So I bit down on the tip of my tongue and avoided eye contact.

"I'll see you at the end of the aisle," he said, before turing and walking out the door.

I felt nerves crawling around in my stomach.

The doors to the throne room swung open moments later, and my sisters, one by one, each dressed in blue kelp dresses, flounced through the entrance, slowly stepping their way down the aisle...my bridesmaids.

I took the biggest breath I could, fighting the constraint of the dress, and stood at the double-doors, my insides churning.

It was time.

A grin of delight was trying not to poke its way upon my face as one solitary, comforting thought rolled around in my head like a marble:

I wasn't really getting married that day.

People stood and a communal gasp of awe escaped their lips as I sauntered forward, into the throne room. As I took the first few sluggish steps toward the dreaded altar, I couldn't help but notice that the throne room was lavishly adorned in huge blue conch shells and shimmery seaweed for the occasion; the tall glass ceiling decorated with painted metallic barnacles and iridescent fish scales.

A choir chanted, accompanied by ceremonial drums, as I took one dainty feminine step after the other.

My five sisters stood in a line in front of me, each with hands held behind their backs. I anxiously studied the clasped hands of my eldest sister, awaiting the moment she would signal and our plan would begin.

Sweat trickled down my temple as the drums' rhythm pulsed through the entire throne room. I could feel Goridian's gaze burning a hole through me as my knees grew a bit wobbly. We were getting close enough to the altar.

Finally, Cela's hands separated at her back, loosening of their clasped position. I took a deep breath, steadying my feet.

Using all the strength in my body, I hooked my hands underneath the corset of my dress and, in one swift motion, ripped the hideous thing in half. The fabric tore under my embrace, and I stepped out of it, revealing my signature outfit of leather slacks, a long sleeved tunic belted at the waist, and laced up boots.

People gaped at me from all different angles, but their stares only fueled me more. Goridian glared at me from where he stood at the altar, taking a stance of combat. I did the same. Surprisingly, as soon as I was out of that horrible wedding dress, I felt no nerves at all. My confidence overruled my hesitance, and I fastened my gaze on Goridian.

"What are you doing?" he hissed, pushing past the line of my sisters and stomping towards me. He was unarmed, and probably believed I was as well.

I felt my own sort of wicked smile beginning to form. "You really didn't think I was going to marry you that easily?" I hissed.

"Yes, and you will," he responded through gritted teeth. His dark eyes flashed silver, and I could tell this was my moment.

I felt the rope belted at my waist and gave it a tug.

The rope went taut, and in a split second, I was pulled into the air, leaving my wedding dress an empty shell below me.

My body was tugged hastily upwards, and through a small gap in the throne room's glass ceiling, I met eyes with the mastermind of this plan. His were sea blue, and could have been mistaken for those of a younger man if not for his torso-length silver beard and pale, wrinkled skin.

His name was Triton, and he was God of the Sea Kingdom. Well, now more accurately, the Overthrown God of the Sea Kingdom.

I untied the rope from my waist. He hooked an arm over mine.

"It is time, my dear Ailith."

I nodded, and in one swift motion, he leapt into the air, and we began floating up, his powerful being lifting us hundreds of feet, through the Kingdom's clouds of aquatic plants and sky of blue ocean being reflected, until we met with The Barrier.

The Barrier was the clear, spherical barrier separating the ordinary ocean from the magical Sea Kingdom where we dwelled, a small but highly important bubble in the massive sea filled with air and intended to be lived in by the God of the Sea and his people.

I reached out, stroking the smooth, spherical wall.

"You must go now," Triton spoke, his voice low and raspy so that we would not be heard. "He will lock The Barrier soon, and you won't be able to get through. None of us will."

I'd never been through The Barrier before, but had practiced breathing water. Our kind had the capability to breathe through our gills, but often, this was a forgotten skill, since our kingdom was conveniently air-filled. However, to venture out into the sea, the ability to breathe water was vital. I began to doubt if I would be able to do it

"Stop doubting yourself. I always had you picked out as the the one to escape," Triton whispered, his eyes peering over my shoulder into the vast blue. If only he could get through, but he was unable without his beloved, misplaced trident; locked in by the malevolent Goridian.

"Go," Triton told me, his tone hurried. "Go, find the Heir of Gaea, find the trident and come back to reclaim the Sea Kingdom."

I nodded. "I will."

With one last quick embrace, Triton pushed me through The Barrier, headfirst into the open sea. As I entered, I saw nothing but blue around me. A shimmer of gold ran across The Barrier, and I recognized it as Goridian locking it—no one would be able to leave. I'd escaped just in time.

With one last wave to Triton, I took my first breath, gills open, and swam upwards, towards the surface. I closed my eyes, finding the will within me, and paddling with all my might. My body began rising hundreds of feet every moment as my powerful legs propelled me upwards, small bubbles escaping my mouth like jellyfish as I continued upwards.

After a few minutes, I could see something I'd never before seen: the ocean's surface.

Just the idea of land sent a shiver down my spine. Like the Sea Kingdom, only not surrounded by a thousand feet of ocean. And bigger...much, much bigger.

I continued kicking my legs and arms, even as they tired, and felt the sugary warmth of relief finding its way into me, my body swallowed up by the miles of indigo and aquamarine.

For just a moment, I forgot everything. The forced wedding, Triton, Go ridian...

My body tilted in the water at an angle, just for long enough that I got a full glimpse of what I'd been anticipating for so long.

A huge bulb of light surrounded by a sea of periwinkle, and cottony clouds. Not the sky of kelp and reflected water within the Sea Kingdom, but the real sky; the sky of the world, of the Kingdom of the Land.

With a few last kicks of my legs, I felt my body bursting through the surface of the ocean. I took in a deep breath of cool air before I sank back into the ocean. I looked around, trying to locate where I was, but was then pulled underwater by a wave the height of a cave. I gasped, ducking underneath its force, and remembering what I'd been told; what Triton had said about the surface.

Once I was there, I was no more powerful than an ordinary human.

My stomach turned. I was gobbled up by a shimmery wave of topaz, and I remembered to swim. Swim east.

I tried to locate the compass on my sleeve, but was blinded by the sea's playing tug-of-war with my limbs. I was curled and tossed underneath the surface, gasping for breath and then being let loose, only to be pulled in again.

I felt panic rushing through me. I couldn't see anything, and I was flailing around helplessly in the water, like someone who wasn't directly from the Sea Kingdom.

Droplets of moisture began to fall from the sky, and, after a few minutes, I heard the most awful noise ever, as if Triton had received his trident and used it to send the Sea Kingdom into explosive oblivion. Light in the shape of an eel flashed across the gray sky, and the waves began to crawl higher, slamming down on me like they sought my death.

I cried out, trying to find my way back into the calm water underneath, but couldn't find the strength to get there. My flesh was humanly buoyant, and I was helpless against the terror of the white tipped waves, gnashing me in between their teeth. I let the water fill my gills and breathed evenly, keeping my muscles clenched as I was spun in imminent circles; my hair creating a tornado around me.

My eyes squeezed shut.

Triton hadn't prepared me for whatever God lurked in the clouds; whomever was trying to poison the sea with such horror.

All of a sudden, I felt something round catch around my shoulders. It felt like seaweed...but stronger. A quick tug, and I was being thrusted through the water, pulled in one specific direction, away from the waves.

I looked up in front of me, and gaped at a large wooden structure the size of the throne room, with large triangular sheets wrestling with the harsh wind. Men—human men—were pulling me with a rope toward their large sea palace...the nerve of them. They had no idea who I was, or what I had come for.

I coughed as a hand gripped the back of my tunic, pulling me onto the surface of the wooden structure. I breathed the cold air, turning over on my side and facing a man with a bushy beard wearing a raggedy black tunic.

"You all right?" he enquired, patting my face as if to make sure I was still alive.

I nodded, flinching at his touch. "Just fine, thank you. Could you take me to where the Sea and the Land merges?"

The bushy man laughed, as if I'd told him the funniest thing in the world.

"Do you mean the shore?" he asked.

I nodded. "Yes, of course. The shore."

The shore. That's what it was called. I remembered now.

The man looked down at me, his eyes skimming over my face. "I'll bet we can have that arranged."

I thanked him, and stood, asking, "Who are you?"

"We're sailors. We work for the King."

"What king?" I asked.

The entire crew of sailors turned to face me, their eyes wide like empty clam shells.

"The King," the bushy-bearded one responded, coiling the rope around his arm like a brown eel.

I sighed. "The Heir of Gaea? The son of the goddess of land?"

"How should I know? We live on these lands as servants of our Gods, not experts on them," the man responded.

I followed him as he answered my questions, simultaneously checking and tightening certain ropes.

"What is this thing, anyway?" I asked.

He laughed, again. "Me ship?"

"A ship? This is...a boat?" I asked, sniffling my nose.

He nodded. "Haven't you ever seen one before?"

I shook my head, slowly. "I come from below the water, not above."

"You're from the land of Triton, then?" he asked.

I nodded. "We don't often come onto the Kingdom of the Land. But, desperation causes unexpected consequences."

"Are you Triton's heiress, then; his daughter?" the man asked,

I shook my head. "No. I'm just...a trainee of sorts. He has educated me in combat and the powers of the sea ever since the overthrow of his kingdom by Lord Goridion."

"I heard about that; the overthrow. Heard we couldn't do anything about it," the man muttered.

I shook my head. "You couldn't without me. But now I'm here."

My sense of purpose, the one burning within me since the day I'd met Triton at age nine, seemed to glow in some part of my chest as I spoke. I always knew I was the one who had to escape, I was the one who had to leave the Kingdom in order to save it.

"Well," the man said. "Welcome to the Kingdom of the Land, sea girl."

"Thank you," I told him, pausing before placing my next request. "Now, take me to this King of yours."

Chapter 2

The ship creaked back and forth, the sea and the rain spraying the deck as the sailors moved around, pulling ropes and bringing down the large triangular sails, letting the ship conform to the powerful sea and the wind.

I shuddered when I realized that this could, perhaps, be Goridian's doing. No...it couldn't be. He was only a sorcerer, and one needed to be a God to cause such an earthly raucous.

Most wouldn't have believed that a God as strong and wise as Triton could possibly be overthrown by a sorcerer like Goridian, but it was possible. In a moment of weakness, Triton signed over his rights to Goridian thinking he had no other choice. The truth was, Triton had simply been tricked by Goridian's conniving games, and for the past nine years had paid the price for it.

"So, all you want is to be taken to the shore?" a voice called from behind me.

I turned, and realized I was facing one of the sailors, his face speckled with the spittle of the ocean and the sky. I smiled, just a bit.

"Yes, if you wouldn't mind," I responded politely.

He appeared amused, his eyes wrinkled slightly. "Did you have a specific place in mind? The shore is a bit vague of a request."

I blinked, crinkling a brow. "Doesn't that make it easier for you, then?"

He roared heartily, his broad shoulders shaking, bending back in laughter before returning to his work with ropes.

"I suppose you're right," he said, coughing down a few last chuckles.

The truth was, I actually had no idea where to go. Triton had simply said 'where the sea and the land merges', which was, I realized in this moment, quite unhelpful. I hadn't thought to enquire with fear simmering within me.

The fear of never escaping, the fear of being forced into marriage with Goridian...

I quivered at the thought.

We sailed into the bright peach morning, the sky clearing by the time the sun rose. The day's events lulled me into a few hours of asleep, and I awoke with tangled hair and the taste of salt on my lips. There was still leftover relief keeping me on a high from the previous day. However, I was guilted in remembering that my task had just begun.

Escape was only the first part, and definitely not the most taxing.

I sat at the tip of the boat as we sailed towards the land, a place I'd been dreaming of for years. Triton had only been once himself, but he often spoke about the feeling of grass rather than sand under foot, and the feeling of being free to move about for miles upon miles. It was a million times more expansive than the Sea Kingdom, and a million times more populated, as well. Gods of all kinds dwelled in the Kingdom of the Land, along with their inhuman and human subjects. Just the thought burned a hole of anticipating angst in my stomach.

As we grew closer, I devoured the sight in front of me. Real trees, and hills and the soft, lush grass I'd heard about. Humans—plan and simple, yet so beautiful—walking around, little furry things scampering about around them. My eyes were gobbling up every detail I noticed; every single observation.

"Never seen the land before?" asked the bushy-bearded sailor.

Slowly, I shook my head no.

He chuckled softly. "Ye must be quite in awe, then."

"Absolutely," I responded. "I can't believe my people dwell in the trenches of the sea when they could live somewhere like here."

A deep, pained breath escaped the sailor's lips. "I can't promise it's going to be as good as you're expecting, girl. It may look like magic, but it's really not."

I didn't believe him.

The enormous boat approached a flat dock of wood stretching from the land all the way into the sea. As we approached, another set of men came close and began anchoring the ship with ropes, tying complex knots as if they did it every day.

I thanked the soldiers for their services, and, unable to contain my excitement, found myself leaping off the ship's deck and onto the dock, sprinting until I reached the earth.

It felt soft and heavenly underfoot, the grass softer than I had imagined it; little blades of rich green. I fell to the ground, expanding my limbs and staring up at the sky, letting myself lie still as I smelled what I thought was dew around me, and a bumblebee buzzed around my face. I lay still, admiring its black and yellow stripes before it hummed away in another direction.

As I let my being go limp, I felt communal laughter escaping the mouths of some highly rude familiar sailors.

"Going somewhere, lass?" one of them howled.

I sat up, sending him a glare. "Yes, actually."

"Well hop up, then!" he exclaimed, gesturing for me to join him with the others. They seemed to be walking in a given direction. Although I was falling in love with the nature of the Kingdom of Land, I stood, deciding it would be in my best interest to follow those I knew I could trust.

We walked down a winding path on the shore. I now knew why Triton called it the place the Land and the Sea merged, because...well, that's what it was, quite literally. Waves rolled out onto the smooth sand and then pulled back, repeating the motion in an almost hypnotizing rhythm. Triton always said he'd created that rhythm for the purpose of pure wonder.

I followed the clan of sailors off the shoreline and down a trail paved by grassy yards and small huts and cottages, people wearing layers of cloth hanging up laundry or washing their toddlers in soapy basins. I watched the humans with pure curiosity, making sure not to stare for too long as I knew they would if they could ever experience my world.

I wasn't exactly human, but I wasn't a God, or even an Heiress of Triton—I was an immortal warrior, trained and christened by Triton as one of his people, but not an equal by any means.

The sailors led me into a small town of buildings and cottages, and helped me locate a group of merchants traveling to the King's palace.

"Ye should be able to make a reasonable bargain with that one," the bushy-bearded sailor instructed me, pointing to a bony, frail elderly woman with silver hair and violet-blue eyes. She was beautiful, even for an old woman, and wore a tan robe knotted at the waist with golden thread. Fake gold, I could tell.

"I haven't anything to sell," I responded, hanging my head.

"You won't need anything." His hot breath tickled my ear, and I turned.

"Thank you, sir. I'm sure once I've reclaimed my Kingdom and Triton has his throne back, I will ensure you are repaid for your kindness."

With a tip of the hat, the sailor and his men were off, and I sauntered over to the merchant woman, watching as she went through a collection of silver clocks.

"Excuse me," I murmured, approaching her cautiously.

She looked up, and a smile spread apart her lips. "Hello, young thing," she greeted me.

"I was told I might find a benefactor in you. I am in desperate need of guidance to the King's palace," I explained.

She continued grinning. "Sit atop my carriage, child."

I gasped. "Thank you, very much. I haven't anything to sell you, but I'm sure I could be of help some way. I could help you count your clocks, or"-

"No need," she responded, her voice cool and silky. "I only have one request, if you would like to travel with me."

I nodded intently. "Anything."

"You must listen, openly, to your fortune being told," she said, reaching forward and taking my pale hands in her wrinkled ones.

I bit my lip. "I suppose there's no harm in that."

Her brightly colored eyes gazed up and met mine. "Of course not. Now, we should be off quite soon. I travel in a group of merchants, if you haven't noticed, but they're all boarish men, as you can see. It should be quite nice to enjoy some female company, for a change."

I laughed. "I should say the same."

"You are so young," she remarked, snapping the reigns of her horse. The carriage was jostled into motion. I felt it rocking under me, and secured a hand on one of the sides.

"I'm only eighteen," I told her.

She inhaled in a long, gradual gasp. "Eighteen," she breathed, allowing some time before she spoke once more. "So ripe and young. Surely you must be married."

I shook my head. "I was...almost married."

"And what happened?" she asked.

Slowly, I stared at the moving road underneath me. "The man trying to force me into marriage was...not right for me. To say the least."

"Yes, I can sense the hate in you," she remarked. "This man did awful things, did he not?

I nodded. "Indeed he did."

We continued in a few moments of silence, keeping to the trail near the shoreline. We were moving parallel to the water, its calming lapping against the sand beckoning me to sleep. However, I chose to remain acute and awake, in case I needed to escape for any reason. This still was a foreign place, and I was my only ally.

"You don't come from the Kingdom of the Land, do you?" the woman asked me, leading her horse steadily down the road.

I shook my head. "I come from the Kingdom of the Sea."

"Triton's land," she inhaled. "You're so human looking, apart from that ghastly pale skin of yours."

I laughed. "We don't get much sunlight down in the depths of the ocean."

"I should say not. You're nearly iridescent," she responded. "Now, I wish to know more about this almost-marriage of yours."

Sighing, I decided it would be better to simply tell the story, and get it out of the way, rather than refusing.

I explained to her how Triton had always kept me close to train me as his warrior, ever since his trident was stolen and his kingdom overthrown by a malevolent sorcerer named Lord Goridian. I told her that, when Goridian found out Triton was training me, he decided to make me his bride in order to separate us. It was a way of insuring his security, I explained, and remove me from Triton's advice and education.

"And so you escaped the Sea Kingdom, at your own wedding?" the woman exclaimed.

I nodded. "Just in time."

"Well, I must say, I'm shocked. I knew about the Sea Kingdom being overthrown, but it was a communally accepted fact that we could do nothing to help. The Gods and Goddesses must sort their own problems out. Humans are irrelevant to them," she said, her voice low and even.

I breathed a few breaths of the tickling breeze, letting my gaze fix on the woman driving the merchant cart.

"You said you wanted to tell my fortune?"

She eyed me for a few moments, before turning and beckoning me to join her sitting at the front of the carriage. I moved forward, seated myself next to the old woman. She kept the reigns of her horse in one hand and took mine in the other, her thumb pressing into the inner part of my wrist, over my veins. Her flesh was wrinkled and paper-thin, but I was not surprised by her warm touch.

"Ah," she breathed, closing her eyes for a few moments. "Your heart beats unevenly. You...you will..."

She paused, for a few moments, keeping her eyes closed and her grip on my wrist. I awaited her words patiently, biting my lip and swinging my legs in anticipation.

"You will fall in love soon," she finished.

I laughed. "Isn't that everyone's fortune?"

Slowly, she laughed as well, and shook her head. "I only will tell you what I feel. And I felt that you would fall in love soon, and..."

Again, her eyes trailed off, and she sat for a few minutes, her grip on my arm still firm, but not frighteningly tight.

"...And beware a man in a mask," she told me.

I nodded, trying to keep the smile from trickling onto my lips.

"You do not believe me?" she asked.

I looked at her, meeting her gaze intently.

"No."

She didn't look offended, but almost as if she had expected my reaction. "Of course," she murmured.

I sat there, waiting for her to mutter something else, but realized that she wasn't going to. I, apparently, hadn't offended her enough to cause a verbal reaction.

"I'm sorry," I whispered. "I simply don't believe in fate, or fortunes."

"But you must," she replied. "You must let yourself be open to such possibilities, or you will experience negative outcomes. Open yourself up, Ailith."

I glanced at her. "Where did you learn my name?"

She shrugged. "You said you were a warrior."

My brows crinkled. "What does that have to do with anything?"

She sighed, almost as if she was disapproving my question. "You are so naive, dear girl. 'Ailith' means 'honorable warrior'. At least...it does in this world. Did Triton not christen you with this name, and tell you its meaning?"

Slowly, I nodded. "He gave me my name, but I suppose never had the time to explain it."

"Interesting," the woman muttered, before she closed her mouth and focused on the trail ahead, our conversation seeming to dissolve into the air like sea mist.

The merchant drove her carriage for several more hours, the land gradually changing from the small port town on the shore to rugged, grassy hills lined with different types of trees and rocky shores that clashed with the water, sending white spray upon us as the trail turned into a still incline.

The carriage rumbled as the horse led us up a mountain slowly and steadily. I let my head tilt back and stare at the sky as we continued, the merchant woman not uttering one word as we travelled.

~

"Ailith."

I opened my eyes, realizing I had fallen asleep on the carriage. I blinked a few times, and sat up in the carriage. We were still, and the merchant woman stood over me, her beautiful blue-purple eyes gazing into mine.

"We have arrived at the King's Court," she said.

Immediately, I stood, my damp boots squishing against the grassy hill. "Thank you for taking me here."

"Heed my previous advice, child," the woman said, clasping her hands over mine for a moment before removing them, and pointing towards an enormous structure in front of me. "The throne room should be right through there, where you may approach the King himself."

I thanked her once again, but then faced the palace and stood there, just for a few moments, gasping at its immediate beauty. It was a dark, gothic structure with large pointed towers and gray-black walls with carved out windows, both glass and stained glass. It was ten times bigger than the alabaster, glass-filled palace in the Sea Kingdom, and just the sheer size and dark color of it sent a shiver down my spine. It was both enthralling, and terrifying.

Slowly, I remembered what I had come to this beautiful land to do, and stepped closer, first taking small, dainty steps and then gliding into a brisk strut, all the way to the front of the palace. I passed dark pillars and approached a pair of metallic double doors, reaching forward and taking a deep breath as I swung them open.

Seated on a silver throne, at the other end of the room, was a man—possibly the handsomest man I'd ever laid eyes upon. He was young; probably a few years older than I; his hair was dark, his eyes piercing and gray. His jawline was noticeably defined, and he wore a silver-embroidered coat, a sword clasped in one of his hands as he sat there, facing me.

"Well, well, well," the man growled, his deep voice toying with the words, his smirk almost amused. "Look who we have here."

Chapter 3

I faced the beautiful man, wondering why is tone suggested that he'd been almost...expecting me. He seemed amused as his gaze flickered from my dark hair to my squeaky leather boots. Trying not to seem completely terrified, I stepped forward. In front of his metal throne was an enormous, stone-floored space. Tall windows lined the dark walls, and sharp metallic chandeliers hung from the ceiling.

"Are you the King of this land?" I asked the man, approaching him slowly.

He chuckled darkly. "Well, let's see. I sit upon a throne, I wear a crown, I live in a castle...what do you think?"

The tips of his mouth curled up ever so slightly, but did not reveal any of his teeth. His face was sharp and pale, but his eyes glossy and dark...warm, almost.

"So you are the King of the Kingdom of Land?" I confirmed.

The man let out a long, annoyed sigh. "Must we keep reviewing this, or are you simply teasing me?"

"Only confirming my information." I reached down to my pocket, lightly touching the dagger sheathed at my side.

"What are you here for, and...," he said, pausing as his nose turned up just slightly. "What are you? You smell of the sea."

I felt a bit offended. "I'll have you know," I began, my voice an irritated scoff, "That I have been sent my Triton himself from the Kingdom of the Sea to save our people. We have been overthrown by an evil sorcerer named Lord Goridian, and I seek the help of someone...in particular."

"Ah, and would this person be me?" the King asked.

I steadied my gaze. "That depends."

"On what?" he asked, standing and leaving his thrown. He strode towards me, his long legs propelling him forward. He was tall, and somewhat built, towering over me. I was immediately more intimidated when he stood so close.

Taking a deep breath, I let my stare level until we were locked into eye contact. He really was one of the best looking people I'd ever seen in my life.

"Who are your parents?" I asked.

The man held up a finger, the corners of his mouth flinching ever so slightly.

"I am a King, but I'll be generous, sea girl," he spoke deeply, shifting his weight from one foot to the other. "Let's think of this conversation as a sort of...quid pro quo. I will ask a question, and once you answer, you may ask me a question, and I'll do the same. But I am not here to simply provide the answers to the world's problems. I have far better things to do."

I rolled my eyes. "And you want to slow the process by asking me questions? Hardly seems valid."

"I need to know who I'm answering to. Take the deal, or leave it," he responded, his stare turning into a slight glare.

Sighing, I responded, "Fine; deal."

The man began pacing a few steps from one side of the room, pivoting on one foot, and pacing back.

"Very well. I'll go first," he said, grinning and revealing a mouth of blinding-white teeth. "What is your name?"

"Ailith," I responded.

"Ailith." He purred my name, spreading out the sounds like butter. "And what are you, Ailith? A warrior, I presume, as that is what your name means?"

How did everyone in this kingdom know what my name meant, when I hadn't known what it meant the past eighteen years of my life?

I nodded. "That was two questions. My turn. What is your name, and what is your mother's name?"

He laughed. "You're frank. I like it. My name is Soren, and, for friendly purposes, I'll let you call me that in private. Most answer to me as 'your majesty', 'your grace', 'your excellence'...it gets quite exhausting to be so highly regarded all the time. Some informality should be refreshing."

I rolled my eyes. "And your mother's name?"

"Why do you care to know?" He stopped in his pacing, standing right in front of me. His gray eyes bore into mine.

"It's very important," I responded, my quiet answer nearly a whisper.

If he responded that his mother was the Goddess Gaea, then I would know I had found her Heir; the Heir whose help I required to salvage the Sea

Kingdom. But something inside me said that that would be too easy for him to admit right away; that fate preferred to present me with a challenge rather than hand me the answer.

He inhaled quickly through his nostrils. I could tell he was contemplating whether or not to answer that question.

"I won't tell you my mother's name. Not yet," he said.

"Fine. What is your father's name?"

Clucking his tongue, he shook his head. "I'm afraid that one's off limits, too."

"Fine. Your turn."

He eyed me playfully, one of his eyebrows going crooked. "My, you are a funny little thing. Tell me, Ailith, what are you? By education, or train-ing—whatever you have in the Sea Kingdom?" He spat the words Sea Kingdom, almost in a derogatory fashion.

"I'm a warrior, by training. I was trained by Triton himself," I responded.

"And are you immortal?" he asked.

I was beginning to have a bit of fun at this. "It's my turn to ask a question."

He held up a finger. "Good catch. Go right ahead."

"How old are you?" I asked.

Slowly, he stopped in his tracks once again. He swung his arms being his back and teetered back and forth. "I'll go with...twenty-two."

"Is that a lie?"

"My turn," he responded, grinning. "Are you immortal, Ailith?"

I bowed my head. "I believe so."

"Interesting," he responded. "You're too young to know for sure. One does not know whether or not they have been blessed with the gift of immortality until their twentieth year. It shall be interesting for you to discover if the Gods cared enough about your existence to extend it indefinitely, or if they preferred you had a more...traditional expiration date."

I scoffed. "You don't know anything about me."

"Ask me a question," he commanded, ignoring my offended remark.

"Are you immortal?" I asked.

Pausing, for a moment, he considered. "Yes," he said, settling on the answer.

"So you're older than twenty-two?"

Slowly, a wry smile spread its way onto his face. "Let's just say I'm ancient, and leave it at that."

"Interesting," I murmured.

He trailed in circles around me, hands still clasped behind his back. "Are you married, Ailith? You are so young; younger than twenty. My, what I'd give to be back at that age."

I shook my head. "I remain unmarried, fortunately."

His brow rose curiously, and I wished I'd never made the comment.

"Fortunately?" his silky voice taunted. "How odd. I have an entirely new set of questions now."

"But unfortunately for you, it's my turn. How old are you?" I probed.

He clucked his tongue, again. "How rude for you to be asking someone like me such a question. I should have your head."

I gazed at him, wide-eyed. "I"-

"I kid, Ailith. Killing you would take the fun out of this," he told me. "Why did you say 'fortunately' when you told me you were unmarried?"

"That question is off limits," I responded, the words escaping my lips faster than they could register in my head.

He chuckled. "I'm allowed to make questions off-limits. You are not. Answer," he demanded, twiddling his thumbs impatiently.

I shook my head. "I refuse."

He let out a low growl. "Just tell me...something about it; anything."

I let out a long, uncomfortable breath. "I was almost forced into a marriage I really didn't want to be in. That is all I will share with you."

His expression remained unchanged, almost as if my explanation was underwhelming. I was confused how someone could find something like forced marriage underwhelming.

"It's my turn to ask a question," I reminded him after a few moments of silence. I opened my mouth to speak, but he held up a hand, signaling me to stop speaking.

Turning to me, he spoke deliberately. "I have heard enough from you, and learned what I needed to learn. If you want my help, or anything from me, then you shall stay here, at my court, for an extended amount of time. In that time, I will assess whether or not I can and want to assist you with your kingdom's overthrow issue," he stated quite diplomatically, then muttering under his breath, "I always knew Triton would get himself into something like this."

I gaped at him, highly offended. "Triton has been King of the Sea Kingdom for centuries. How could you say such a thing?"

Again, his lips curled. "You do remember that I never stated my age? How are you sure I haven't been around a long as Triton?"

I shook my head slowly, trying to comprehend all I was being told.

"You expect me to live here with you while my Kingdom suffers under the rule of a horrible sorcerer? I must do something—I must do something now. I cannot wait for your help," I told him, turning to walk out.

He spoke from behind me, his voice warning.

"But what if you need it?"

I turned again, facing him in exasperation. "You won't tell me what I need to know. I need to know"-

"From whom I descend?" he finished.

I blinked a few times, nodding. "Yes. That information is critical, Soren."

Using his name seemed to soften him a bit. His taut muscles loosened, and his neck bent forward, his face titled toward the ground.

He looked up at me. "I need time. But if you are who I think you are, then please be sure that I will not fail you."

His tone was strict and commanding, yet somehow compassionate at the same time. I did not understand him, but at the snap of fingers two female servants, both dressed in leather much nicer than mine, emerged from seemingly out of nowhere. They both approached me and took my arms in their soft, maternal hands.

"You'll be provided quarters in the palace," King Soren told me blankly. "Please do not hesitate to ask for anything you might require."

"Fine, then I will. I require some answers," I told him, my voice even, but beginning to crack. I was going to run out of time. Lord Goridian could potentially find me, and if he did, I wasn't sure what would happen.

"I cannot answer you now, but take comfort in the fact that I very well could, someday," he told me, moving his fixated gaze to the servants. "Take her away."

"Wait, I wasn't finished"-

But as I tried to fight my way out of their grasp, the two women, both in their sixties, but with strong grips, led me out of the throne room, away from potentially the only source of help I would come across in this foreign land.

After a few steps, I realized King Soren wasn't going to tell me anything if I did not cooperate. So I let the servants lead me through a door at the side of the throne room and through dark corridors, up steep stone stairwells and across dank, cold passageways. Although everything was medievally dark, it was also clean and modern with its silver, metallic touches and glassy decor.

The servants led me to one of the enormous stairwells that led to the top of a tower. I began to ascend the staircase, but, before I could take my first step, felt my body floating into midair. I gasped, feeling the shock of magic pulsing through my body as I realized the stairs were under a magic spell, probably cast by the person I was seeking...the Heir of Gaea, her son—the God of the Kingdom of the Land.

I wondered if that was King Soren, but had my doubts. He'd been strangely secretive about hiding the identity of his parents. It concerned me, and I decided not to settle. I would review all possible options of who could be Gaea's Heir, as I needed to make sure I was getting into business with the right person.

I determined that I would stay at Soren's court for a week before I determined if I would stay there indefinitely because Soren was who I thought he might be—or leave, in pursuit of Gaea's real Heir. At this point, I had no idea if Soren was who I was searching for, but it wouldn't hurt to have him as an ally, as, God or not, he was the Land's immortal King.

I felt my body dropping to the ground after I floated up all the twisty stairs, not having to touch a single one. The two servants floated behind me, right at my ankles, as I twisted the doorknob right in front of me, assuming it led to my chambers.

As I opened my door, I gasped—for two reasons. One reason was the sheer luxury that greeted me in my tower chambers, and the second was the man seated on my bed.

Chapter 4

I gasped, taking a few steps back.

"Who are you?" I exclaimed.

Seated in front of me was a man with tousled dark-auburn hair, blue eyes, and an amused grin on his face. He was handsome, yet not as good-looking as Soren, but held some uncanny resemblance I couldn't put my finger on.

"Ailith, I know who you're here for. And that person is me," he said.

I crinkled a brow. "How do you know my name?"

He laughed. "Soren told me. My brother, King Soren."

I quirked a brow. "You're Soren's brother?"

He nodded. "So I see you two are on a first-name basis. Well, I've come to tell you that my brother won't be the help to you that I will. I am the Heir of Gaea, Ailith, the God you have been looking for."

I shook my head in confusion. "What are you doing in my chambers?"

A smile crept upon his face. "I thought it would be funny to surprise you. Nothing to scare a woman like a strange, handsome stranger in her bedroom."

"I wish I could say you're wrong," I muttered in response. "Hold on...you're Gaea's heir? Wouldn't that make King Soren Gaea's heir too?"

Slowly, he shook his head. "Soren and I are only half-brothers. Gaea was my mother, not his."

Slowly, I exhaled in satisfaction. "Great. Well, thanks for clearing things up. Can we go now? Because I have to save the Sea Kingdom. I promised Triton I would do things as quickly as I could."

He clucked his tongue, similar to the way Soren did. "I wish, warrior sea girl, but we're going to have to follow my brother's orders for now. He is king, and he did order you to stay at his court for an indefinite amount of time."

I rolled my eyes. "Great. So you're going to be just as helpful as he was."

"I'm assuming that he was insurmountably helpful," the man responded sarcastically, extending an arm. "I'm Lazarus."

"Ailith...," I responded, shaking his hand as Triton told me the people of the Land might do. "But, of course, you knew that."

He smiled. "Will I see you at the ball tonight?"

I smirked. "The ball?"

"Of course," he responded. "King Soren only throws the most magnificent balls in the Land. Tonight we celebrate the Summer Solstice."

Slowly, I shook my head. "I don't think I'll be able to attend."

He rolled his eyes. "Just come. You know you want to see what humans act like."

Unfortunately, he was correct. I did want to see how humans acted, and I did want to see if I could talk to Soren, perhaps convince him to make his decision sooner rather than later. Perhaps, however, Soren wasn't the one I needed to convince. Maybe it was Lazarus.

My head spun as I thought about getting intertwined with the two of them, trying to figure out who to believe.

Soren hadn't denied being Gaea's Heir, but he hadn't directly said he was, as Lazarus had.

"I'll be there," I told Lazarus. "And...how did you know I was looking for you?"

He grinned. "Remember—Soren and I spoke briefly."

"How"-

He pointed to his temple. "We're both the offspring of Gods. We don't need to use our mouths and ears to speak."

I nodded, inhaling deeply. "Thank you for introducing yourself, even if the manner in which you did was highly unconventional, and nearly scared me back to the sea."

He spoke softly, his breath tickling my face. "Well, I'm glad I didn't frighten you that much. It'd be terribly less fun if you'd run away."

With that, Lazarus was gone, and I was alone in my chambers, my head seeming to swim with secrets.

I wondered if the man named Lazarus was telling the truth, or if he was try-ing to convince me he was Gaea's Heir so I wouldn't know that Soren—or someone else—was. Perhaps, however, it would be this easy. Perhaps Soren had just been messing with me that day, and Lazarus was the truthful one.

"Ugh," I groaned aloud, thinking about all the ways this situation was unmistakably messy.

~

The two female servants, whose names I learned were Cleo and Nela, fussed about possible colors of gowns I could wear to this Summer Solstice ball all afternoon.

I cringed, turning to them and asking, "Do I have to wear a dress? Can't I wear what I have on now?"

They both eyed my wrinkled belted tunic, leather slacks and lace-up combat boots and shook their heads furiously.

"The event is much too formal to have something like that on," the woman named Cleo told me, furrowing a brow apologetically. "We'll let you see a selection of gowns. What is your favorite color?"

"Black," I responded.

They both hung their heads, disappointed that I hadn't said something like seaweed green or parrotfish rainbow, for heaven's sakes.

Cleo and Nela came back with an assortment of heavily, floor length gowns that would drape over and weigh down my body.

"Well this won't do at all," I muttered.

"We could bring you another selection," the woman named Nela offered.

"No need," I told them, my gaze solely focused on one of the lace dresses in front of me. It was easily the lightest material of all of them, and had a nice sweetheart necklace with thin, sheer three-quarter-length sleeves. I slipped the dress on in another room by myself, and examined it in a mirror. It did look quite nice, but awfully long for Summer Solstice. If I remembered correctly, Summer was supposed to be the warmest season on the Land. I was still getting used to the idea of seasons.

I retrieved the dagger from the sheath on the side of my leather slacks—which I had folded and hidden in a special place to make sure the servants did not try and hide them away somewhere when I was gone—and bent down. The gown's material was far longer than floor length, draping around me in a three-foot circumference. I took the dagger and slowly began cutting the material right above my knee, carefully spinning the knife around myself before I'd successfully cut away almost half of the gown.

What was left was a beautiful lightweight dress, and the best part was that my beloved lace-up leather boots were visible.

I lined my eyes with eyeliner, let the servants apply some lipstick, and rouge to my unusually pale skin, and unbraided my long, dark hair. It sprung into waves like the ocean, cascading down my back to my tailbone. I smiled in the mirror.

"This is more like it," I said aloud, grinning to the servants.

"You look wonderful," Cleo cooed. "Just gorgeous."

"If not, a little unconventional," Nela added. Cleo elbowed her.

I laughed. "Does no one else wear lace-up boots here?"

"No one else cuts their dresses here," Nela responded.

Cleo hushed her. "I think the crowd shall enjoy some change, for once. Go and have a good time at the ball tonight, Miss Ailith."

I floated down the enormous spiral staircase, letting the spell carry me down the stairs midair. I had to say, I enjoyed the sensation of flying almost as much as I had the sensation of floating through the calm blue sea.

I followed some party-goers dressed in long gowns (I had been warned this was the more traditional trend) and suits of shiny armor to the throne room. In the time since I'd been there that morning, it had been transformed into a ballroom, the chandeliers lit, flowers adorning the walls and huge glass vases in each corner of the room. Arrays of steaming food lined the walls...roasted pig, hen, turnip soup and roll filled the tables. My mouth watered.

As I entered the throne room/ballroom, people began to grow silent as I walked in. I realized now that my pale skin, blue-black hair, short dress and leather boots probably were drawing attention to me. However, I brushed off the stares.

I noticed, as I walked in, that King Soren his bother Lazarus were both seated at the front of the room together, Soren on his throne and Lazarus close by.

In the blink of an eye, Lazarus had teleported himself to my side, taking my hand.

"Ailith," he greeted me, a grin spreading across his face. "I knew you'd show up dressed to impress."

"Am I really making such an impression?" I asked.

"Yes, you really are. You come from the sea, and everyone seems to know it," he responded. "I think it's quite interesting."

I felt my eyebrows twisting. "Thanks?"

"I meant it as a compliment," he admitted. "Soren has been asking to speak to you."

I felt relief rushing through me like a drug. "Thank goodness. Perhaps he's made up his mind."

All of a sudden, Lazarus let out a deep belly-laugh. "As if! Sor, you'll never believe what the sea girl just said."

He pulled me forward faster. With a quick burst of magic, we were standing right smack in front of Soren.

"Enlighten me," Soren responded, his face still intensely serious.

"She thinks you've made up your mind about her already," Lazarus laughed.

Soren's facial expression remained unchanged. "Stop teasing the girl, brother. Dear Gods and Goddesses, Ailith, what are you wearing?"

King Soren's dark eyes trailed over my body, from the tip of my head to the boots on my feet.

I shrugged. "Just thought I'd change up your traditions around here."

As he was taking a sip of his wine, Soren nearly spat it out.

"I can see," he responded, gulping the wine uncomfortably. "And...do you sea people often show your bare legs in public?"

I shrugged, nodding. "I suppose we're a bit more informal. I'm not one to usually wear dresses."

"I see," he responded, the words seeming forced on his tongue. He kept his gaze on me, but every so often glanced away, as to make sure I didn't notice. Despite his efforts, I most definitely noticed.

"So...," I said to the brothers, trying to break up the awkwardness. "Is there any way we could get this whole thing cleared up, because I'm really dying to know which one of you is the real Heir"-

"LADIES AND GENTLEMEN," a hugely loud voice boomed from a different spot in the room. "BEHOLD...YOUR REAL KING!"

"Damned Zeus," Soren growled, standing from his throne. He and his brother both pushed me behind them, facing an enormous man standing at the other side of the room.

"Zeus," I breathed, knowing exactly who this was. "King of Kings."

As I spoke, a rush of wind passed through the hall and, all of a sudden, Zeus was standing right in front of us.

"Well, it seems like I don't need a proper introduction," Zeus cackled. "Who said that?"

He looked to be in his mid-thirties, with a thick beard and an enormous frame. He was both exceptionally tall and muscular; everything I'd ever thought Zeus to be.

"How are you doing, my sons?" Zeus said to both Soren and Lazarus.

Lazarus shrugged. "Fine, dad."

Zeus laughed. "It's been...what, seven hundred years since you last called me dad? Come on!"

"This isn't the time to be crashing a ball," Soren said through gritted teeth.

"What is that thing standing behind you?" Zeus asked, ignoring his son's questions. With the flick of a hand, I was standing in front of both Soren and Lazarus.

"How cute," Zeus murmured, tugging on a lock of my hair. "What is it?"

"This is Ailith, a warrior from the Sea Kingdom," Soren introduced with a nervous scowl, his tone remaining level but warning. "She was sent here by Triton."

"Oh, yes, I know. Poseidon's incredibly dramatic and careless son. Let that stupid sorcerer overthrow him. Without that trident of his, he stands no chance. And he was cowardly enough to send up this mortal," he murmured, continuing to play with my hair.

Soren snatched me away from Zeus, sending me flying back into Lazarus's grasp.

"I will not have you picking through my ball guests for another wife, father," he seethed.

"Oh, I'm just playing, my son! I already have...," Zeus pretended to count on his fingers, as if numbering them each. "Two hundred and twenty-four. But they've been spread out over the past three million years, give or take a few."

Lazarus snarled. "You're not trying to claim her, are you?"

Zeus laughed. "No, no. I mean, I might at some point"—- he afforded me a wink—"but definitely not tonight. Aphrodite and I have this thing going right now, and I don't want to mess it up with some mortal sea girl."

"I could be immortal," I muttered.

Zeus laughed, and I felt Lazarus's grip tightened. Soren grasped my arm, too, warning me not to speak further.

"She is feisty. Well, I suppose it is time you come to terms with your fate, Soren. You do know that that is to be your future bride, do you not?" He roared with laughter as he sauntered across the crowd of shocked people, back to the entrance, where a purple tornado was beginning to form.

"Until next time, my sons!" Zeus called, waving goodbye before being swept up by his own tornado.

In just a moment's time, he was gone.

I stepped back, facing Soren and Lazarus.

"What was he talking about back there?" I exclaimed. "He said I was fated to be someone's bride. I don't know about either of you, but I haven't heard about any of that."

Soren looked at Lazarus, and Lazarus looked back. They seemed to be staring at each other for a few moments, but as their facial expressions hardened, I realized they were exchanging thoughts through the telepathy they shared. Those damned Gods.

"Take her upstairs," Soren ordered, turning to me. "We'll talk after the ball, Ailith."

"Wait, but"-

Before I could say another word, Lazarus was grabbing me around the waist and hoisting me into midair, and in the blink of an eye we were gone.

Chapter 5

After flying through the palace at lightning-speed, Lazarus plopped me down onto the sofa in a dark room, lit only by the flames of a gargantuan stone fireplace nearby. I moved toward the fire, immediately fascinated by its heat and colors. I'd never seen a fire before in my life, since, obviously, we didn't have fire in the Sea Kingdom.

I reached out to touch it, but suddenly felt Lazarus's hand grabbing mine.

"Don't touch that." His voice was low and warning.

I quirked a brow. "Why not?"

"You'll burn yourself," he responded. "Especially that paper-thin, alabaster skin you've got covering your frail sea bones."

I rolled my eyes. "I'm simply paler than you Land people, not frailer!"

"You look fairly frail to me," he teased. "What did they do back in the Sea Kingdom, starve you?"

I licked my lips, staring into the fire. "Something like that."

Lazarus's face fell from across the room, realized he'd reached a sensitive subject. "I...I didn't realize"—

"It's fine," I snapped, turning toward him, keeping my face blank. I sat down, letting the fire warm my back, resting my face on my palms. We sat in silence for a few moments, before I felt the overwhelming urge to ask him about this bride business.

Sighing, I asked, "Why did Zeus say I was destined to be Soren's wife?"

Lazarus shook his head. "I'm not going to be the one to answer that. You're going to have to let Soren explain that one. It's his fault, after all."

I groaned sarcastically. "Of course it is."

"Yes, it's so unfortunate. You were destined to fall in love with Soren, when you were so close to getting with me, the better-looking brother," he joked, a cheeky grin appearing on his face. I couldn't help but laugh under my breath.

"You don't think he'll want to...to actually marry me, right?" I asked Lazarus after a few moments of silence.

Slowly, he stood, sauntering over and nestling his large, Godly frame in front of the fire next to me.

"I don't know, Ailith. Soren can be stubborn. However, he is sensible. And he isn't malicious. He's not going to force you into marriage, if that's what you're asking," he said, following his answer with a nervous sigh.

I stood, the hair on my body standing straight up.

From the look on Lazarus's face I could tell that he barely knew more than I did. And if he did know more than he was letting on, he was doing a damn good job of hiding that, even in his facial expression.

It only took a few minutes before Lazarus was slumped over on the floor in a fetal position, fast asleep, and I decided that this would be my best chance of escape. I could find Triton's trident and seek help of another God; I didn't necessarily need Gaea's Heir. Right?

The idea of being possibly forced into a marriage again twisted my insides into knots as I opened one of the huge glass windows in that dark room.

Triton had trained me for years in combat and escape, and I knew exactly what to do.

Slipping out of the window, I was careful to close it behind me as I lowered myself onto the edge of another window, cautious not to peer down, for I could feel the great height I was at. I carefully slinked my way down the row of windows, climbing carefully down floor after floor of the castle. Luckily, the walls were made of stone, and easy to cling to, rather than being completely smooth and unclimbable.

After around a half-hour, I reached the ground, and took a deep breath of the midnight air. The moon hung low in the sky, casting a milky-blue haze over the land. I didn't know where I was going, but I assumed if I followed the trail down to the shore, I would be able to find my way back to the town in which I had arrived, and start from scratch trying to figure this all out. I knew, in my deep subconscious, that it would be too easy if Lazarus was Gaea's Heir and willing to help me. It was just too easy.

As I walked along the moonlit path, listening to the crunch of my footsteps against the rocky dirt, I couldn't help but feel a looming presence nearby. I looked behind me, and found no one there. In fact, when I stopped, I couldn't hear any additional footsteps.

I kept walking, trying to convince myself that I was being paranoid. As a means of distraction from my own crippling paranoia, I decided to speak to myself.

"I can't believe I thought I would find the Heir of Gaea that easily," I muttered under my breath, kicking my feet into the dirt. "No wonder Lazarus was quick to trick me...it had to have all been a trick! Fate wouldn't just nestle the one I need help from into my palms like that, would it?" I sighed, continuing my solo rant, "And just when I thought perhaps those two brothers could be some form of help, they turn out to be half-brother offspring of Zeus. Not that I'm surprised; everyone knows Zeus typically pops out a few babies each year thanks to his creepily ambitious life of polygamy . I'd like to know how many of us aren't Zeus's spawn. Perhaps that's what is so messed up about our world. Perhaps we're all Zeus's children, and some wacky inbreeding stuff is messing us all up."

I was stopped, dead in my tracks, as I noticed dark figure looming in front of me.

"Interesting theory," the familiar, silky-smooth voice teased. "But I have to remind you that most of Zeus's children were mortals, birthed by mortals, who have all died by now. Except for those of us lucky enough to have goddess mothers, in which case, we're still around."

My blood ran cold. "Soren?"

He stepped close to me, a small grin apparent on his face, even in the dark of night.

"I can't believe my idiot brother fell asleep," he remarked. "You know, I've been out looking for you for hours."

Biting my lip, I responded, "I..."-

"You don't have to explain your escape," he told me. "Look, Ailith, I want to help you. But we need to speak to one another first, and we need to do so safely, inside the palace. You need to be protected."

I snorted. "Why are you so concerned about my protection?"

He inhaled slowly, glancing up at the sky in irritation. "Why? You have to enquire why I consider your safety a priority?"

I shrugged my shoulders. "Yes."

Shaking his head, Soren wrapped an arm around my waist. "Well, I suppose you're just going to have to figure that one out yourself, sea girl."

With that, we were midair, floating in the opposite direction. I let out a gasp as we flew through the air, along the shoreline, all the way back to the palace.

We were back inside the dark room, through the window out of which I had escaped, before I could think about what to do. Soren had grabbed me back before I could make up my mind about whether or not I wanted to continue with my escape, or surrender. I realized, now, that my choice had been made.

As we entered the room, we both noticed Lazarus slumped over on the floor, snoring next to the flickering fire. I covered my mouth to hide a laugh.

With a quick kick to the shin by Soren, the man was awoken, muttering a bit as he stood.

"Wake up," Soren ordered, and, with a look of irritation pinned on his face, Lazarus stood, wiping the drowsiness from his eyes.

Soren took me by the arm and guided me to the sofa, where we both sat down and he contemplated silently for a few moments, his words coming together in a calm, calculated fashion.

"Ailith, I have to admit that, when we first met, I wasn't being completely honest with you," he told me. "I knew exactly who you were, and who you were destined to be." He inhaled slowly, creating an awkward pause.

"Your father said we were destined to marry?" I exclaimed.

He nodded, slowly. "Yes. Unfortunately, there is a prophecy a couple hundred years old (that I take full responsibility for) that states that this specific year, I am going to fall in love with Triton's mortal Heiress. The Heiress of the Sea."

His eyes stared into mine with pure concentration. However, I couldn't help myself from letting out a snort.

"That's hilarious," I told him. "Thank the Gods and Goddesses, this isn't my destiny."

"What are you"-

"I'm no Sea Heiress," I explained. "I'm just one of Triton's warriors. I was sent here to salvage my overthrown kingdom, not become queen of this one."

Soren's eyes trailed over me for a thoughtful second, before he suggested, "What if you were sent to do both?"

I shook my head. "I'm not the Heiress of Triton. The Heiress of the Sea would have to be his daughter, and I remember both of my parents, before they died. Triton is just a close ally, not my father."

Soren breathed through his teeth. "Then explain to me how you have come along, bare legs, pale skin and all, exactly when the prophecy says the Heiress of the Sea would show up to become my bride?"

I half-laughed, half-scoffed. "I'm sorry to burst your bubble, King Soren, but I was never sent here to marry anyone. In fact, I was escaping my wedding when I came to the Land Kingdom. The wedding I was narrowly almost forced into. Triton sent me as a warrior to help save his Kingdom. There were no additional motivations for my escape."

Soren sighed. "The prophecy says that I would meet you this month. It says we will marry by the time the first snow of winter falls."

"And if we don't?" I asked.

He shrugged. "We can never know until it's too late. There could be a horrible natural disaster. A war could break out. Or nothing could happen. You never know the stakes with prophecies, which makes them all the more dangerous and tricky."

"So, essentially, you're telling me that you think we should get married because the world could possibly fall apart if we don't, but maybe not—and we're not even positive I'm this sea girl you're supposed to be marrying?"

He blinked. "I suppose that's one way to put it."

Shaking my head, I said the words bluntly. "I'm not going to marry you, Soren."

He threw his arms to his sides in exasperation. "Why not?"

"Because, one: we've known each other barely two days, two: we don't love each other, and three: I was almost just forced into a marriage, and I don't intend on running out of another wedding I'm not keen on having."

Lazarus speaks lowly from a corner of the room. "It's interesting how the sea mortal reasons in lists."

"Yes, I should try it sometimes, it's quite convincing," Soren responded nonchalantly, before realizing that Lazarus was still in the room. "Get out, you fool." With the wave of a hand, Lazarus was sent sprawling through the door, which was then slammed and locked after him.

"Harsh," I muttered.

"We need privacy," Soren growled.

I rolled my eyes. "Why?"

"Ailith, if my father says you're the mortal Heiress I'm destined to marry, then mark my words—he isn't wrong."

"Why are you destined to marry a mortal Sea Heiress?" I asked.

Soren walked across the room, locking each of the windows as he trailed across the wall, his stride confident but slow.

"Seven-hundred years ago, I got into a fight with Zeus, my father, and Poseidon—Triton's father...God of the Sea," he began explaining.

"What kind of a fight?" I enquired impatiently.

"The kind of fight that causes the world to explode, that's what kind," he growls in response. "They were fighting over a mortal woman they each loved, and wanted to marry, and I had the stupid audacity, as a young God, to trick the woman into falling in love with me instead. I joked that a God could never love a mortal woman the way he could love a fellow Goddess, thinking I would be teaching the two men a sort of lesson. My father, Zeus, was quick to forgive me for stealing the mortal, but Poseidon was beside himself with rage as he mourned her straying from him. He cursed me, creating a prophecy that stated that I would fall for one of his own mortal descendants (basically as a means by which to get revenge) seven hundred years in the future, so I would have all the time in the world to dwell on my future doom. Now, the time has come, and I accept my fate."

I laugh. "You what?"

"I accept my fate. Now, please say you'll marry me," he said, rolling his eyes.

I shook my head. "No way."

His face suddenly turned sour, and he stood. "Fine. But remember, you need my help, and you need my brother's."

"Are you saying you're not going to help me if I don't marry you?" I exclaimed.

Silently, he shook his head. "I'm not saying that. It's not so black-and-white. I'm simply telling you that, if you were to accept our fate and get this over with, I'd be much more inclined to help you with your overthrown kingdom."

"So you want to marry me, just in case something terrible will happen if you don't?" I confirmed.

Slowly, he nodded. "I have to accept what Poseidon wrote into the book of fate."

I grimaced. "There's a book? For fate?"

"Yes. Only certain Gods can get a handle on it, but mostly it resides with Poseidon, since he likes to collect things, even though it technically belongs to my father. However, Zeus is a cunning man. He never really forgave me for stealing away that mortal woman either, so he didn't care to reverse the prophecy, even though he could technically steal the book back and do so."

"Why don't you try and steal the stupid book, and rewrite your fate?" I asked.

Slowly, he hung his head. "I can't. Because Poseidon burned it five hundred years ago, to make sure I couldn't ever steal it and do just that."

Slowly, I took a deep breath. "So there's really no way out of this? Our only options are risking the safety of the entire world, or getting married?"

He shook his head. "I'm not asking you to decide right now. I mean, that would be helpful and efficient, but I understand your hesitance. I simply encourage you to consider it...seriously. And to realize the benefits that would come your way from such a union."

"How romantic," I responded, my tone soaked in facetiousness.

A hint of a smile flickered on Soren's face as he reached forward to brush a hand against my pale cheekbone. "I'll see you tomorrow, sea girl."

And as fast as I could open my mouth to respond with an equally witty nickname, he was gone.

Chapter 6

Cold, white fingers ran down the length of my arms as I heard a snicker escaping the man pressing my body to his.

I tried to scream, but I felt my shriek catching in my throat like bile, and my body flinching as he reached for my neck, bringing my lips to his as he snickered.

When he kissed me, I was able to glimpse his icy eyes, eyeing me like prey. He grinned, before he spoke against my mouth.

"Your move, Ailith," Goridian growled.

I awoke in a sea of sweat, tears running down my cheeks as I gasped for air, trying to stop myself from shaking. I felt my stomach slowly stop its churning and my arms stop shuddering every time I breathed.

Standing, I made my way over to the window in my chambers and rubbed my eyes, looking over the sliver of sun just beginning to peak over the sea. I noticed the water dancing and roaring; creating waves that climbed up tall and then crashed down relentlessly. Goridian was angry, and he wasn't going down without a fight.

He knew Triton had always planned for me to escape the Sea Kingdom, and he'd thought he would be able to control me by marrying me. He was just a few minutes too late. If he had married me, I wouldn't have ever gotten out of his sight, and the Sea Kingdom's fate would have been sealed.

I realized, that night, that I might have removed myself from Goridian's realm, but I couldn't manage to remove him from my nightmares.

I couldn't fall back asleep, so instead I dressed myself, pulling on my stowed away leather slacks and boots, and apologetically sliced one of the simpler gowns Cleo and Nela had left in my closet. I cut it right below the hips, creating a more comfortable tunic that I tied around the waist with some silver string. I looked at myself in the mirror, and smiled.

I didn't look particularly pretty. I was horridly pale, dark-haired and smaller than a typical-sized human. My gills hid discreetly behind my ears, the lines only noticeably appearing when I got close to water, as if in preparation. I snickered, realizing that I could probably pass for a human, if Soren and the rest of his court didn't already know my true origin.

I left my chambers, quietly letting my body float down the stone-lined spiral staircase, all the way into the deserted corridors of the palace.

I knew nobody was probably awake at this time of day, so I wandered through the stony castle, admiring all of the glass decor and the broad, gold-framed windows facing the sea that lay just a half-mile in front of the palace.

As I awoke to the sunrise that morning, something I hadn't really seen before in my life, I remembered Triton's words in my head.

"Go, find the Heir of Gaea, find the trident and come back to reclaim the Sea Kingdom."

It appeared I had successfully accomplished the first part. However, Lazarus didn't really seem like the type to fight the battle against Goridian that I knew would be monstrous.

"I heard my name being thought?"

I turned around, and was immediately shocked to realize Lazarus was standing right behind me, a fresh morning smirk plastered onto his face.

I nodded. "I was just thinking about...you know."

Laughing, he responded, "I don't know, actually. All I heard was my name being thought a few times, and after that nightmare of yours, I don't think I want to know how I'm related to...that."

I shuddered. "You were able to see my nightmare? You can read minds?"

This time, he bent back and pretended to roar in laughter.

"Ailith, you're really hilarious. Read minds. As if. I can sense thoughts, in pieces. I don't know exactly what you're thinking, but I can feel how you're feeling."

"And you can do this with...everyone?" I asked.

He nodded. "Pretty much."

I sighed. "I was thinking about something that has to do with reclaiming my kingdom. I've found you, Gaea's Heir, but I have something else I need to locate as well."

"Which is?"

"Triton's lost trident," I told him. "Goridian stole it, and hid it somewhere on the land, and Triton told me I will need it in order to defeat Goridian."

"Goridian is the evil dude who overthrew Triton, right?"

I nodded silently, avoiding eye contact and staring at the floor.

"And...he is the man from your dream?"

I quickly looked up at Lazarus. "Y-you said you could only sense things. Not see them."

He shrugged, sending me a grin. "I can see a few things, too."

I felt my face burning like fire. "I...yes. Goridian was the man in my dream. But you can't tell anyone. And don't talk about it. Ever."

"Fine. I won't," he responded, clasping his hands in front of him and remaining silent for several moments, before turning to me.

"I just want you to know that what happened to you was horrible"-

I swung my head around. "What part of 'don't ever talk about it ever' don't you get?"

Again, he went quiet, before letting the pause dissolve and speaking once more.

"Triton's trident is lost forever, Ailith."

I glared at him. "How would you know?"

"When Goridian stole Triton's trident, he sent it to the shore, and Hades took it."

I rolled my eyes, groaning. "Not Hades!"

He nodded. "So, you see what I mean?"

Taking a deep breath, I told him, "I do. You're saying that I'm going to have to go to the underworld in order to get that trident."

"No, I didn't mean"-

I sneered. "I can take Hades."

Lazarus raised a brow. "Have you met him before?"

"No, have you?"

He nodded, his voice cautious and low. "Yes. Once. Three hundred years ago."

"Damn," I responded, poking him in the bicep. He grunted, folding his arms in front of his chest.

"How do I get in touch with Hades?" I asked him.

Lazarus looked at me, his blue eyes bulging a bit. "You can't."

"There has to be some way."

He snickered, shaking his head. "None that I can tell you. Sor would murder me in the snap of his fingers."

"Why does Soren care?" I asked, rolling my eyes.

This was Lazarus's turn to poke me. "He's trying to marry you. Remember, sea girl?"

I titled my head back and groaned. "I'm trying to steal back my kingdom. Remember, cherry-head?"

He snorted. "Cherry-head? Really? That's clever."

"Lollipop. Your-Almost-Majesty. Strawberry tart."

He clasped a hand to his heart and feigned offense, dropping his mouth open and gasping dramatically. "How shall I ever forgive you? Insulting my hair color and the fact that Sor beat me out for the throne of the Land? Unforgivable."

I glared. "Go away."

"I would, but that would be too easy."

"Not for me. That would be nice for me."

Lazarus clapped a hand on my shoulder. "No-can-do seaweed. I was told I'm supposed to make sure you don't try to escape again. Or, assumably, try to dig your way down to the underworld."

I grouched. "I can't take another minute of this."

With that, I was walking briskly down the hallway, hearing Lazarus calling behind me, his list of nicknames ever-growing.

"Come on, it's four in the morning, kelp-hair. Don't you Sea people ever sleep?"

I didn't respond.

"Where are you going, seashells?"

"Hell," I replied.

"Cool," he responded, following me to the first floor of the palace, where I found an open window and crawled through it, hoisting myself onto the ground. Lazarus followed me, grunting as he lifted his considerably larger frame through the window.

"You could have just used the entrance"-

"Let's march, pumpkin-head," I told him, walking briskly in the direction of the seaside. I felt my legs dropping downhill, away from the palace, towards the water. I could hear the lapping of the waves against the sand, considerably rougher than when I had arrived.

So I was being missed, was I?

I approached the shore, my boots crunching against the rocky sand. I felt Lazarus's looming presence as I stepped forward, gently reaching forward and touching the water. I knelt at the shore, holding out my palms. I let them fill with seawater, and then tilted my head, drinking the contest of my palms and doing so again.

"Do you really drink that stuff, scale-tail?" Lazarus enquired. I turned, and saw him quirking a disgusted brow.

I nodded. "I can't drink that freshwater you Land folk drink. It burns my throat."

"I could say the same about your ocean water. Have you ever been concerned about your sodium intake?" he joked.

Just as Lazarus was talking, I felt the water drip from my hands and recede back on the shore, the water forming a mountain-high tower in front of me, curling just over my head. I was standing a few feet away as the wall of water seemed to grow. I kept stepping back, and felt Lazarus's inattentiveness had caused him to wander off again.

Cursing that fickle redhead, I watched as the wander began to glow ever so slightly, and then turned painfully bright.

And all of a sudden, I could see a familiar face through the barrier of water, grinning at me.

"Goridian?" I gasped.

He spoke through the water, his gills appearing and reappearing, the slits on his throat filtering the water.

I knew he wasn't able to physically leave the water, but he could always try to drag me in.

"Come on, my little Ailith. Do really didn't think I wouldn't be able to sense your presence near the water, when it came time for you to rehydrate? You cannot survive without seawater, and I've just been waiting for you to come and take a sip."

His eyes were wide and devilish; flickering icy blue-green.

"I'm not coming back to the Sea Kingdom, Goridian," I growled, taking a few steps back.

"Oh, but you are," he responded. He thrust an arm forward, and the water surrounding it did as well.

I shook my head. "You can't just..."

"Can't just what? Invade your every dream?" He cocked his head tauntingly.

"How did you know about that?" I breathed.

He shrugged. "I may have had some play in making sure you remembered me last night."

I felt my throat tightening. "I...no. I hate you."

"How unfortunate," he responded, clucking his tongue. "Well, time for you to return. We'll go right back to the palace, get married, and forget this whole thing ever happened."

I sunk my feet into the sand, ready to run. "No." I realized that, at this point, it was useless. I wouldn't outrun the water. I was surrounded by a ginormous wall of it; it could crash down upon me the moment I decided to run.

Come on. Think. What could I do?

"I won't ask again nicely, Ailith," Goridian said, his gaze dead serious. "You will come back to the Sea Kingdom with me now, or I will be forced to take you against your will."

I pretended like I was contemplating, before saying, "Fine," as convincingly as I could. His stance seemed to loosen, almost as if he was relieved, before I added, "Just right after I say goodbye to my friend."

With that, I turned and took of sprinting.

I felt the wave of water growing behind me as I sprinted, Goridian's body lifting to the height of at least two of the palace's floors. I gulped.

Well, now what?

"You're really not as intelligent as I thought you were, Ailith," Goridian teased from behind as I continued to run, realizing it was pointless. Finally, I stopped, panting and realizing I was done.

This was it. Goridian had me trapped, and Lazarus was somehow nowhere to be found. Where was that stupid pumpkin-head?

"If you ever want to see your friend again, you'll come with me," Goridian teased. All of a sudden, I saw he held a limp, unconscious body in one of his arms.

My breath caught in my throat. It was Lazarus.

"How did you"—

"You underestimate me, wife," he growled.

I felt my rage building. For trying to marry me, for taking Lazarus, for tricking me...for everything.

I clenched my fists, a feeling I'd never felt before in my lifetime building up in my palms. "I. Am. NOT. Your. Wife!" I yelled.

Before I could react, my arms sprung forward, and Goridian went sprawling back. The wall of water seem to lower a bit, too. I pulled at Lazarus's limp body, and found that, the more I beckoned, the more his limp body moved through the water. Before Goridian could grab him, Lazarus was pulled out of the water-wall. He sprawled onto the sand and immediately began coughing, his breaths heaving as he coughed up seawater.

I would have helped him, but I knew I needed to concentrate. I'd never before known I had this skill.

"Go away," I growled, before thrusting my arms forward, this time, ten times harder than I had before.

I sent the water wall receding all the way back to its original state, and Goridian's body flying backwards, until I couldn't see him anymore.

In just those few moments, the ocean went back to looking the way it had just minutes before. I was shocked at my new ability, but more concerned about my friend.

"Lazarus!" I gasped, running over to the man. He was still coughing as he shivered, soaked in the chilly water.

"Thank you, Ailith," he breathed. "For saving me."

"Come on," I said, wrapping my arm around his, and helping him to his feet. "Let's get off the seashore."

"Agreed."

We turned, and began making our way back in the direction of the palace, but were both stopped by a familiar face. Handsome, but highly intense.

His voice was warning and low.

"Lazarus, get inside, you fool," King Soren ordered. "And Ailith, you come with me."

AUTHOR'S NOTE:

Hi, everyone! I've been absolutely blown away with all the kindness and support from all of you. This story is very important for me and I'm really excited it to share it with you. Please comment your thoughts, and don't forget to vote if you enjoyed it!

Again, thank you all so much for your growing support and adorable comments and feedback!

Xoxo,

L.K.

PS: Feel free to ask me questions! They can be about my story, or author/writer/reader questions...anything you want. Speaking of questions, here are a few I have for you:

-Do you trust Soren?

-Do you like Lazarus or Soren better?

-What do you think of Ailith so far?

<h1 style="text-align:right">Chapter 7</h1>

"Don't blame Lazarus; I was the one who decided to go to the shore," I exclaimed as Soren led me through a wing of the palace I had never before been his, his arm stiffly looped around mine.

"You almost died," he snarled.

I sighed in exasperation. "I almost died getting to the Land in the first place. So what?"

"Ailith, I'm warning you not to intensify my anger."

"Anger towards who?" I gasped.

"Lazarus."

"But I told you, it wasn't his fault!"

He gripped my arm tighter. "You could have been easily killed back there. Luckily, you must have some form of inherited strength you had yet to discover that happened to become of use when you most needed it," he responded, seeming a bit annoyed at the spontaneity of my new skill. "If you hadn't been able to do any of that, Lazarus would certainly be dead, the Sea Kingdom would be doomed, you would be forced back into marriage, and the prophecy of our marriage would never be fulfilled, meaning corruption of the entire world."

He stopped in his tracks, breathing heavily as he stared at me for a few moments, his dark eyes looming upon my face.

"Why are you so worried about me?" I whispered.

He inhaled slowly. "Why do you think? Because you're my fiancee, Ailith."

"No, I'm not. I said I'd consider your outrageous proposal. Mostly out of politeness," I grumbled.

He glared. "Well that's comforting to hear."

"I'm sorry, but nobody proposes to another person when they've only known them for a day." I folded my arms in front of my chest.

"They do if they've been destined to wed for seven hundred years," he responded, stepping closer.

"Can we please put this behind us?" I asked.

He nodded, slowly. "Under two conditions. The first: you must promise not to go back to the shore. Ever. I can get you seawater to drink, or I can send a servant. No one else is to go, not Lazarus...and especially not you," he said, pausing. "And the second is that you really consider the proposal. Consider that you could be saving our whole world immeasurable pain by marrying me. I promise, I will make a good husband."

I snorted. "You think I'm going to take you at your word at this point?"

"Take me at my word, and I will take you at yours," he said. "Promise you will seriously consider the proposal."

I rolled my eyes. "Um...no."

"Well, I'm glad to see you really thought it through," he muttered, before turning and walking away.

As he was halfway down the hall, I could hear his shoes screeching to a halt before he turned around and faced me again.

"Oh, and Ailith?" he yelled.

I glared. "Yes?"

"Don't expect any help after this, for your kingdom. From me, or Lazarus."

With that, he slammed the door at the end of the hallway, and I sighed.

"What a drama king," I mumbled, before strolling off to the opposite side of the hallway, leaving this strange wing of the palace.

Soren was so irritating, which made my blood simmer a bit. However, I was even more upset when I realized he was right. I did need to consider the possible consequences of not fulfilling the prophecy.

Okay, but he could have gone about the whole proposing thing a little more smoothly, and not the day after I arrived at his court.

So it was decided. I was indefinitely mad at him.

~

Cleo and Nela looked overly excited as I entered my chambers that morning, exhausted after the run-in with Goridian and angered by my conversation with Soren.

"What are you going to wear tonight?" Cleo asked me as I plopped, face-down, only to my freshly made bed.

I shook my head. "I'm not going anywhere tonight."

"Oh, but His Majesty told us to prepare you for a special dinner for some of the Gods' and Goddesses' other heirs," Nela said.

I groaned. "Dinner my ass."

"A young woman shouldn't speak like that," she muttered.

"So, I have to restrain myself now, but once I start getting all old and wrinkly I can swear as much as I want?" I responded sarcastically.

Cleo was the one that spoke this time.

"We'll leave you with a selection of gowns to choose from, Ms. Ailith. And you should know that we've had to confiscate your dagger. His Majesty told us that it is not appropriate for you to be cutting up your gowns and showing your bare legs at formal gatherings."

I let out a low, highly annoyed moan. "Are you kidding me right now?" I exclaimed, rolling over on my bed. "This is not hosting me, this is controlling me."

"Well, you are meant to be the next Queen of the Land," Nela said.

I could hear Cleo muttering chastising comments.

Quickly, I sat up on the bed. "You know about that?"

Nela nodded. "Everyone here knows, Ms. Ailith."

I flopped back down on the bed. "That's it. I'm dead. My life is over. Time to go back to the Sea."

"You can't go back, miss"- Nela began.

"I know I can't!" I snapped.

As I lay there, I listened to the noises of Cleo and Nela shuffling out of the room, Cleo quietly hissing at her counterpart.

I groaned, standing in the deserted space. I slowly paced around in circles, considering my few options. I could try to escape again, but I found there wasn't really a point in that. If I needed Lazarus's help (which I did), then I would have to compromise my own comfort to get Soren to agree, once I wasn't seething at the idea of speaking to him.

I could try to skip the dinner, but I knew that would probably make things worse between Soren and I. And, although I found pleasure in pushing his buttons, I knew my kingdom had to come first. So, I decided I would go—no matter how much I didn't want to.

The array of gowns set out for me was an ocean of colors—pink, blue, green...even a nauseating pink. I went through every single dress, and not a single one wasn't either heavy or brightly colored. I quickly eliminated all with color, which left me with silver. It still counted as a color in my book, but I really had no other choice.

The dress had simple, wrist-length sleeves, knotted at the waist with some silver string, and cascaded into a long, narrow skirt that flickered iridescent silver and reached my ankles. I was dissatisfied by the weight of the skirt, so I reached down and tore the dress so that it hit my mid-calve. At least now I could walk without tripping.

I kept my boots on, even though there were a pair of black heeled shoes left in my closet. I couldn't fathom wearing a pair of shoes so unbalanced.

An hour later, I heard a knocking at my door.

"Who is it?" I called, cringing at the idea that it could possibly be Soren.

"It is I, pumpkin-head. Your royal escort."

I let out a long exhale of relief, and swung open the door.

Lazarus was dressed in a dark charcoal suit and a dark red tie that complimented his auburn head.

"Wow," he said, his gaze trickling over me.

"You clean up nicely yourself," I remarked, letting him in the room.

Lazarus pointed to my boots. "You're wearing those to the dinner?"

I nodded. "Do you have a problem with that?"

He snickered. "I don't, but Sor might."

"Well you can tell him to shove his problem right up"-

He held up a hand, silencing me. "Okay. I get it. You're not gonna budge on the shoes. Okay." His tone was surprised, as if he was expecting his comments would get me to put on those pointy death traps.

"Shall we leave?" I suggested.

He nodded, biting his lip. "Let's."

Lazarus and I floated down the stone stairs, and then he led me across corridors, through different passageways...all practically unrecognizable due to their similarity in decor and structure: stony and dark, with glossy glass touches.

"Here we are, seaweed."

Lazarus opened a heavy door, letting me inside. When I got in, I saw an enormous dining table, dark and wooden, piled high with game hen and boiled potatoes and carrots. I felt my stomach grumbling.

The room had golden walls adorned with blue and purple flowers I recognized had been brought in from the fields surrounding the palace. Huge crystal chandeliers the size of small cottages hung from the ceiling, which was painted with ancient depictions of how the Gods and Goddesses had created our world. Zeus and Hades were painted at opposing sides of the room, facing one another in battle.

I gaped at the dining room, in all of its glory.

As my eyes trickled down from the ceiling, my stomach turned when I noticed Soren seated at the far side of the table, tightly clutching a wine goblet, his gaze fixated on me. I couldn't tell if he was confused or angry, but his intense stare seemed to include some combination of both.

Lazarus bent down, and whispered in my ear. "He's not angry at you. He's just always like that. But be careful, because he was angry a few hours ago."

I nodded, wondering how he'd known I was questioning Soren's expression when I remembered that Lazarus could practically read my mind.

I glared at him. "Stop reading my thoughts, strawberry."

He shrugged. "Sorry, kelp girl, no-can-do."

I groaned. "You really are a piece of work."

He chuckled from behind me. "I could become a bigger piece of work, you know."

"ENOUGH."

We both peered across the table. Soren's eyebrows were intertwined, and a scowl played at his lips.

"You both are acting like monkeys," he remarked, slamming his wine goblet onto the table.

"Well, I don't understand why I had to be here tonight," I mumbled.

Soren stood, and began walking across the dining hall. I noticed he was dressed in a long black long-sleeve tunic embroidered in silver and gold thread, along with black slacks and tall leather boots. The metal crown he only wore in formal events sat effortlessly on his tousled dark hair. I didn't like admitting it, but Soren was attractive.

Dammit. Stop, Ailith.

"You have to be here," Soren said, his low voice warning. "Because all the other Heirs and Heiresses think that we're engaged."

As if on impulse, I reached forward and struck him right across the face. I didn't mean to do it, but I had to admit, it felt good.

Immediately, I felt his hands gripping my forearms. He pulled me forward, his dark grey eyes boring into mine.

"You underestimate me," he growled, before pushing me to the floor. I felt my feet slipping out underneath me, and I toppled over.

Soren hovered above me, breathing heavily. "I am the son of Zeus and Hera. I am thousands of years old, and have capabilities you couldn't even fathom. You are a mortal. If you think hitting me is going to make any sort of impact, then you are highly mistaken. You're just a sea girl, and I am a God—you should be honored I want to marry you."

I glared at him. "If you think boasting about yourself is going to put me in my place, then you're a fool. And also, if you hurt me, Goridian will have war."

"Whose side are you on?" he breathed.

"My own," I responded, before jutting out my leg, kneeing him in the stomach and slipping out from underneath his embrace.

"My, you are a little warrior," he grumbled, a taunting grin tickling his mouth.

I noticed, as Soren stood and got into a stance of combat, that elegantly dressed people, all bearing crowns of some sort, were beginning to trickle into the space, watching this exchange happen.

"Brother, I urge you to put an end to this," Lazarus warned.

Soren shook his head, grinning just slightly. "No, Lazarus. This is only just beginning."

With that, he sprinted toward me in an attempt to push me over, but I simply leapt into the air, letting him slide to the other side of the room. We now faced each other again. We both ran towards one another, and this time, nearly collided.

He began throwing punches, which I expertly dodged. He then grabbed onto my waist, pulling me against his chest.

"Ready to give up, sea warrior?" he taunted, quirking a brow.

I shook my head. "Like you said, we're just getting started."

With that, I felt him flipping me onto the ground. I scrambled to get up, and swiftly somersaulted between his legs as he reached forward, about to grab me.

We faced each other once more.

In this pause, I felt a hundred gazes fixated on me.

Soren felt it too, and, as he turned to face those people, I stepped forward and tackled him in his moment of distraction. I pinned him down with my arms and legs, and, all of a sudden, his muscles seemed to lose their tenseness.

"So you do know how to fight," he murmured, the grin still toying at his face. "Just not as well as I do."

With that, he flipped, sending me sprawling onto my back. He grinned, his breath husky and deep, as he held me there.

"I've had a few thousand more years to practice, so we'll call this one even. Fair, sea girl?" he growled.

With that, he removed himself, standing up and adjusting his crown.

"No," I whispered, the words too quiet for anyone else to here, but enough for me to contain myself for those few moments. "Not fair."

AUTHOR'S NOTE:

Hey, everyone! Thank you so much for checking out my story. If you enjoyed it, please don't forget to vote and comment (if you'd like). :)

Again, thanks for being here. I appreciate every read, and I love it when you guys comment!

UPDATE ANNOUNCEMENT ---> If you didn't see my announcement earlier, I have decided to make my official update days every Monday and sometimes one more day of the week, either Friday or Saturday.

Xoxo,

LK

Chapter 8

The dinner party went on as if nothing had happened.

I was both perplexed and angry about that—I wondered, did any of these people care that Soren and I (who, as far as they knew, were engaged) had just fought one another in front of all of them?

I sat between Soren and Lazarus at the party, carefully toying with the food on my plate and avoiding the glass of horrible freshwater in front of me. Instead, I opted for some of the wine, gulping it down quicker than it could burn my throat.

Hundreds of people were seated at the enormous mahogany dining table, talking amongst themselves. They all seemed to be in their twenties, even though I knew they were all easily a thousand years old. Soren had said he was thousands of years old. I couldn't even imagine living for that long.

"Hey, kelp hair," Lazarus whispered in my ear. "I think you should put down the wine goblet."

"And I think you should reconsider your hair color," I mumbled into my glass. "It looks stupid."

However, after one final sip, I did as he told and put the goblet down. He did seem tense that night...probably because of the fight. It was quite strange seeing Lazarus anything but easygoing, as he normally was.

As I went over the possibilities for the cause of Lazarus's tenseness in my head, Soren stood, goblet in hand, and looked out over the dining table, at all of the other children of the Gods. Everyone seemed to grow quiet as he did, putting down their silverware and looking back at him.

A nerve rolled around in my stomach like a tumbleweed as I remembered that, technically, he was all of their King. He didn't seem so powerful until he was so up-close.

"Hello, everyone," he addressed them cordially. "It is my great pleasure to welcome you here this evening. I hope you are enjoying the feast and conversation, but I am afraid I must remind you why we all have gathered here. There are many issues we must discuss to keep our kingdom safe, and the problems aren't going to fix themselves. So, I declare that this conversation must commence."

People began murmuring amongst themselves, the whispers creating a buzz throughout the room. I watched everyone, and waited for something to happen. I had no idea how this worked.

I peered over at Lazarus, and he whispered, "You're not required to participate, although I doubt you'll be able to resist."

I quirked a brow. What did that mean?

"We're going to be discussing the issues of our world," he told me, before turning to the crowd.

The first to speak was the Heir of Persephone. His hair was curly and blonde, mimicking Persephone's famous golden locks, and he had big, beautiful green eyes.

"The underworld is a growing threat," he spoke to the crowd. "Hades, God of the underworld, is trying to keep my mother, Persephone, in his territory longer than he ever has before. He is growing in power, and eventually will want to keep her with him full-time."

"But Hades and Demeter agreed to share Persephone," Soren responded. "He cannot keep her longer than they agreed, or he will suffer the consequences."

"Not if he's ready to fight whomever is supposed to deliver those consequences," the man said, his tone becoming impatient.

Soren held up a hand. "Enough. I will deal with Hades when and if he formally breaks the treaty."

Everyone on Earth had heard the stories of Hades and his wicked, conniving ways. However, I never really had believed him to be a true threat; more of a trickster from underground.

After that, a woman spoke. She was small and sprightly looking, and had big, buggy eyes.

"I come from the land of Poseidon," she spoke, her voice high and raspy. "I am here to enquire about one piece of information, and to deliver another."

"Let's begin with whatever you've come for. Go ahead," Soren directed.

The woman nodded. I recognized her small frame, blueish skin tone and big eyes—she was a water nymph. We had a few in the Sea Kingdom, but they generally dwelled with Poseidon, in his estate.

"Poseidon enquires how your engagement to the Sea Heiress is going," the woman spoke. "Is she here?

My stomach turned.

Soren stood. "No, she isn't."

I felt both relief and confusion bubbling in my stomach. I quickly gazed down at my plate, trying to hide my gaze. Apparently, Soren thought my presence needed to be hidden, which communicated to me that this nymph was a threat.

"Where is she?" the nymph asked.

"She hasn't arrived yet," Soren responded quickly.

"Interesting...Poseidon heard she had escaped from the Sea Kingdom. I'll have to look into this," the nymph said, clicking her tongue impatiently.

"And what information did you have to deliver?" Soren asked, changing the subject expertly.

"That was part of it. That your future bride has escaped the Sea Kingdom," the nymph explained—the word 'bride' made my blood boil—"and that the man who overthrew Triton, Lord Goridian, is building an army. The Sea Kingdom is in turmoil, and Triton is being held captive, without any means of defense."

"And you're saying I should come to this kingdom's rescue?" Soren spat. "Triton was stupid enough to trust Goridian. I thought I'd let him learn his lesson; let the kingdom be overthrown for a couple of centuries before stepping in."

I wanted so badly to roll my eyes.

The nymph appeared irritated. "Well, your majesty, Poseidon is seeking your help now. And he expects you to fulfill the prophecy of marrying the Sea Heiress as well."

"I will set a date for the wedding as soon as I happen to come across her," Soren responded through gritted teeth.

The nymph nodded, sitting down.

I believed the conversation was over, when I heard another person speaking. This time, a man's voice.

"How much turmoil is the Sea Kingdom in?" he asked.

The nymph wasn't slow to respond.

"The predicament is quite horrible. Lord Goridian is in a fit of rage at the moment. Triton is being held against his will, and without his trident, he cannot do anything to help his people," the nymph spoke. The entire group seemed interested in what she was saying, and so we all listened.

"Lord Goridian was expecting to marry the Sea Heiress to be sure the prophecy of the girl and Zeus's son marrying could never be fulfilled."

So that's the real reason he'd wanted to marry me.

"What was he thinking; trying to interrupt a prophecy? Does he want to corrupt the world?" another voice growled.

"Aye," the nymph explained. "We believe he is a much bigger threat to us than we first believed. He has been honing his capabilities, and his only limitation, as of now, is that he is incapable of physically leaving the water. He cannot come onto Land, but even that limitation could be shattered, if his powers continue to grow."

"Where does this Lord Goridian come from?" a woman exclaimed.

"Goridian is the son of Hades; an underworld demigod, born of Hades and one of his lovers. He worked as Hades's consort for many years, until he betrayed him. As soon as he entered the sea and took over, Hades cursed him for the betrayal, making sure he would never be able leave the water as long as he lived. However, he was successful in taking over the Sea

Kingdom. We thought Triton and his people would eventually be able to fight him off, but it appears they have been unable."

"Are you saying that I am their last hope?" Soren snorted.

"Yes. And, with your brother, the Heir of Gaea and Zeus, and the Sea Heiress, it could be possible to defeat Lord Goridian," the nymph explained.

"Why am I expected to do everything around here?" Soren muttered under his breath. I could tell no one had heard him.

"Will you be willing to help the Sea Kingdom?" the nymph asked.

"Why can't Poseidon do it? He's supposed to handle all matters of the sea." Soren accidentally knocked over an empty wine goblet.

"Poseidon is dying," the nymph responded, her voice catching in her throat.

Suddenly, a communal gasp escaped the room, along with a buzz of one question: the question that I myself was thinking.

If Poseidon was immortal, how in the Land and Sea could he be dying?

"How is this possible?" Soren asked.

"It has been discovered that Poseidon has been poisoned continually for the past two hundred years, without his knowing," the nymph explained. "Unfortunately, the antidote to try and counteract the poison isn't making up for the centuries Poseidon went without knowing what was happening. He will die, in time."

"Who poisoned him?" Soren asked.

"We are still searching for the culprit. Whomever they may be, may they hang by their bowels," the nymph growled.

"Agreed," Soren murmured. I could see an idea flickering across his eyes, but I couldn't tell what it was.

Next to me, Lazarus stiffened in his chair.

I looked at him with wide eyes, wondering what was going on. He only shook his head, signaling me not to speak, and continued picking at his plate.

"Well, I will think about what to do about the Sea Kingdom," Soren told the nymph, the conversation seeming to come to a close.

"Please do. You are the most powerful Heir in the world. Child of Zeus and Hera. How couldn't you help?" she said, her voice calm and level.

He didn't respond, only let the conversation dissolve into the air like sea mist.

~

When the dinner finally ended that night, I wondered why I had been expected to attend as Soren's fianceé, but stay quiet as he hide my presence at the same time. It didn't make any sense.

Lazarus walked me to my chambers again, my silver dress feeling heavy against my body as I strolled beside him. We were silent for the majority of the time. I really wanted to be able to hold in my questions and ask him the next day, but after minutes of silence, I simply couldn't contain myself.

"Lazarus," I murmured as we floated up the spiral stairs.

"Don't ask, Ailith," he warned.

"But I have to know," I told him.

"You don't have to know anything," he responded.

"It's my kingdom that's in danger!" I exclaimed.

Suddenly, I heard a familiar dark voice behind me.

"Laz, you can go. I need to talk to Ailith alone.'

I turned around, and saw Soren standing at the bottom of the staircase. Lazarus grabbed my hand and pulled me all the way back down, floating until we halted in front of his brother.

Lazarus then left with a huff, and Soren and I stood at the base of the stairs in silence, studying one another.

He looked at me with what was either indifference or pity. I didn't like the idea of either.

"I wanted to apologize," he said, his gaze fixated on mine. "For how I acted earlier. The fight I initiated was...childish, to say the least. Especially for a man who has fought much bigger fights over many years."

Surprising myself, I found his apology genuine.

"I accept your apology," I responded. "And I'm sorry as well. I shouldn't have slapped you."

With that, a faint smile tickled his face.

"What?" I asked.

He shrugged. "It was kind of adorable."

"I could have done much worse," I scoffed.

"I'm not going to question that, but I will second it in saying that I could have done much worse, as well," he replied. "I hope we can have a bit of a start-over, Ailith. I do like you, and I think this could be the beginning to a long and beneficial"—

"Don't you dare say marriage, or I will sucker-punch you," I warned.

He sighed. "Fine. A long and beneficial relationship."

I smirked. "That's vague."

"Fine. Friendship. Are you happy now?"

"I'm on my way to content."

He took a long, deep breath, clasping his hands behind his back. "Well, I still hope you will agree to consider my proposal."

I bent my head, staring at the ground timidly. "I...I need time."

"We have some, but not much," he told me. "I hope you'll realize that."

I looked up at him. "Wait," I said, shifting my weight from one foot to the other. "If Poseidon is dying, couldn't he die before he has the chance to see us fulfill his stupid prophecy?"

Soren furrowed his brows; shaking his head. "Although Poseidon's death will mean that we do not necessarily have to fulfill every aspect of the prophecy, the prophecy isn't connected to his satisfaction. Its fulfillment is independent of him, and needs to be taken care of whether or not Poseidon is still alive."

I shuddered. "What becomes of a God when they die?"

He took a long, deep breath. "A constellation, in the sky. Poseidon will always look over us, as a God, but will never have his power or bodily form again. While his flesh may be diminishable, his soul is not."

"How is he being poisoned?" I asked.

Soren shrugged. "I'm not sure. The nymph knew more about it than I do."

"Speaking of the nymph," I added. "Why did you lie? Why did you pretend like I wasn't there?"

Soren took a long, deep breath. "Because I was afraid you were going to make a scene if I told everyone you were there."

"Why would I make a scene? Lazarus told me in advance that I was attending the dinner as your fianceé," I responded. "I wasn't happy about it, but I suppose I understood why you needed me to pretend."

"Yes, but...there are some norms they would have expected us to follow, as engaged people," he responded, his face looking awkwardly pained. "I was anticipating that we could dodge the subject of engagement entirely at the dinner, but it came up."

There was definitely something he wasn't telling me.

"What norms?" I asked. "What are you talking about?"

"Well...," he said, scowling. "They would expect you to be noticeably...un der my influence."

I quirked a brow. "What?"

"It's something to do with Gods and their lovers," he explained. With that, he grabbed my hand and pressed his lips to it.

I felt a surge of something in my flesh, and pulled my arm out of his grasp, slowly examining it.

My hand seemed to glow...no, not glow. Sparkle.

"That's just the first part. They would expect your whole being to look like that," he smirked, pacing in circles around me.

Suddenly, I understood.

"I see," I responded, keeping my stare on the ground as he placed two hands on my shoulders.

"And that's just the beginning, sea girl," Soren whispered, leaning over me and slowly brushing his soft lips against the side of my neck. I felt a flutter of nerves in my stomach, and then the tickling, glowing sensation where his mouth had touched. I heard him snicker, and say, "This is going to be more fun that I initially thought."

I spun around to slap him again, but he was gone.

Author's Note:

Hey, everyone!

1K...I don't even know what to say. To me, that's unfathomable. Thank you guys from the bottom of my heart! I really appreciate every read, vote, comment, and message.

If you enjoyed what you read, don't forget to vote and comment, if you'd like! :)

Updates every Monday and Friday/Saturday (one or the other).

Thank you to everyone, again--

Xoxo,

LK

PS: I want to know everyone's predictions. What do you think is going to happen next?

Chapter 9

I awoke the next morning feeling well-rested for the first time in a long while. The sun glowed through the open windows in my chambers, kissing my face as I awoke and congratulated myself for begin capable of sleeping past dawn for the first time since I had arrived on Land. After all, I still wasn't really used to the idea of day and night.

Stepping out of bed, I sauntered over to my closet to dress for the day—and nearly yelped when I looked in the mirror.

Turning to examine myself, I realized the place on my neck that Soren had kissed was still sparkling.

I rolled my eyes, gritting my teeth and cursing myself for letting him do that. I hadn't known that my skin was still going to continue to glimmer so showily all these hours later, or I would have stopped him.

I sneered. Soren had known that what he was doing would cause me to be on showcase in front of everyone.

I felt my fingertips tingling, and by blood simmering in my veins.

That bastard.

I dressed in my usual leather pants, boots and tunic—even as Cleo and Nela attended to my hair and brushed makeup over my face, saying what a pity it was that I refused to wear the lovely dresses provided for me. I grumbled internally when I heard their coos. After all, my choice of wardrobe was much more practical.

However, there was something else about their tones; something hushed and secret, as if they knew something I didn't.

After several hissed and whispered comments, I couldn't contain myself.

"Okay, what's going on?" I asked both of them.

"Nothing, Ms. Ailith," Cleo murmured softly, her gentle fingers stroking my scalp as she pulled my hair away from my neck. I could tell they were trying not to look at the spot where it sparkled, but it was unfortunately quite flashy.

I felt a growl formulating in my throat, but I choked it down.

I didn't ask any more questions, even though I didn't believe Cleo and Nela for a second when they assured me that nothing was going on that I wasn't aware of.

Luckily, they didn't pull my hair up that day, so I didn't have to worry about the shiny patch on my skin being completely bare. As soon as they were finished curling my long locks, I pulled some of my hair to the side of my face in an attempt to hide the shimmer.

My maids seemed to know what I was doing, but neither of them said a word about it.

~

I ventured out of my chambers alone, intending to confront (and probably pummel) Soren about his shine-inducing mouth at some point. However, I had more important things to do first.

First, I wanted to meet with whomever was in charge of Soren's army that morning, and see if they would be willing to help me form a small army of warriors to assist in my reclaiming the Sea Kingdom. If I was going to defeat Goridian, it would be much easier with some backup.

I still needed both Lazarus and Soren to agree to help with my cause. However, I knew Lazarus would be quick to assist—Soren, however—he was a different story.

Truthfully, I was considering his proposal. I didn't like to admit it, but every day it seemed to make more and more sense on a logical level, yet I was quite adamant about refusing for the time being. Especially after he'd turned me into a shiny fish scale without the slightest of my knowing or consent.

After asking a few servants, I learned that the head of Soren's army was named Caspian, and that he was a demigod who dwelled in the east wing of the castle. I was given directions by a kitchen boy, and immediately took off in the direction of the east wing, winding my way through the palace.

As soon as I made it to his private study, I knocked on the door impatiently. I could hear a buzz of murmurs within the room, and was surprised to recognize Lazarus's voice on the inside, along with an unfamiliar woman's voice, and another man's I assumed to be that of Caspian.

Heavy footsteps grew closer to the door, and soon it swung open, revealing a tall, bald man with enormous upper body muscles. He was probably seven feet tall, and had a cold, icy blue stare. Veins popped out of his biceps and neck. He eyed me up and down with a scowl before he spoke.

"Yes?" His voice was a deep baritone as he greeted me at the door. I blinked a few times, taking in his monumental aura.

"Hi," I said, my voice a bit squeaky. "My name is Ailith, and"-

"I know who you are," he responded, his stone-still facial expression unchanging. "What can I do for you?"

I peered in the room and saw Lazarus, seemingly quite content compared to the previous evening, and a woman I hadn't ever seen before. She was tall and blonde, and watched me with an evaluating gaze as I entered.

"I was hoping to speak to you," I told the man, taking a deep breath as I realized I was going to have to do this in front of Lazarus, "about building an army. With me. To help me reclaim my kingdom."

"Your kingdom?" The man raised a brow.

I nodded. "The overthrown Sea Kingdom. That is where I come from."

"Does his majesty know about this?" he enquired.

Dammit. My stomach turned.

I opened my mouth to explain that King Soren was not directly aware of it, but heard Lazarus speaking first.

"Yes, Caspian," Lazarus quickly said. "Soren has given her the go-ahead."

I felt both relieve and surprise flooding through me. I gave Lazarus an appreciative glance, and he nodded his head as if to say, no problem. However, his eyes did not meet mine. Instead he was looking at my neck, where it shone.

I blushed, and turned away—knowing Lazarus probably knew exactly how I'd received sparkling skin.

"What kind of an army?" the man named Caspian asked, letting me into the study and closing the door behind me.

"Fairly small," I responded. "I was thinking maybe one hundred warriors."

I couldn't gobble up the grandeur of the room quickly enough. The walls were wooden and polished; glossy marble statues complimenting every corner and bookshelves lining the walls. A huge, round wooden desk stood in the middle of the room, and a monstrous stone fireplace held a crackling fire nearby. I couldn't tell if the space was more cozy or intimidating.

"One hundred?" Caspian confirmed, flipping his hand nonchalantly. "I have thousands of warriors. One hundred shouldn't be a problem at all."

"Is there any way that I could train them myself?" I asked.

The man looked a bit taken aback, his eyebrows shooting up to his forehead.

"You train them?" His eyes skimmed over me once more. He folded his muscled arms across his broad chest.

I nodded. "I know the opponent best."

"And who would that be?"

I took a deep breath. "Lord Goridian. Hades's traitor son who took over the Sea Kingdom."

"Oh yeah, I heard about that," Caspian said, his tone growing a bit more informal.

Lazarus and the blonde woman stayed where they were, still as statues, watching this exchange with keen interest.

"I escaped the Sea Kingdom in order to salvage it, sir," I explained. "And I really need the help of this kingdom, and of your army."

"If his majesty has given approval, then I see no reason why I cannot help you. I would like to support your noble cause," he said, gruffly clearing his throat as he brought out a piece of paper. "Write down the specialties you would prefer in these warriors, and I will have a group collected by the end of the week."

"And I can lead them in training?" I asked.

Caspian's muscles went taut as he looked up at me, his glare almost a warning.

"You can talk to them. But—and I hope you do not find this offensive—I think I am better equipped to prepare an army for battle than you," he said, his gaze fixated on the piece of paper in front of him.

I furrowed a brow. "What is that supposed to mean?"

He shook his head. "I don't mean to insult you, but you're a little sea girl. I am a master of war. A demigod; the Heir of Ares; God of war. Do you honestly think you're more of an expert on fighting than I am?"

I shook my head. "Not at all. But I think I'm more of an expert on fighting Goridian. I know him, and I know what these warriors will need to be capable of in order to perform offense and defense at the same time. I know what we need to win."

He sighed, his huge frame inhaling an exhaling quite visibly.

"We'll lead training together," he huffed.

I nodded coridally. "Thank you. That sounds like a perfect compromise."

He sneered a little under his breath, but I didn't mind if it meant I'd received what I'd come for.

I was going to build an army, and reclaim the Sea Kingdom before Soren could think to try to stop me.

I thanked Caspian and left his study, strolling down the long corridor; feeling like I had finally done something useful since I'd arrived on land.

However, as soon as I crossed into another passageway, I saw two familiar figures standing in front of me.

It was Lazarus, and the blonde woman.

"Lazarus?" I murmured, stopping in my tracks. "What's wrong?"

"We have to talk," he responded gruffly. Taking my arm, he grabbed me into a nearby room, and the blonde woman followed behind us.

"What's going on?" I exclaimed, as Lazarus shut the door behind us. "Why did you just pull me out of the hallway?"

"Laz, calm down," the woman told him, rolling her eyes. "I'm sorry, he can be quite dramatic. I'm Juniper."

"And...who are you?" I asked.

She laughed, nodding towards Lazarus. "I'm his sister. Soren's half-sister. I usually live with our mother, Gaea, but I've come for a visit."

"Can you please stay out of this so that I can get my point across before it's too late?" snarled Lazarus.

"Fine. Have fun," she told him, giving him a sisterly pat on the shoulder. "Ailith, if you ever need anything, don't hesitate to find me. We can t alk...or just rant about my brothers and their obnoxious behavior." She shot Lazarus an irritated glare, before flipping her golden locks over her shoulder and strutting out of the small room, gently closing the door behind her.

I faced Lazarus.

"You two don't look alike at all," I remarked.

Lazarus didn't chuckle once. Odd, I thought.

"What's going on?" I asked him, my tone growing serious.

He sighed, his tone commanding. "Move your hair, Ailith."

"What?"

"Pull your hair away from your neck."

I folded my arms in front of my chest, planting my feet sturdily against the ground. "Why?"

Lazarus reached forward and grabbed the hair that covered the sparkly patch on my neck, letting it fall past my neck, onto my back. He seemed to grow a bit angrier when he saw the shine.

"Where did you get that?" he growled.

I glared at him, whisper-hissing my response. "Where do you think, genius?"

This time, his expression turned perplexed. "You...you let him do that?"

I snorted. "Sort of. He was trying to explain something to me last night; something about the expectations of our engagement. He did the same thing to my hand. It was more of a demonstration than a gesture of affection. Don't worry yourself, strawberry."

"You're right," he said, his voice low. "It wasn't a gesture of affection. It was something else entirely."

I quirked a brow.

"Sor didn't mention this to me. Which makes it worse," he said, beginning to pace back and forth in the small room.

"Lazarus, what's going on? Is this...is this bad?" I asked.

He shook his head. "No, it's worse than bad. Do you love Soren?"

"What?! No," I responded.

"Do you think you might fall in love with Soren anytime soon?"

I shrugged. "I don't know. Why?"

"Well, that mark...that shine on your neck...," he breathed, his breath becoming raspy and his mind seeming to flood with different ideas. He was hyperventilating a bit, and I wondered what could possibly so horrible that he couldn't even speak properly.

"What, Lazarus?" I gasped. "Calm down."

"That mark on your neck means more than you think, Ailith," he told me, his hands shaking a bit. "The fact that Soren did that—dammit, I can't believe he would do that. He knew you don't know what that means. But he still did it."

"What does it mean?" I asked.

He shuddered. "You don't want to know."

I glared at him. "Tell me. Now."

"It's a marker," he explained, throwing his hands to his sides as his freakout seemed to reach its breaking point. "Ailith, Soren is...he's dangerous. He's a God; possibly the most powerful God ever born. He's the son of Zeus and Hera—and he's not human."

"What does that have to do with him kissing my neck?" I asked.

He shook his head. "He wasn't kissing your neck to prove a point. He was marking you, Ailith. He was...he was marking you."

"For what?" I exclaimed.

He took a deep breath. "You're not going to like it."

"I already don't like a lot of things. I'm a big girl. You can tell me," I muttered in response, nerves beginning to tumble in my stomach.

"Ailith, amongst the Gods and Goddesses, the mark of glowing skin, or erat arida cutis amans,is a sign of a chosen mate," he explained. "It has to do with a God's animal instinct. His...feral instinct."

"What?"

"Soren is aware of what he's doing. But he's not fully aware," he explained, continuing to pace in circles.

"Wait," I said, holding out a hand, trying to get Lazarus to calm down. "Soren did this why?"

"Because it's his mark to all the other Gods to...to back off, basically," he explained, his voice reaching a breaking point. "He—he wants you, Ailith. He has chosen you."

"Chosen me? As what?" I gasped.

"As his mate; his wife. His companion forever. Whatever you want to call it. He is falling for you," he explained.

"How is that possible? We've barely known each other a month."

"The prophecy must be doing this to him, or something," Lazarus breathed, his eyes focused on my neck. "But it's only a matter of time now."

"A matter of time until what?" I gasped.

Lazarus spoke softly, his low tone threatened.

"Until he claims you."

Author's Note:

Hey, everyone! As always, thanks for all the continuing support from all of you. I appreciate each and every one of you readers!

If you enjoyed what you read, don't forget to comment and vote (if you want)!

Xoxo,

LK

PS: Do you guys want me to do a 'song of the week' thing with each chapter? I noticed some authors do it, and I could totally do that. I listen to music when I write, so...let me know!

Chapter 10

"Wait. Hold your seahorses. What do you mean claim me?" I asked.

Lazarus was still breathing heavily. It was apparent that it had taken a lot for him to explain this.

"Claiming is an ancient ceremony, and a means by which Gods and Goddesses declare their forever lovers. Their spouses; mates—whatever you want to call it. Once Soren has claimed you, you're his forever," he explained.

I grimaced. "What if I don't want to be his forever?"

"Trust me. If he claims you, you will."

"Why?" I exclaimed.

"He'll know what to do. He'll know exactly what to do," Lazarus breathed. "He'll do anything necessary to get you to fall in love with him."

"And this is some innate part of him, or something?" I confirmed.

"It's in his nature. Every God has the instinct to claim someone when they're very attracted to them. It's like falling in love, and getting married, only on an amplified scale. The love, commitment and level of devotion you will get from Soren will be a million times more meaningful and intense than you could receive from any mortal. When he says he will love you until the end of time, it is both a literal and a binding statement. And...," Lazarus took a minute to let out a sharp exhale, "he will be very willing to love you, Ailith."

"Why?" I murmured.

"If you didn't know already, you're kind of perfect for Sor. You put him in his place. You can handle him," he explained. "I haven't seen that in a woman before. Ever."

I groaned. "Why does this have to be happening right now? I have a kingdom to save; I don't need some messed up love life."

"If you let him kiss you like that last night, then you mustn't be completely disgusted by the man," Lazarus teased. "Maybe you should let the tide push and pull as it will." He winked, trying to combat his internal anxiety.

"Stop being weird," I commanded, rubbing my temples. "I have to think."

Although I would confess I was attracted to Soren, I definitely was not in love with him. I wasn't in love with him, and I wasn't close to falling in love with him, as far as I knew. I needed to do something to slow this whole thing down, or he'd be 'claiming' me before I had the chance to save my kingdom.

"Do you think," I said to Lazarus, "that if Soren fell in love with me, and claimed me—he would be more likely to help me reclaim my kingdom?"

Lazarus snorted. "That's an understatement. He'd probably fight Goridian for you."

I sighed. "What would you do if you were me?"

Het took a deep breath, placing a hand on the doorknob of the tiny room we were hiding in.

"I don't know. Figure out what you want, Ailith," he told me, his tone both instructing and warning. "Figure out what you want, do so quickly, and then do something about it. Because it seems that Soren is getting ahead of you in that regard."

With that, he opened the door and stepped out, leaving me to my thoughts.

~

I couldn't think about the sparkles on my neck or Lazarus's warning words about Soren trying to claim me for any longer, so I set out to help Caspian with building the army.

I felt all this unnecessary meddling with romantics was just getting in the way of my ultimate goal, so I vowed to focus on the Sea Kingdom and my real purpose for the rest of the day.

I knew I was probably way in over my head.

I found Caspian on the palace outskirts, near the stables, where he was practicing his own skills in combat. As I watched him throw punches and shatter a stone statue to the ground, I had to admit that I was impressed. However, strength was no match for cleverness when it came to fighting someone like Goridian.

"Hey, Caspian," I greeted the man, careful to tuck my neck behind locks of my dark hair. "Can we talk?"

He nodded, sweat rolling down his neck. "Just let me finish up here."

Caspian and I walked through the grassy fields surrounding the palace. They were filled with blue and purple wildflowers; hummingbirds and bumblebees creating a harmony of buzzing. We could hear the sea nearby, whispering as it pulled and tugged at the sandy shore.

"So, how is forming the army going?" I enquired.

He shrugged. "I've found a few candidates."

"How are you going about finding them?" I asked.

"By the skills you specified. Gills, knowledge of the sea...we have a decent number of warriors with such attributes. It should only be a matter of time before I have one hundred," he explained.

"Thank you," I told him, pausing. "I really appreciate you doing this."

Slowly, he nodded. "It's a great thing you're trying to do. Although, I'm surprised King Soren would be attempting to claim you and let you fight Goridian simultaneously. Seems...unlike him."

I took a deep breath. I felt my face flushing. "How did you know about the claiming thing?"

He snorted. "Your neck glimmers. Haven't you noticed?"

I shot the man a scowl. "It wasn't like that. He was...he was trying to explain something to me."

"That's what they all say," he muttered sarcastically.

I bumped him on the bicep. "Are you saying there's been lots of girls before me?"

He laughed, shaking his head. "No, of course not. Have you met Soren? Lazarus is usually the one bringing women to the palace, left and right. Sor, though—he's a special one. He hasn't really loved someone for a long time."

I sighed. "Does everyone know? Is it really that obvious?"

The man continued chuckling. "Ailith, I don't mean to burst your bubble, but this is an ancient sign. Gods have marked their intended beloved this way for millions of years...since the beginning of time. It means a lot."

I shuddered. "I wish it didn't."

Furrowing a brow, he asked, "So you do not appreciate the king's advances?"

I shook my head. "I barely know him."

"That doesn't make a difference in our world," he responded, looking at me with an expression that told me that he thought I was naive. "We have so much time, that it becomes irrelevant to everything."

"Look, I really need this army. I need Soren's help, and the help from his kingdom. What I don't need is a marriage, or to be claimed, or whatever," I exclaimed, feeling my face heat up at the word 'claimed.'

"But you are attracted to him?" teased Caspian.

"No."

"Yes, you are. I can feel it," he mumbled, a playful smile tickling his lips.

I groaned. "So what if I am? I'm definitely not excited about this claiming business. If you want to know my opinion, it's kind of creepy."

"And if you want to know my opinion, Ms. Ailith, being claimed would be advantageous to you. King Soren will do anything he can to help you salvage your beloved kingdom if he claims you; if he falls in love. I think he is falling in love, but if you make it clear to him that you're uninterested in being claimed, then he will not persist. He's a good person, and he's sensitive. He won't continue this if it's not what you want."

"But what if I don't know what I want?" I whined.

He laughed. "That's your problem. You need to figure it out. However, for the time being, just see where this goes. You'll never know how something feels if you don't try it," he told me. "I have to get to training for the day. I'll see you later, Ailith."

I nodded. "Thanks, Caspian."

He then took off, leaving me in the warm field alone. I listened to the sounds of the birds, and the seaside nearby, and wished I could visit the water. It was the only place I felt really comfortable, yet I knew going would be a recipe for disaster. Instead, I forced myself to watch from afar as the sea rippled with the wind. It was calming down; almost as if Lord Goridian was finally considering me a real threat.

He was building an army.

I walked back to the palace, my head seeming a bit unappreciative of all the new ideas and thoughts swirling around in it, when I felt a striking grasp on my arms, one unfamiliar arm wrapping around my shoulders and the other over my mouth before I could think to scream.

I struggled, flailing around as I felt myself being thrown to the ground. As I hit the earth, I felt an unknown source of power pinning me to the ground, keeping me from fighting back as I might have normally. Whomever was doing this knew of my capabilities as a warrior.

I looked up, eyeing the face of my assailant, and gasped.

"Hello, dear Ailith." His dark face twisted into a grin.

I quirked a brow. "Hades?"

The man in front of me was tall, built and had twisted eyebrows, and a mouth pinned into a seemingly permanent smirk. He looked to be in his twenties, which made his immorality quite noticeable. His hair was jaw-length, wavy, and bright red, as was his thin stubble, and he wore a fur cape big enough to fit my bed.

"It is I. Don't worry, I don't intend to hurt you," he explained.

I scoffed. "Then why did you tackle me to the ground?"

Shrugging, he responded, "It seemed more efficient than trying to explain myself. Plus, I need you not to try and combat me. I really don't feel like wiping blood off my clothes today." He sighed, and brushed a piece of dandelion fluff off his shoulder.

I rolled my eyes. "What do you want, Hades?"

"Well, I'd love to have us a little chit-chat. We're very similar in many ways, Ailith, and we have things to discuss," he responded, smirking.

I glared. "What things?"

"Oh, I'm sure I could spend the entire day listing them, but it will be a much better use of time to just take you with me, to somewhere we can share a private moment," he told me, his grin uncanny.

I groaned. "You're not taking me to the underworld, are you?"

"I could, if you wanted me to," he taunted. "But...,"—he clicked his tongue—"I think I should prefer to just have a word with you in this kingdom. Plus, poor King Soren will have a hissy fit if I were to remove you from his territory."

With that, Hades reached forward and grabbed my arm, helping me up.

"Where are we going, then?" I asked.

"You'll see," he responded, wrapping an arm around my waist and taking off into the midday air, the sky seeming to gobble us up as we soared to higher heights, passing clouds of fluff and squawking arrays of birds.

"This is kind of the antithesis of your home," I remarked as Hades continued upwards, his grasp loosening.

"I want to go somewhere Soren will never think to look for me," he responded.

I looked up at him. "Why do you seem so concerned about Soren?"

"Have you not noticed? You're marked, you lucky little sea waif," he remarked.

I growled. "Why does everyone have to notice?"

"It's cute how you're trying to cover it up with your hair. Really. Adorable," he snickered.

As he spoke his last sentence, we stopped—landing on a big, snowy mountaintop. Around me, the atmosphere was swirls of softness; we were so high up, I couldn't see the land through the thick marshmallowy clouds.

"So," Hades spoke, his wicked smile unable to keep itself from his face as he ran a hand through his thick red locks. "You were involved with Goridian, weren't you? Tell me about that."

I gulped. "What about him?"

"He's my son," he responded. "Well...he was. Until he ultimately betrayed me, all those years ago."

I felt my breathing falter. "You're not here to...to kill me in his name, or something, are you?"

He laughed. "Never in a thousand years, child. In fact, I am quite fond of you. You escaped him. And you're attempting to defeat him."

"And you're not mad about that?" I asked.

He shook his head. "Not at all. I hate what Goridian is trying to do. He'll never be able to take over the world as long as Zeus is patrolling it."

As I looked into Hades's flaming eyes, I suddenly recalled a critical piece of information that Lazarus had told me the first morning I spent in the Land Kingdom.

When Goridian sent Triton's trident ashore, Hades took it.

"Where's the trident, Hades?" I growled, changing the subject of the conversation very abruptly.

"Whoa, sea girl...I didn't think you knew about that," he responded, clicking his tongue. "I can't tell you. If I tell you, you won't believe me, and you'll never find it."

"Conch shells."

"Is that your idea of a swear word?" he teased.

Actually, it was a swear word in the Sea Kingdom.

"Just tell me where it is, Hades," I pleaded.

"Sorry, sea girl. I can't. It's mandatory that you find it within yourself," he told me, lowering his gaze. "Just remember that."

I groaned. "So did you just drag me all the way up onto this mountain for fun, or do you actually have something helpful to say?"

"Actually, I was going to tell you that"—

Before Hades could finish his sentence, we heard a deafening crack in the distance. I shuddered, remembering the sound from the first night I had arrived at the sea's surface; one of the most terrifying sounds in existence.

Thunder.

"HADES!" a familiar voice called. "WHAT DO YOU THINK YOU'RE DOING?!"

I felt my insides turning, and my heartbeat quickening. Nerves crawled around in my stomach and a shiver trickled down my spine. The shimmer on my neck tingled as I made a realization.

The voice was Soren's.

AUTHOR'S NOTE:

Hey, everyone! Thank you so much for reading! 2k...that blows my mind!

Thanks to every single person who has read my work only once, to every single person who has voted, commented, and supported me from the beginning. I appreciate all of you more than you know. You guys are the greatest!

If you enjoyed the chapter, don't forget to vote and comment your thoughts, if you want to! :)

Xoxo,

LK

Chapter 11

Soren approached us, his body soaring through the cloudy sky and smoothly landing on the top of the mountain as it began to rain. I could tell there was some correlation between his mood and the weather. ..there had to be. It had gone from sunny and calm one minute, to cloudy and dark when he arrived.

"King Soren," Hades exclaimed, scooching himself in front of me. "How good it is to see you. We haven't crossed path in...oh, it must have been three hundred years ago when we last met."

Soren peered past Hades; at me. I could tell he was eyeing the glimmering flesh hidden behind my hair.

"Don't lay a finger on her, Hades," Soren warned, his eyes looking more annoyed than concerned. I wondered, if the two fought, who would be the winner—who was more powerful. I knew Hades was much older than Soren, but Soren was Zeus's son.

My head was spinning with the possibilities.

"I'm not here to hurt her," Hades responded, his tone a bit offended. "Geez, Sor, who do you think I am?"

"You're the ruler of the underworld. You're dangerous, and infamously conniving. Plus," Soren added, snarling the last few words. "You have a tendency to take concubines."

With that, Hades broke out into peals of laughter, roaring so loudly I could swear the thunder in the distance was responding with a deafening crack. I covered my sensitive ears, rolling my eyes.

"What is that supposed to mean? You honestly think I can stand spending only half the year with my Persephone? She is my beloved, and I do only see her when she is with me, but I cannot wait for her all the months that she dwells on Land."

"I heard you're attempting to bring her into your world full-time," Soren said, stepping closer.

Hades shrugged. "I've discovered a few loopholes. I won't break the treaty, if that's what you're wondering. But Persephone loves me. She would choose to dwell in the underworld forever, given the choice. But her mother is greedy, and wants her for half the year. So we suffer through it."

"Are you trying to guilt me into breaking the treaty?" Soren exclaimed. "My father put that in place nearly two million years ago. I wouldn't touch it with the longest tree branch in the world."

"Which is the problem, Son of Zeus," Hades taunted. "You think you're ready to take your father's place, once he decides he is ready to really settle ...but you're not. You're only what, four thousand years old? So young. So naïve." Hades was now inching closer to me, his feet nearly reaching mine.

"Don't touch her," Soren warned.

Hades snorted as he twirled a lock of fire-red hair. "Or what? You'll kill me?"

"I could," Soren threatened. "You know I could."

"Possibly, but that would be terribly unfortunate. My people would have war, and that—I'm not sure you could win," Hades responded, his wicked smile returning.

"Just return Ailith to me, go back to the underworld, and don't come back," Soren growled, clasping his hands in front of him.

I wanted so badly to roll my eyes—as he spoke as if I belonged to him—but knew this wasn't the time to make a retort.

Hades clicked his tongue, seemingly amused by this painfully tense dynamic. For some reason, he seemed to have more confidence in himself than I thought he should, if, in fact, Soren could kill him.

I didn't doubt that he could.

"Not so fast, majesty," Hades snickered, reaching forward and placing a hand on my shoulder. I shuddered.

Soren sprung forward, ripping him from the soft touch.

"Sor, stop," I commanded. "He's just messing with you."

"You don't know him like I do." Soren shot me an intense look, his eyes reaching out and begging me not to get involved.

For once, I complied. I feared Hades, and, as much as I didn't like to admit it, I trusted Soren...at least, to a certain extent.

"I was just in the middle of having a conversation with Ailith. We weren't getting involved in anything inappropriate," Hades sneered.

"I don't appreciate your teasing. Say what you want to say, then leave," Soren told him, his voice turning raspy...more of a feral growl than a human's voice.

"Or what? You're not going to try and kill me, are you?" Hades murmured, a fake frown appearing on his face. "That would be highly ungodly. Geez, Son of Zeus, haven't you any manners? No wonder your people fear you so much; you probably scare the hell out of them."

"I won't ask again. Say what you came to say, and then leave. Or, better yet, just leave," Soren responded.

I could tell he was reaching the brink of impatience.

"Fine," Hades responded, sighing in irritation. "Ailith, I just wanted you to know that I find your actions heroic."

I scoffed. "You don't know anything about my actions."

"Fine. I find what I've heard about you heroic. And I might have over-heard you talking to that bastard Caspian earlier today. About building an army?" he said.

"You did what?" Soren exclaimed.

"Thanks." I shot a glare towards Hades.

He put a hand to his mouth, feigning apology. "Oops. Sorry. I didn't realize there were so many secrets between you two, especially if you're doing what I think you're doing." He seemed to laugh internally, as if he'd made a joke only he could understand.

I felt Soren's gaze burning a hole in my flesh. My cheeks flashed crimson.

"Now," Hades said. "I'm sorry I let the cat out of the bag about your secret army-building. But, if his majesty here tries to halt your little plan to get rid of my traitor of a son, then I want you to know that you have the support of my armies."

I gasped.

"Really?" I exclaimed. I didn't even notice the rage in Soren's eyes when he heard this statement.

Hades nodded, his stare playful. "Yes. Of course, for a price. But, we can discuss that later—when Soren tells you he won't let you fight. That is what you were going to do, isn't it, majesty?"

"Get out of here, devil," Soren seethed.

"Fine. I think this is a good time for me to take my leave," Hades murmured, sighing once more before turning to me. He took my hand in his. I felt his unfamiliar flesh, and noticed it was strangely warm.

Soren growled from afar.

"Ailith, if and when you need me—which I know you will—you know where to find me," he said, gesturing downwards and grinning before floating back, off the mountaintop, into midair where he began to hover. I thought he was finally going to leave, but was surprised when he stayed another moment.

This time, he turned towards Soren.

"She is adorable," he told him. "I'm genuinely upset to see you've already marked her, or I would have done it myself." He shot me a wink, and I felt my blood boiling underneath my skin.

"Get out." Soren's breath was husky; unforgiving.

"Alright. I suppose I'll see you sometime in the near future, won't I?" he murmured. He ran a hand through his hair. "So long, dear Ailith. I sure will miss seeing that pretty little face; that pale, pearly skin...those delicate bones." His thoughts seem to trail as his eyes did, traveling up and down before he disappeared in plain sight.

Soren had been a hair away from lunging. I sighed.

Silence overcame us for just a few moments, before I spoke.

"You marked me?" I exclaimed, turning my head to face Soren.

He turned towards me. "I had to."

"Um...no, you didn't," I spat.

"Ailith, you're destined to marry me. We need to figure out if there's anything between us," he said, walking towards me and grabbing me by the arms. "You have to agree."

"I don't have time to deal with this prophecy. My people are in turmoil, and I must help them. And if you won't, I now have another option." I yanked my arms from his grasp, crossing them in front of my chest.

"Did you hear what he said? If I hadn't marked you, he would have. Hades would be horrible to serve as a God—especially in the way I'm sure he was implying. And I'm certain there would be several others willing to take you that would be much worse than Hades," he growled, before he pulled me close, a hand secured around my waist. He began sprinting, and suddenly leapt off the mountaintop.

We floated downwards as it began to rain, thunder cracking in the sky. Soren didn't bother to stop it.

"You didn't tell me I was going to glitter," I muttered into his ear. I nearly blushed as I realized how I must have looked; pressed up against him, arms wrapped around his neck.

He snickered. "Why did you need to know about the glittering part?"

"Because I was on display all day. I felt like...I felt like an object. People viewed me as as sign; as a thing. It was awful. How long does this last?"

"Only a few days." He chuckled under his breath.

"I don't appreciate your smug attitude towards the fact that I'm your shiny new fish scale."

"Ailith, listen"—

"No, you listen. I am not an object. I am not yours to claim, or to toy with for fun. I am a person—a mortal—and my time, unlike yours, is limited. And when I say that, I do not only mean my lifespan, but also the time in which I have before Lord Goridian builds up too much power for me to be able to defeat him. I made a promise to Triton and to my people, and no matter this prophecy, I can't let them suffer."

"But you can let yourself feel," he murmured. "Or, at least, be open to feeling."

I shook my head. "No, I can't. I just narrowly escaped another marriage; one that was forced upon me. I...I still have nightmares. He still haunts me, and I'm not ready to even consider anyone else."

He looked frustrated as his face twisted into smugness. "You do realize that you can't stop me from claiming you." He shot me a smirk.

I glared at him. "Watch it."

"I was kidding," he murmured.

"Good. Because, if you're worth marrying, then you'll accept that I'm not ready to dive into anything quite yet. We've known each other barely six weeks."

He took a deep, long breath.

"Okay," he said, his voice suddenly calm. "I will try and understand your situation. If I have to wait, then I will."

I sighed. "Why are you so eager, after such little time?"

"I don't quite understand it, either. Four thousand years and I've never felt such adherence to anyone."

I felt my stomach flutter.

"Is the prophecy still as urgent as it was before?" I asked.

He nodded. "Its deadline approaches faster every day."

I knew the dangers of agreeing to a marriage I was unsure of. However, I didn't want the entire world to corrupt on my account. My kingdom was my biggest purpose. And... if this would get Soren to help me save my kingdom, wasn't it the right thing to do?

"I'll marry you," I told him, taking a deep breath. "By the time the prophecy is supposed to expire."

He looked at me with keen curiosity. "I don't understand."

"The last thing I want is for the world to suffer because of my selfishness," I muttered. "I'm ready to accept my place on this earth. If that means being your wife, due to a centuries-old prophecy, then damn the galaxy...I'll do what I need to do to fulfill the role made for me by the Gods and Goddesses. But, please, do not mistake this for me being ready for you. I'm—I'm definitely not ready for you."

He was grinning. "We'll have to do something about that, now won't we? Your denial is just so pleasant, Ailith. Your words and actions seem to have no logical correlation, and I love it."

With that, he tilted me forward and pressed his mouth to my jaw, his warm breath tickling my skin as I felt myself go shaky.
I jerked my head back, instinctively smacking him on the face. Bastard.

He groaned. "What was that for?"

Glaring at him, I responded, "I don't need to continue this glittering business, asshat."

He chuckled under his breath.

We returned to the palace, and I could feel the shimmery tingle on my jaw, where he'd kissed me. I could picture how it would gleam the next morning.

Nerves tossed around in my stomach like little jellyfish.

AUTHOR'S NOTE:

Hey everyone! Hope you enjoyed this chapter as much as I enjoyed writing it. If you enjoyed what you read, don't forget to vote and comment! Seriously--I love each and every comment I get.

Thank you, everyone, for all of your support! I appreciate every single read, vote, and comment that I get from you guys. It's seriously mind-blowing how many nice people have reached out to give me feedback, comment on my work, or just say hi! I love it all!

Again, thanks everyone :) Toodles 'til Friday!

Xoxo,

LK

Chapter 12

The sun was beginning to rise over the grassy fields surrounding the palace, the sea surprisingly calm that day as Caspian and I walked the newly formed army of one hundred men into the meadow, where we would begin training.

It had been three days, and I hadn't seen Soren once. I missed him, but was also glad to not have to think about us for a little while.

In other news, my skin had finally stopped sparkling...much to my relief that morning.

"So...what are you planning on teaching today, General?" Caspian teased as we continued walking, a trail of warriors following us.

I smiled under my breath. "You'll see."

Caspian scoffed. "Is there a reason you won't tell me?"

"No," I responded.

He sighed. "Are you sure you can't just go back to the palace and leave the army-training to me? It is my job, you know."

"Why are you prejudice against me?" I asked. "I don't know who trained you in combat, but I was trained by Triton. If you forgot, he's the God of the Sea."

He shrugged. "The overthrown God of the sea," he corrected. "And I was trained by my father; Ares. If you forgot, he's the God of War. Look, Ailith...you're a breakable mortal, and, not to mention, it's pretty obvious my boss wants you. My boss being Soren."

I turned my eyes into glaring slits. "Shut up, Caspian."

He chuckled under his breath, throwing up his hands. "I'm just saying."

I took a few steps in front of him, finally reaching the edge of the field, right before it met with the sandy shore.

I called to the army to stop walking. They all were somewhat familiar looking, each with almost-noticeable gills tucked underneath their ears. I knew they were all somewhat experienced in underwater combat, as I had asked for warriors with such attributes, but none were experienced in fighting Lord Goridian. That--I knew for a fact.

Just thinking about Goridian sent a shiver down my back.

I shuddered, shaking off the nerves, and faced the army before me.

"Hey, Caspian, get over here," I called.

He sauntered over to where I was standing, in front of the army, a smirk plastered on his face. I could tell he wasn't sure what was going on, but he had pretty obvious confidence that what I had planned would miserably fail amongst these other well-built warriors.

However, as soon as he was close enough, I kicked him in the shin, sending him sprawling onto the ground.

Luckily, I knew how he would react, and stood still, waiting for him to drag me down with him. We began wrestling on the ground--he was twice my size, and exceptionally strong, but that didn't stop me from kneeing him in the stomach, which, I had to admit, seemed to be becoming my trademark when it came to fighting men.

We both got on our feet, and began throwing and blocking punches. The army, as I had expected, seemed to watch as if this were a classroom lesson. Finally, I let Caspian grab ahold of me, keeping me in a chokehold.

"I surrender," I muttered, and he let go, stepping back and grinning, hands clasped behind his back.

"First lesson," I told the army, stepping back and kicking Caspian in the stomach, knocking him over. "Never believe a claimed surrender."

Caspian gasped for breath, wincing as he attempted to crawl to his feet. "Not nice, Ailith."

I felt a wicked grin pulling at my lips. "Unfortunately for you, I didn't come here to be nice."

The army of men before me stared with wide eyes, each of them nearly gaping.

"Lesson number two," I said, panting a bit. "Which you all failed, by the way. Always, no matter what, defend your allies."

"What are you talking about? We didn't fail to defend anyone," exclaimed one of the soldiers.

"None of you defended me against Caspian," I pointed out, pacing back and forth, facing each and every one of them. "And, in this particular battle we will be fighting, I am your closest and most important ally. Now, which one of you wants to take me next?"

~

Caspian and I sat on a rock near the seaside, staring at the water. To my surprise, he was allowing me to teach my lesson freely, even though he maintained a sort of tenseness about it that I couldn't understand. However, I decided not to push him on the subject—just the fact that he was allowing me to essentially take over part of his job was asking enough of him.

In that moment, I began a conversation, to break the loud silence.

"I wish there was some way I could knock the pride out of all of them," I told Caspian, nodding my head to the army of soldiers off in the distance, playfully wrestling one another.

He sneered. "What are you talking about?"

"You know exactly what I'm talking about," I responded. "I bet they all think they could beat me in a fight, given the chance. Their own pomposity is going to get them killed."

"I can't say I disagree," he admitted, reaching forward to retie my unlaced left boot.

"Thanks," I muttered, peering out at the sea. "How many of them do you think I'll have to beat before they'll take me seriously?"

Chuckling, Caspian sneered, "All of them."

"Great." My voice was drenched with sarcasm.

He grinned, sliding off the rock and offering me a hand. "Come on, sea warrior. You're really not going to get discouraged now, are you? It's only day one."

I shook my head. "You're right."

"Wow," he remarked. "If I thought you were going to listen to my advice, I'd have pushed you to go back to the castle in the first place."

I elbowed him. "Like I said before. Shut up."

- -

The day ended with the sun setting at the opposite side of the field, and my having fought pretty much every warrior of that damned army.

"You okay there?" one of the soldiers remarked as I limped across the golden meadow, legs feeling like jelly and arms like cake.

My muscles were so sore after that day of training, I thought I would be bedridden for the remainder of the week.

I glared at him, a smile making its way onto my face. "Only because I beat every single one of you."

He nodded. "Hat's off to you, Ailith."

I laughed softly, not bothering to respond.

We arrived back at the palace a little while later, where the soldiers began to return to their respective quarters.

I collapsed in front of the palace, laying down in the grass and smiling up at the orange sky, letting my heavy eyelids fall.

I could have sensed Caspian's smirk from one hundred miles away.

"You good to go again tomorrow, sea girl?" he enquired facetiously.

I nodded, my eyes still closed and a goofy smile stuck on my face. "Sure thing."

"Are you sure?"

"Caspian, I'm fine," I responded, laughing.

"You don't look fine," another voice said.

I opened my eyes, and was pleasantly surprised to see Lazarus standing above me, opposite Caspian. He stared down at me, his hair blending in with the fiery sky.

"Hey, Laz," I murmured.

"Is she drunk, or something?" he asked Caspian.

"Of course not," I answered for Caspian.

"She's just tired," Caspian added, his voice low.

Lazarus reached down, taking my hand. "Let's get you up, then."

"No, I like the grass," I responded, yanking my hand from his grasp.

"You sure she's not drunk?" he whispered.

"Who's drunk?"

I felt all of my nerves tingling as a familiar presence approached from a distance: powerful footsteps, dark glare and all.

I opened my eyes, only to watch him sauntering over to where the three of us were clustered.

"Ailith," Soren murmured, leaning over me. His eyes flickered with concern.

"I'm fine," I told him, holding up a hand. "I'm just tired. Geez, do you people ever need to lie down?"

"No," the three of them responded simultaneously.

"Damn," I muttered under my breath.

I did realize, in the moment, that all of them were Gods.

"Why is Ailith on the ground? I thought I told you to make sure she never got injured," Soren growled.

Caspian stuttered. "I...I don't know what's wrong. S-she isn't injured, your majesty, she's just tired."

"Exactly," I added, sitting up in my spot and rolling my eyes. "Let's not get all dramatic, boys." I shot them all a cheesy grin.

"Are you sure?" Soren asked.

"I'm fine," I reassured him once more, standing on my wobbly, sore legs. "See? I was just taking a little rest. It's something we mortals do from time to time."

"I know, but...," Soren responded. "Ailith, I'm not sure combat is the best idea for you at this point in time."

I groaned. "What? Why? I just beat one hundred different warriors in combat. I'm kind of exhausted!"

Soren's eyes grew wider...angrier.

He turned to Caspian, his mouth trembling, his sharp jawbone locked. He looked like he was about to throw a punch himself.

"You let her fight?" he snarled.

Caspian's eyes widened. "I-I didn't think it was a problem. She just...s-she is really good, majesty"—

"I don't care if she could win fighting Zeus himself. She is not to be touched. By anyone. She is your future queen; my future wife. You can't be putting her and your soldiers up against one another for fun."

"Soren," I exclaimed. "It was not for fun. Caspian agreed to let me help him with training our army for the fight against Lord Goridian. I have knowledge of the opposition; of Goridian. I will make sure we have the best chances of winning against him."

"I don't care," he seethed. He took me by the arms. "If anything happens to you, I don't know what I would do. Honestly...I have not one clue, and I don't care to find out." He shot a dirty glance at Caspian.

"Enough," I gasped. "Caspian didn't do anything wrong. I wasn't hurt, and neither was anyone else."

"But you could have been," Soren responded, taking a few steps back, and then stepping back forward, almost in a pacing motion. "Caspian, I told you not to let her fight."

I felt a snarl festering in my throat. For the time being, I choked it down.

"You're too important to risk injury. You don't even understand what you're getting yourself into by agreeing to marry me," Soren said, somehow calm but seething beneath the surface. "You'll be my wife, Queen of the Land, mother to the future rulers of the Land. Do any of those titles mean anything to you?"

"Soren, I know exactly what I'm getting myself into," I told him. "But none of those titles are as important as my own title. The title of being who I am, fundamentally; of being a warrior of the Sea Kingdom. It's where I come from, and what matters most to me."

He smiled ever so slightly, reaching forward to graze a hand over my cheek-bone. "If only it were that simple."

Lazarus stepped between us. "Brother, I believe you're being too protective. Ailith can do as she pleases. She is a good warrior, and needs to be protected as a person, rather than an artifact to be hidden away in the palace."

I crossed my arms in front of my chest. "I second that."

"I don't care what any of you think," Soren grumbled. "Ailith, you're my fiancée. You will be Queen, and may do as you please—within obvious reason. Which means that I will protect you when protection is necessary, such as in this instance. Lazarus, you're my subject, and therefore, I can order you to leave. Same with you, Caspian. For the love of Mother Gaea; subjects should learn to obey their kings."

I turned to leave as well, but felt a tug on the back of my tunic.

"Not so fast, sea girl," Soren mumbled, a grin toying at his lips. "I didn't tell you to leave."

I hated that he could do that; tell me what to do and then smile, and brush it off as if it meant nothing.

"No, but I want to leave," I responded, removing his grasp from my shirt. "And you're right. Subjects should really learn to obey their kings. But you're not my king, and this is not my kingdom. I serve the Sea Kingdom, first and foremost, and Triton as my king. And, therefore, I must attend to some battle plans to ensure that I do exactly as I was asked, and save my kingdom, and my king. As his subject."

I was spitting the words at this point. I wanted nothing more than to tackle Soren to the ground and give him a run for his gold, but I knew that wouldn't solve anything.

So, with that, I walked away, my blood boiling.

AUTHOR'S NOTE:

Oooohhh...things are heating up between Soren and Ailith. Can any of you guess what's going to happen next? ;)

As always, thank you to everyone who has read, commented and voted! Y'all are the best.

If you enjoyed this chapter, don't forget to vote, and leave me a comment telling me your thoughts! Comments are my favorite! [Insert meme of Buddy the Elf saying 'smiling's my favorite!']

Until Monday...

Xoxo,

LK

Chapter 13

Cleo and Nela were waiting for me when I returned to my chambers, a ridiculous pile of flouncy gowns clutched in their arms. Their excitement could be sensed from the bottom of the floating staircase; however, when they saw my face as I entered my room, they both seemed to recede a bit.

"Do you have plans for tonight, mistress?" Nela asked hopefully.

I shook my head. "No need for one of your death traps tonight. Thanks, though."

I huffed in anger, muttering curses under my breath as I lay down on the freshly made bed. The blue-black nighttime was beginning to take over the orange sunset sky as they placed the gowns back in my closet and began lighting candles so the room wouldn't be completely devoid of light as it grew darker out.

I reached down to unlace my worn leather boots, but stopped mid-reach.

"Actually," I told the maids. "I'm going out for the night. On personal business. Both of you; take the night off. It's too nice an evening to waste tending me."

I could feel a wicked smile beginning to spread across my face at the same time a genius idea crossed my mind.

I was going to go exploring.

My maids left soon after I assured them I didn't need any help getting ready. I changed into a clean shirt, quickly brushed out my dark wavy locks, colored my pale lips and cheeks, and lined my seafoam-green eyes.

As I looked at myself in the mirror, I saw a woman I hadn't before.

My skin was a shade darker than usual—due to the time I now spent in the sun, my physique stronger than it had been in months, and the fear in my eyes seemingly diluted. It was incredible how one month out of Goridian's kingdom had impacted me. I actually appeared to be healthy, for once.

For a moment, I smiled at myself, thinking I might look nice. Pretty, even.

I laughed. Now I looked truly ludicrous.

I floated down the spiral tower staircase, then meandered down the main corridor of the palace, finding my way to a connecting hallway through a small wooden door.

The palace was so full of hallways and corridors that I could have gotten lost for a week in all the intertwining passageways.

The hallway was dark and dank, and, as I wandered, I was able to see flickering orange light at the other end of the tunnel, along with famil-iar laughing. There were several people behind that door...several people whose voices I recognized; however, I could not place them.

I stumbled down the rockily-paved ground and pressed my ear to the door, clasping a hand to my mouth as I realized who was there.

"I really can't believe you proposed after one day, Soren," a familiar saccharine female voice laughed teasingly. "You really are stupid."

"Don't taunt me, Juniper," Soren's dark voice snapped.

"He knows what he wants," Lazarus roared, before I heard a slapping noise, which I assumed to be Lazarus clapping Soren on the shoulder.

"The only problem," Soren responded, taking a pause, I could tell, to sip from a goblet, "is that she doesn't know what she wants. She's incredibly complex."

"Do you think she wants you?" Juniper enquired.

A pause. My stomach twisted.

"I don't know," Soren murmured. "It's so difficult being around her. She is wild and free, and I like that about her. But I can't seem to restrain myself when it comes to her safety. It's a curse, because I know that I will lose her if I cannot control myself."

I mouthed into the darkness, "You got that right, buddy."

"You can't take away who she really is, Sor," Lazarus's voice calmly stated. "She is a warrior, and if you try to strip her of that title, she will run."

"I know," he grumbled. "It's so difficult, though. Letting her roam around like a common warrior, when she really is so much more. Even though I know that's what she enjoys doing."

Lazarus cleared his throat. "Do you love her?"

Again, silence.

"Sor, if you're not sure you love this girl, then you can't be serious about marrying her," Juniper murmured.

"You're horribly impatient, Juniper," Soren scolded. "I think...I think I do love her. In fact, I think I love her very much."

I squeezed my hand closer to my mouth. I couldn't believe he'd just said that. I could feel my heartbeat all the way in my thumbs.

"She's close by," I heard Soren muttering.

"How do you know?"

"I can feel her heartbeat," he responded. "It's thumping like a goddamn drum."

Lazarus coughed uncomfortably. "I can feel her thoughts."

"What is she thinking?" Soren was quick to exclaim.

"Wow," Lazarus murmured...evidently a reaction to how I was thinking and feeling. I felt myself blushing in the darkness of the hallway.

He knew exactly what was going on in my head, and I didn't like it.

"What?" Juniper gasped.

Lazarus was silent for a few moments. I knew he was going to spill my guts out to both of them if I didn't stop it, so this was my chance.

With all my might, I swung my leg against the wooden door, sending it toppling over with a cloud of sawdust.

I stood in front of all of them, gaping at the normalcy of this exchange.

For some reason, I was expecting some cult-like gathering, but, instead, it simply appeared like three friends sharing supper. No mortal sacrifice or strange hooded robes.

I took a deep breath.

"Ailith," Soren whispered. He said my name like a spell.

"I don't appreciate being talked about behind my back," I muttered through my teeth. "And, Lazarus, I sure as hell hope you weren't about to tell these two my innermost feelings. Because, if I can fight Caspian, I can definitely fight you. And if you were going to do what I think you were going to do, then know that I can—and will—fight you. One word about it, and we'll have us a little chit-chat outside; you and me." I stared him down relentlessly, and he seemed to quiver.

I felt my breath thickening.

"There's no need for threats, Ailith," Juniper said, standing and placing two comforting hands on my shoulders as she led me to the table, pulling up a chair for me between hers and Soren's.

"My entire conscience was about to be explored by someone quite unwelcome. I was simply letting them know that they were unwelcome," I growled, glaring at Lazarus. He pretended not to notice.

"Why are you so defensive?" asked Juniper. "We're all here to help you through these emotional barriers, Ailith, but you need to open up to us."

"What are you talking about?" I exclaimed. "I didn't want all of you knowing exactly what I was thinking, that's all. No emotional barriers here." I cringed at the statement, knowing it wasn't true.

"I can feel your tenseness," Juniper murmured. "Could this have something to do with your recent engagement?"

Dammit. He'd told them.

I shook my head. "Don't analyze me." My words were so quiet, I wasn't sure if she even heard them.

She ignored my comment. "Because, everyone here knows about your almost being forced into marriage before, with Lord Goridian. And I can tell that's causing some difficulty for you. You should share your story with us. Let us help you."

Her voice was so silky-smooth. However, her words were jagged and harsh.

"I don't want to," I whispered.

"Why don't you have something to eat?" Soren murmured. He handed me a plate of roast beef and peas. I took it, nodding appreciatively. I set it down in front of me and played with the peas, blobbing them together in a shape with my fork.

There were a few moments of awkward quietness as we all sat there. Lazarus stood and picked up the broken door, nestling it against the stony wall. He then sat down, took a few sips of wine, and stayed silent.

"If you at least told us something—" Juniper said, breaking the peaceful silence.

I shook my head. "It's not the time or place, Juniper."

"Why not?" she seethed. "What happened between you and this man that you feel you must hide? Is there something we don't know; something horrible? Did he...did he ruin you, or something?"

I looked up at her, my eyes widening. I gulped.

"Juniper, leave," Soren growled. Suddenly, I felt a warm hand gently grazing mine. He took my clenched fist and unrolled it in his fingers, and I only realized then how tense I truly was.

Even though I'd wanted to rip Soren's throat out just that afternoon, I was now appreciative of his protectiveness.

However, Juniper seemed to have different sentiments.

"If she can't talk to the three of us—her closest allies—then I don't know how she'll ever manage to be your queen, and talk to the people of the Land," she hissed, gathering her long gown in her hands and moving towards the doorway, her shoes clacking against the stony tunnel until we heard the slam of a door.

"Thank you," I muttered, daring a glance at Soren. I almost flushed when I realized he'd been watching me the whole time.

He nodded, clearing his throat. He chose his words gently. "I've just received news, that I was waiting to tell only to you two," he said, leaning in. I looked over at Lazarus, who seemed significantly calmer now that his sister was gone.

"Is it Hades?" Laz asked.

Soren shook his head. "No, it's worse. Father is coming."

"Zeus?" I whispered.

I felt my hand being squeezed once more. I did not object to the touch.

"Yes," Soren responded. "He sent a message, saying he wishes to come to my court and congratulate us on our engagement."

"How did he find out?" I muttered.

Lazarus laughed. "He's known for seven hundred years, kid. He's just been eagerly waiting until now."

"Which, unfortunately, means he's going to be particularly flamboyant when he arrives," Soren grumbled.

I laughed. "You're kidding, right? More flamboyant than he was the first night I was here, on Summer Solstice? You do remember that entrance he made, don't you, and the exit; with the purple tornado? That seemed just about as flamboyant as it gets to me."

A grin played at Soren's lips. "You don't know Zeus, my dear."

I let out a sharp exhale. My dear.

A few moments of quiet passed.

"Well, I'm going to let you two lovebirds have some alone time," Lazarus snickered, picking up his wine goblet and sauntering over to the broken-down entrance of the room. We heard him chuckling all the way down the echoey tunnel, before the door on the other side closed gently.

Soren gripped my hand again. "Finally," he joked. "I was wondering when those two idiots were going to leave."

I stared down at my plate, trying not to smile.

"Really?" he murmured playfully. "Not a single witticism or insult tonight? Is there something terribly wrong with you?"

I laughed. "I'm sort of tired."

"I heard you fought off one hundred warriors in your kingdom's name today," he murmured, leaning forward to brush a stray lock of hair from my face.

I looked up at him. "You're not still mad about that?"

"Oh, I was never mad about that," he responded, standing and grabbing the bottle of wine from across the table. "I was mad at Caspian for letting you do that."

I rolled my eyes. "You know you don't have to worry about me, right?"

"Ailith, that's like telling my father not to practice polygamy," he explained, pouring himself more wine. "The chances of both happening are impossible. But, I do suppose I owe you an apology. I acted like an ass today. And I'm sorry."

A smile flickered on my face. I gazed at him softly. The only sign of forgiveness I could muster.

"I want you to know," I told him, sitting up in my chair and cutting the roast beef that was beginning to get cold on my plate, "that I will tell you about what happened with Goridian. Just not...not yet. Not today."

"Take the time in the world, if you'd like," he responded. "In fact, I've got more time than you could even fathom. Time is meaningless to someone like me."

Someone immortal.

"It's funny you say that, when you're kind of in a hurry to rush this marriage," I remarked, popping a bite of food in my mouth. As I began to eat, I realized how hungry I truly was.

"I only rush because I have to," he explained. "Not because I want to."

"I'm just going to stop talking about the engagement for now," I informed him. "I'm too tired, and, unlike you, my days are limited. So I'm going to end this one on a calm note."

He chuckled. "You're just so—so..."

"Nonsensical?"

"Not what I was thinking, but perhaps."

"Pale?"

"You've grown tanner while being on Land."

"Stubborn?"

"True, but not what I was thinking of." His grin only grew.

I smirked. "Majestic warrior to beat all?"

"I was going to say young," he murmured, adding, "but those things aren't entirely untrue, either."

I glared. "Is it my turn to call you old now?"

"My, my my—I think it might be."

We both turned from our locked gaze, feeling our stares drawn to the entrance of the room. My stomach turned at the same time Soren stood, facing the enormous man standing in the doorway.

"Father," he breathed.

AUTHOR'S NOTE:

Well wasn't this chapter just scrummy? [If you get this reference, then I love you forever] [It's the Great British Baking Show]

Uh-oh...Zeus is in the house!!! What do y'all think is going to happen next? ;)

I can promise you this: there will be drama, there will be insults...and there will be ALL THE FEELS. [Sorry guys, my brain is kind of shot right now]

As always, thank you to everyone who reads, votes, and comments. Especially to you special people who vote and comment. Thank you, thank you, thank you!!!

And if you enjoyed what you read this time around, don't forget to vote/comment, if you want to!

Until Friday...

Ta-ta, my steadfast acolytes!

Xoxo,

LK

Chapter 14

- -

THREE WARNINGS BEFORE YOU READ THIS CHAPTER:

WARNING #1: This chapter is a bit longer than usual. So sorry for the extra time it will take to read.

WARNING #2: You might experience "the feels" while reading this chapter. Don't say I didn't warn you.

WARNING #3: The song I pasted is the I imagine one Soren and Ailith dance to. I'm an orchestra nerd, so this was a hard decision! If you listen to it, you won't regret it :)

OKAY--let's get into this!

"My son," Zeus responded, a grin appearing on his face, turning to face me. "Oh...I remember you. The little sea warrior. Gods and Goddesses, you look so much better now than you did before. Now tell me, son, how long have you been married? Is she pregnant yet? I want the details. You know better than anyone that I'm quite the romantic at heart. Tell me the whole story."

His grin widened as he seated himself across from me, swinging his legs up onto the table, crossing them at the ankles and grabbing Soren's wine goblet.

"Actually," Soren responded, through his teeth. "We're not married yet."

Zeus's face molded into a scowl. "Oh. Well...no, no, no; that just won't do. Poor Poseidon won't be happy about this at all. Soren, I thought you'd be handling this much better than you are," he said, eyebrows furrowed, turning to me. "I'm sorry, sea girl, but you and my son are going to have to marry tonight."

"What?!" I exclaimed. "The prophecy states that we must marry before the first snowfall of winter. Doesn't it?"

I turned to Soren.

Relieving me of my immediate stress, he nodded. "Yes. Stop trying to mess with us, father, because it won't work.'

"Aw, you're really no fun. And I find it humorous how you call me 'father'," Zeus remarked. "You're soon going to be so much more powerful than I, yet you still address me like I am your superior."

"What do you mean he's going to become more powerful?" I asked.

Zeus's gaze turned to me, and he grinned.

"You didn't tell her?"

Soren shook his head. He looked sick.

"Once we marry," Soren explained, gulping down nerves, "I will take my father's place as King of Kings. I will inherit all of the power I was ever meant to have. There are still some skills that have yet to be unlocked, as I am unwed."

I raised a brow. "Wait...what does marriage have to do with unlocking extra power?"

"It brings on the prospect of an heir," he responded matter-of-factly, and I felt my eyes widening. "Which—which will unlock my full potential."

I hadn't even thought about that. I mean, I had, but never seriously. I felt myself wincing and flushing at the same time.

"In the distant future," he added, to which I felt a bit relieved.

Zeus chuckled. "You know, when I first met Hera, my first wife, and your mother, Soren, we conceived you the very day we met."

Soren cringed. "Thank you for letting me know, father."

"What can I say? We're both people of passion. That's why I've had to take many other lovers in my lifetime, as you know." Zeus sighed, sipping out of his wine goblet.

"Can we please stop dallying with the revolting details of your polygamous habits and skip to the part where you explain why you're here?" Soren growled.

Zeus smacked his lips. "You really are protective, son. I see the way you clutch her hand, like she might be snatched away if you don't. Now, I really am happy for the pair of you. Most arranged marriages don't work out so swimmingly. I'm just here to oversee the wedding, and to see the dynamic between my son and his mortal lover, throw you an engagement party and be on my way."

Soren glared at his father. "I didn't invite you."

Zeus bended back, roaring with laughter. "My son, I would have still come if you had uninvited me."

He then stood, taking the bottle of wine, and sauntered down the tunnel. Soren and I sat in silence, waiting to hear the door close.

"He's absolutely mad," Soren muttered, as soon as we knew he was gone. "Don't listen to him."

"Then who do I listen to?" I enquired.

Soren almost grinned. "That's a question you're going to have to answer for yourself."

~

Layers of black satin folded out from my waist, which was cinched so tightly I could barely breathe. My arms were luckily freed, as the gown was sleeveless, but I did, more or less, feel like I was in my wedding gown again.

Luckily for me, this gown was black; my favorite color. When Nela and Cleo had asked what color gown I wanted, I told them I wouldn't attend the ball if the dress was anything but black.

I was fortunate they had listened.

After arriving the previous day, Zeus had insisted on throwing Soren and me an engagement ball, which meant a thorough amount of my personal humiliation was in store. I was sure, as I heard a knock at my door, that this was going to be embarrassing.

"That must be Lazarus," I muttered, pulling away from Cleo and Nela as they put the finishing details on my face. My hair was pulled back a bit, and curled as it cascaded down my back, blending in with the dark-colored dress. My eyes were lined with kohl, my lips plumped and colored and glossed, and my hair sprinkled with glitter— fake glitter.

My flesh was not glittering naturally that day, which I was quite thankful for.

I opened the door to my chambers, and grinned as I saw my favorite redhead standing at my doorstep, waiting to escort me to the ballroom. He wore a black and white suit, and his hair was brushed back with product.

"Hi, cherry head," I greeted him. "You're looking spiffy, as always."

He laughed quietly. "You look stunning, Ailith."

I blushed a little, not expecting the upfront compliment. "Thank you."

"Shall we go?"

I nodded. "We shall."

Lazarus walked me to the throne room, which was adorned with wildflowers painted gold, intertwined with seashells painted aquamarine blue--obviously to represent the union of the Land and the Sea through this marriage.

"Hold in your squeals, sea girl," Lazarus joked as he opened the doors for me. "Zeus throws a hell of a party."

As we stepped into the room, I gasped. "I'll say."

Hundreds of people flounced down the marble-floored throne room, women dressed in dresses made of clouds of tulle and chiffon; men dressed in sharp uniforms adorned in respective medals and pins; swords sheathed at their sides.

Long tables stretched down the huge length of the room, holding silver platters piled high with roast chicken stuffed with chestnuts, steaming rolls and huge bowls of blood-red fruit punch.

Large ribbons of blue and gold stretched from one side of the room to the other, creating an array of color overhead. A small orchestra played lively dancing music at the front of the room, in one of the corners, and in the center of the other side of the room were the thrones, and seated on the tallest was Soren.

I could tell Lazarus had brought me through the entrance at the opposite side of the room for a reason. As I entered, people seemed to begin staring at me. My cheeks heated up as the guests grew silent, either curtsying or bowing as I stepped in. As I walked, Lazarus at my side, the people moved out from the middle of the throne room, stepping to either of my sides, forming a walkway in the middle of the room.

I realized, at that moment, that I was supposed to walk all the way across the room, to where Soren sat on his throne.

My heart began to rush, and I felt my mouth go dry as people watched me take one small step after the other.

It almost was like an aisle.

I gulped.

"Don't worry," Lazarus whispered, close enough that no one but me would hear him. "Remember, this isn't your wedding."

I took a deep breath, feeling the tenseness in my shoulders.

"Just keep walking," he urged me. "And try not to look as if you're about to be sick."

I loosened up a bit at his encouragement, and continued across the throne room, eventually making it all the way across, to where Soren was standing, his hand outstretched, anticipating my touch.

"Hello." His greeting was informal, and polite.

"Hi," I responded.

"You seem a bit out of your element," he commented.

I felt my face flush an even darker shade of crimson. "I am."

He pulled me towards him, his dark eyes trailing over me. "Well you look ravishing, if I do say so myself."

I scoffed. "You're such a flirt."

He shrugged. "What can I say?" he grinned, before leaning forward and whispering in my ear. "You really do look lovely, Ailith."

He stepped back as we were approached by a familiar enormous figure, a snide grin printed shamelessly upon his face.

"Well if it isn't the Land Kingdom's most beautiful couple?" Zeus remarked as the musicians began playing a lively waltz. "Is this not the most beautiful, aesthetically satisfying engagement party a father—and father in law—could throw you?"

I felt Soren's hand between my shoulder blades.

"Thank you for your generosity," Soren responded coldly.

"The idea of the golden wildflowers and the blue seashells joined really is creative," I added, trying to lighten the mood and deliver an insult at once. "I wouldn't have guessed the King of Many Wives would have the time to think up something so original."

With that, I felt Soren's hand pulling at my waist as Zeus bent backwards, roaring in laughter.

"Well, she is feisty," he said, his face bit red as he coughed through a few last laughs. "I take it you're not open to the idea of an open marriage?"

"No, I'm not," I responded, my tone calm and serious. "And neither is Soren. We plan on living up to a set of morals, which I know could be a foreign concept to you."

"Oh, completely foreign," Zeus responded, apparently not at all offended by my comments. "Soren, as much as I'd love to stand here and listen to your bride's opinions of me, I think she would much prefer sharing a dance with you, as she does seem to prefer your company over mine. I'll have the musicians play something special."

"That's a good idea," Soren said through his teeth. He took me by the arm and pulled me across the room, into the middle of where people were dancing. Couples moved out of the way as we passed, finding a spot in the middle of the room.

A slow, minor-keyed song began softly drifting through the throne room, and Soren took my hands, placing them on his shoulders.

"This is how Land people dance," he murmured, placing two hands at my waist.

I laughed. "It's how people of the Sea Kingdom dance, too."

"Oh." A smile played at his lips.

"I'm sorry about how snide I was around your father," I murmured. "Something about him just...gets to me."

"That's the point, Ailith," he responded. "He's trying to make you feel insecure about me."

"Should I?" I asked as he spun me slowly, his touch as delicate as a feather. People were beginning to watch us, and Soren's voice was growing quieter and quieter.

"No," he responded gruffly. "We have to trust each other, if this is going to work. And you can trust me."

He looked around, as did I, and we realized all eyes were on us. Soren stopped speaking, and pulled me closer to him, so that we were lightly touching. I could feel the embroidered fabric of his jacket underneath my cold, nervous hands.

His breath was so close to my ear that I heard every time he breathed, and as we danced, I could feel his inhaling growing a bit shallower and his exhales a bit less calculated; a bit more rugged and raspy.

My heart was beating quicker by the minute as I felt his fingers pressed into my waist, his forearms lightly brushing my elbows; my hands clasped behind his neck.

My breathing seemed to quicken with my heartbeat, and I bit my tongue, my entire body seemed to go taut at the hundreds of people watching this intense moment.

Soren leaned in close to speak, his whisper tickling my earlobe.

"It's okay, Ailith. I feel it too," he breathed.

I didn't respond.

We finished dancing a few minutes later, even though when we were released from the dance, our fingers seem to linger upon one another.

I didn't know what was going on within me, but I felt my legs moving me towards the door as Soren was swallowed up by the crowds of people. When I looked back for a few moments to make sure he wouldn't notice my freakout, I bumped into someone familiar.

"Excuse me," I muttered.

"Ailith?"

The voice was warm and sweet. I felt dread simmering within me.

Slowly, I peered up, and was both surprised and a bit nervous to realize it was Juniper who stood there. She was dressed in a heavenly white gown that flowed to the floor in a few simple but stunning satin layers. However, it wasn't the fabric of the dress that was so shocking. It was, in fact, the fact that the dress was insanely low-cut, exposing her chest on almost full display to the entire ballroom. I felt a bit dizzy.

"It's nice to see you," she said, her big smiled seeming forced.

"You as well," I responded, beginning to step away, but feeling her hand on my forearm.

"Wait, Ailith," she murmured. "Are you alright? Is everything okay?"

I nodded, forcing a small smile. "Of course. I'm just going to ask a servant to retrieve me some seawater. I can't drink freshwater."

She nodded, buying my made-up excuse, and I dashed for the exit before anyone else could think to watch me.

I felt my legs moving quicker and quicker, down the corridor, and through the main entrance of the castle. The warm late summer air greeted me as soon as I stepped outside, as did the nighttime sky, stars blocked by layers of fog.

I walked through the fields of wildflowers and grass, moving away from the palace, keeping my huge skirts lifted with my hands as I ran in the direction of the sea. I knew I couldn't get too close, but I needed to see it; to be able to feel its presence. It was the only thing I thought would comfort me.

I approached a small cliff that looked out over the ocean, its waves clapping against the rocks below and sending familiar white spray into the air. I sat upon the cliff, watching the peaceful movement of the water.

"Ailith."

I turned, and saw Soren standing a few feet behind me, a bit out of breath.

"Did you follow me?" I gasped.

He nodded. "I saw you leave."

I bit my lip. "I'm sorry."

He didn't respond, but rather took a few steps forward, taking a seat next to me. We both looked out beyond the small cliff; at the daunting black sea beneath.

"It's okay...it's okay to feel," he murmured.

Slowly, I nodded my head. "I know, Soren. It's hard for me; that's all."

"Why?" he asked. The question was neither forced nor careless. I could tell, with all that was in me, that he was genuinely curious.

"Because of where I come from," I mutter. "Because...because of him. What he did to me."

"Goridian?"

I nodded, letting a sob catch in my throat.

After a few moments of silence, he spoke softly, his voice as effortless as one of the waves in the ocean.

"Tell me."

I took a deep breath, staring out at the blurry moon in the sky; barely visible through the thick fog overhead.

"It all started with a trident."

AUTHOR'S NOTE:

OKAY. THAT DANCE THOUGH.

AND ALSO JUNIPER...?

I hope you guys enjoyed this chapter as much as I enjoyed writing it. If you did, please don't forget to vote and leave me a comment telling me your thoughts down below.

Thanks everyone!

Until Monday...

Xoxo,

LK

Chapter 15

WARNING: There are some sensitive subjects mentioned in this chapter.

"Before Goridian arrived in the Sea Kingdom, it was a beautiful, peaceful place. No one ever left, and no one ever came from the outside. I was raised by my parents; a pair of Triton's sea warriors. I was the youngest of five sisters. Although my parents were trained to fight, their skills were never required, and they were free to pursue their real interests in the meantime. As long as Triton had possession of his trident, his power couldn't be taken away from him."

"I take it the trident got taken away?" Soren murmured.

I nodded. "I'm getting there. Anyway, when I was a very small child, Lord Goridian arrived in the Sea Kingdom willing to serve Triton, in his army. He surrendered to Triton, took an oath of loyalty, and even fought for him. He was considered an honorable warrior for many years."

"One day, Triton's trident went missing. No one knew what happened. One minute it was there, and the next it was lost. I was nine years old at the time. Lord Goridian overthrew Triton and his government in a matter of days, after a short and easily won war against Triton's loyal army.

He was a God, and the mortal warriors couldn't defeat him. He soon sat atop Triton's throne. The adults of the kingdom knew he was a traitor, but young children, such as myself, didn't realize it. My parents had been training me and my sisters in combat since we were old enough to stand upright. They always assumed we would continue their legacy of fighting for King Triton, but once he was overthrown, they stopped. One day, they were telling us to hit harder; to jump higher, and the next they just let us play with toys, like normal children. It was strange, but but we were young; we didn't question it."

"One day my parents mysteriously disappeared. They were known for being loyal to Triton. Many others like them disappeared too, and, well... none of them ever returned. My sisters and I were taken in by an orphanage meant to train the children of the kingdom as warriors, to one day serve Lord Goridian, in his army. We were told our parents had just moved away temporarily, and that they would come back if we put everything we had into becoming warriors. It sounded, to me, like something my parents would have wanted—after all, they had always told me I was meant to be a warrior in Triton's army. None of us knew the difference between fighting for Triton and fighting for Goridian."

"Most of the other children hadn't been trained on a daily basis as I had, and, as soon as the instructors realized I was excelling at a much higher rate than the other children my age, I was separated from all the others, and put into private training," I said, taking a few moments to breathe. You can say his name, I told myself.

"At the age of ten, I began training one-on-one with Goridian. He introduced himself to me as a teacher...a friend. I believed him, of course. He was kind to me. He complimented me; told me I was gong to be the best warrior in his army when I grew up. He trained me, every day, for two years. I began to like him. In fact, I viewed him as a replacement for my parents;

as an older brother, or uncle. Someone I could trust. People blamed him for being evil, and I defended him."

"By the age of twelve, I was known as the warrior whom would lead Goridian's army for the entirety of my mortal life. Then, one day, Goridian stopped showing up for training. And he didn't show up the next day, or the day after that. Eventually, I realized he wasn't coming back. He left me—just as my parents had: in the blink of an eye, without an explanation or warning. I felt betrayed, and so I turned, as any angry adolescent probably would have, to Goridian's sworn enemy: Triton."

"At first, I thought I was going to hate Triton. We were taught to view him as this blood-sucking, fish-eating wizard of the sea. None of us could remember that life under his rule had been better, and freer, than it was under Goridian's. We were too young to remember it at all. I found Triton in a small cottage, where he dwelled alone, forever in hiding from Lord Goridian. I told him of Goridian's betrayal, and he offered to train me until I was eighteen years old, in exchange for my loyalty."

"In a fortunate fit of hormones and anger, I agreed—and it was probably the best decision I made in my adolescent years. Fortunately, Triton was someone I could truly trust. He not only trained me in combat, but in knowledge. He taught me to read; to write...he educated me in the history of our world, in the Land and its dialects. I learned everything other than fighting, and I loved it. For once in my life, people around me weren't valuing me for my skills in combat. It was a wonderful, secretive few years. Triton was my second father; the one who truly brought me up and showed me how blind I had originally been to Goridian's manipulation."

"It was sad that my education by Triton didn't go unnoticed for the entire six years. On my fifteenth birthday, unbeknown to me, Goridian followed me to Triton's dwelling, where he watched us and grew jealous of my loyalty. However, he knew it was too late to try and earn my loyalty back, so he decided to try and force it back."

"He started speaking to me again. I was wary of his flattery, knowing that he was a master manipulator. However, when he ordered me to come and live at his palace (which, he said, was supposed to be an honor), I couldn't refuse him. It would have landed me in a lot more trouble than it was worth. So, I promised Triton I would sneak out of the palace at nighttime, and come see him then. It worked...for a time."

"Ailith," Soren told me, reaching forward to take my hand. "You don't have to continue, if you don't want to."

I shook my head. "I need to put everything out there. And I think you deserve to know, if you're going to marry me."

"Very well," he murmured.

"I continued nighttime training with Triton for a year, and about two months after I turned sixteen, I was in his cottage, studying the geography of the Land, when I heard knocking at his door. Triton told me to hide, and so I hid in the closet where he stored grain. I heard the door being knocked down, and Goridian found me not a minute later in the storage closet. He asked me, politely, to return to the palace. I wasn't sure why he was treating it so nonchalantly, but I agreed."

"Goridian demanded that I end my training with Triton. And for a time, I agreed. I assumed I would go back eventually, once Goridian forgot the events of that night. I anticipated that he would lock my doors at night for a few months, and eventually forgot to one night, and let it go. I was right, about him locking my doors. However, I was wrong about him forgetting. He still acted casually towards me, yet every night I heard him lingering at my door, before he locked it. It was torture, not being able to see Triton. He and I were like a father and daughter, and he meant more to me than anything else in the world. But Goridian kept me locked up; separated from visiting Triton and my sisters. He forced me to work in the kitchens and the fields during the day, and wouldn't let me eat. He starved me to keep me weak, and he controlled me, every moment of every day."

I took a deep breath. Just breathe, Ailith. You need to say this.

"One night...," I said, my gaze meeting Soren's. "One night, after a few months, the door to my bedroom wasn't locked. Goridian opened it, and came inside. He asked me if I would marry him. I said I wouldn't, and he asked why. He told me that if I married him, I wouldn't have to work any longer, and that he would stop starving me. And I told him that I would rather starve to death than marry him. That made him angry. Really angry. He told me that he didn't need my permission to marry him, and that he would kill me if I tried to flee the castle. He then...he...he forced himself on me." I blinked back little droplets of moisture, but they still snuck out of my eyelids.

"I tried to fight him, but he used magic to make sure I couldn't move. He anticipated everything," I breathed, a sob catching in my throat. "That night, he gave me this." I held up my arm, where a white scar could be easily noticed in the milky moonlight: a bite mark on my forearm, where Goridian had sunk his teeth. Soren took my arm without saying a word, and gently examined the scar.

"I never told anyone," I added, before going silent, wiping away tears.

Soren sat there, in silence, running his fingers over the scar, his gaze fixated on the white mark.

He looked up at me, his stare both apologetic and burning with rage, before he spoke words that made my very spine tingle.

"I vow to the Gods and Goddesses—I will kill him."

I took a deep breath, letting my shoulders loosen. Soren reached forward to take one of my clenched fists and unravel my fingers, his touch gently running against my palm. I sighed.

"I'm sorry," he murmured, his voice silky and smooth. "I don't really know what to say to you."

"Makes sense." I afforded him a close-mouthed smile.

"I suppose there's a fair amount of realization within me," he admitted, pausing for a moment, before adding, "but not enough to overtake the overwhelming sense of anger. Goridian should be eternally grateful he isn't here right now."

I laughed. "I'll say."

"I understand now," he whispered. "Why you want to reclaim your kingdom. It's not just for your people. It's personal."

I nodded. "Exactly."

"It makes sense, why you're hesitant to marry me," Soren said, tracing a line up my forearm. "How could you trust another man, after Goridian betrayed you in so many fundamental ways?"

"But that's what doesn't make sense," I told him. "Goridian was a monster. But you're different."

He chuckled softly. "Different, hm?"

I nodded. "But, I still find myself with doubts."

"Understandably," he added. "And please know that I would—never—even fathom behaving in such an animalistic, disgusting manner."

"I know, Soren," I murmured.

"Good," he responded, his fingers tickling my elbow. "You should be married to someone who respects you. Someone who can love you without trying to control you. I can try my best to do that—although I can't promise I won't be in some form of disarray whenever you decide to fight the man in charge of my army."

I smiled. "I only did that once."

"Well, I hope you won't attempt it again," he responded. I wanted to roll my eyes, but noticed a grin trying not to creep its way onto his face.

"I won't...for now," I told him.

We sat for a few minutes, listening to the sound of the water climbing the rocks, and then receding again.

"I think you should know something," Soren said, moving closer, his dark grey eyes boring into mine.

"What?" I breathed.

There were a few moments of silence before he spoke, his voice deliberate and calm.

"Do you remember when I told you that I feel an adherence to you that I'd never felt to anyone else before in my life?" he asked.

I nodded. "Yes."

"Well, I want to reiterate that I do have a certain sense of...uncanny protectiveness."

I couldn't help from smiling. "That's not obvious at all."

He reached out to run a gentle hand through my hair, his fingertips stroking my scalp. I closed my eyes, shivering at his touch...wanting more.

"Hey, Soren, what's going on, dude?!"

A familiar voice, perhaps a bit squeakier than usual, called from just a few feet away. I rolled my eyes and quickly pulled away from Soren's grasp, peering up to see a wobbly-legged Lazarus sauntering our way, a wine bottle clutched in his left hand.

"Are you drunk?" Soren exclaimed, scrambling to his feet and pulling me up with him,.

Lazarus shrugged sloppily. "Probably."

"Great timing, brother," Soren muttered under his breath. His hand slipped over mine and he pulled me towards where Lazarus seemed to be teetering back and forth on his feet.

"What were you two talking about?" Lazarus joked, his words slurring together. I held back a laugh.

"Nothing," Soren responded, letting his brother slip a hand over his shoulder.

"Let's go back to the palace," Lazarus muttered.

"Good idea," Soren responded. "Why did you wander out of the ballroom, Lazarus?"

"Dad told me to come find you two," Lazarus responded, a sly smile creeping upon his face as he pointed to the two of us.

"Great," Soren whispered.

"I don't know, I kind of like you drunk," I joked, tapping Lazarus on the nose and snatching away his wine bottle.

I took a swig and then handed it to Soren, who did the same. Lazarus began to mutter under his breath, and he was nearly asleep on his brother's shoulder by the time we made it back to the palace.

As soon as we entered, Zeus was standing right in front of us. His frame was barely taller than Soren's, but towered over mine by several feet. I felt my heart catching in my throat for a second.

"Soren," he said, clapping his hand on his son's shoulder. He shoved Lazarus out of the way, sending him flying onto the floor.

"What did you need?" Soren growled.

"Well, first of all—it is kind of rude to leave your own engagement party," Zeus told us, sending me a wink. I felt Soren's grasp tighten on my wrist.

"What do you need?" Soren mumbled again, speaking through gritted teeth.

"Well, there was something I needed to ask you," Zeus responded, taking the bottle of wine from my right hand and sipping from it. "I have just received word that there is conflict, in the mountains. A revolt of peasants, who have pledged loyalty to Hades and his arm...against me and mine. I need to go and show them who their real king is."

"And you want me to come with you?" Soren guessed.

Zeus nodded. "Precisely. Rally your armies, son. We have a less-powerful God to overpower." A grin began to spread upon his face.

Soren nodded. "We'll leave tomorrow, at dawn."

Zeus pointed at me. "You coming with, sea girl? You're a warrior, right?"

I shrugged. "I don't see why not," I said, feeling an evil smile creeping its way onto my face. "I could use a good, old-fashioned skull-smashing. Let's do this, boys."

AUTHOR'S NOTE:

Okay, so that was a lot.

How do you guys think Soren will react to Ailith wanting to go fight in the mountains with them? Hmm....

ALSO. THAT MOMENT THOUGH. WHERE HE STROKED HER HAIR. GAHHHH.

I hope you guys enjoyed this chapter, and if you did, please don't forget to vote and comment!

Thanks to everyone who reads and supports, as always!

I would like to dedicate this chapter to @LightAva01 for the awesome "Wattpad party" and the super cool banners in celebration of Heiress of the Sea making the top 100 rankings on Saturday. Thank you so much!!!

Also, a huge shoutout to @AlyDevinator for volunteering to bring booze to that party :) AND for being a cheerleader for me since Chapter 1. I really appreciate it.

And one last announcement--since school is starting up for me again, I won't be able to post during the mornings anymore, so please don't be disappointed when you don't find my updates on Mondays and Fridays until a little later (since I will have to upload them after school, in the afternoon).

Sorry for this huge author's note.

Au revoir, my unwavering grasshoppers!

Xoxo,

GOSSIP GIRL (jk it's LK)

Chapter 16

S oren's gaze immediately switched from Zeus to me. "No."

"Come on," I groaned. "I can defend myself. I successfully combatted one hundred of the men in your army. Surely I can fight off some peasants."

"Let her come along, son. Once she gets this out of her system, she'll be fine hanging low for all the other fights, in the future," Zeus said.

I furrowed a brow.

"No, she won't," Soren responded, eyeing me quickly, before turning back to his father. "If she comes with us, she could get hurt, or worse. She is only mortal, and so young."

"I'm old enough that I can keep myself safe in a fight. I'm just as good at fighting as one of your men, if not better. You could use my help," I told Soren. "Your father is okay with it. If he thought I was going to die, I don't see why he would let me come. He wants the prophecy fulfilled just as much as you do."

Soren nodded, sighing gruffly. "May I speak to you privately for a moment?"

He grabbed me by the wrist, and pulled me a few yards away from Zeus, and out of the palace, where he spoke in a hiss-whisper.

"What are you thinking?" he exclaimed.

"I want to come help you and your father. I don't understand why you're so against that," I responded, crossing my arms in front of my chest.

"Because you could get hurt. You don't know what to expect form this revolt—I don't even know what to expect."

"Exactly," I replied. "So you need all the help you can get."

"Not from you, Ailith," he gasped.

I narrowed my gaze. "Oh really?"

"You matter more to me than anything else," he said. "If anything happened to you, I would never forgive myself."

"If anything happens to me, it'll be on me. Not you. Now, you can take me with you, or I can just follow you. And if you try to lock me in my chambers, I swear to the Gods and Goddesses"—

"I won't do that," he interrupted, shifting his weight from one foot to the other. "I just...I wish you weren't so stubborn."

"Are you saying I can come?" I asked.

He nodded. "Yes. But under one condition."

"Yes?"

"You have to stick with me," he said, gruffly adding, "the whole time."

I sighed. "You won't regret this."

"I'm sure I will," he muttered as I sauntered back into the palace.

~

The early morning sky was a color combination of hazy blue and iridescent orange. The moon was barely visible through the fog looming around the horizon, dancing on the surface of the sea.

I awoke naturally, my heart seeming to ricochet off the sides of my ribcage as I smiled and dressed. My cheek glowed that morning, sparkling from where I had been kissed. I pulled my hair into a long braid that hung over my shoulder limply, and found a fur coat in my wardrobe that I slung over my shoulders. Its heavy weight draped over me, but I knew it would keep me warm in the day's journey.

I floated down the spiral staircase, and was met by a newly sober Lazarus. His auburn hair was tousled and messy, and his face pale. He rubbed at his temple as I approached, letting out a pained moan.

"Hey, pumpkin-head," I greeted him, with a smile.

"Hey, seashells. Oh, I see I was too late last night to save you from whatever happened to your cheek," he responded, his voice cracking.

"How are you feeling?" I responded, ignoring his comment.

"Hung over. Obviously," he grumbled in response, looping his arm around mine as he pulled me away from the staircase and into the main corridor of the palace.

We approached the entrance of the palace, where we were greeted by a cool late summer breeze.

Soren and Zeus stood at the entrance, waiting for us. They were also dressed in long fur cloaks. I knew that we would be venturing up into the mountains, where it was snowy year-round.

Soren meandered over to me, smirking as he ran a finger over the sparkle on my cheek.

"Wonder where that came from," he mumbled playfully, before changing the subject. "Ailith, have you ever ridden a horse before?"

I shook my head.

"Well, you're going to have to today," he muttered. "It isn't difficult. If you want, you could just come with me."

"I'm sure I can figure it out," I responded as Zeus wandered over, leading a black horse by the reins. He grinned.

"I see you've embraced the idea of being shiny all the time," Zeus remarked.

I pretended not to hear, and asked, "How do I mount this beast?"

"Put your foot here," Soren instructed, guiding my leg to one of the stirrups. "And, um, swing your other leg around, and sit in the saddle."

"Oh," I exclaimed. "We do this with dolphins in the Sea Kingdom."

I quickly stepped into the stirrup and sat in the saddle, reins in hand.

"So you are familiar with this?" Zeus asked.

I nodded. "Somewhat."

"Good. That means you won't be slowing us down," he muttered, wandering off to his own horse, which was bigger than mine, and snow-white.

"Follow me," Soren said, squeezing my left hand before wandering off and mounting a chestnut stallion.

Lazarus followed behind us, mumbling and groaning the whole time.

Members of Soren's army seemed to appear out of nowhere, all on horseback and fully armed, ready for battle. Most of these warriors I'd never seen before in my life, except for one familiar face.

"Caspian!" I exclaimed, waving my arm enthusiastically.

He flashed his trademark smirk before snapping the reins of his horse and trotting over to me, his grin growing bigger and bigger.

"I see you're still glittering," he remarked.

"And I see you're still smirking," I responded. "Are you here to help with the retaliation against Zeus?"

"Against Zeus? Sea girl, people aren't worried about Zeus. He's old enough to retire at this point. It's his son they're worried about. The one who made your face all shiny," he seemed to hold in a giggle at the end of his explanation.

"Why do they fear him?" I asked, ignoring his silliness.

"Because," Caspian replied, leaning close to me so he could whisper. "Soren is rumored to be more powerful than his father. No God has ever been more powerful than Zeus. Soren could very well be the single most powerful being to ever grace this world. This universe, even."

I tried to hold in a laugh. "I haven't seen any of this power myself."

"Oh, but you will," Caspian responded, his voice now deadly serious. "I'm surprised he has allowed you to tag along on this little skirmish hunt. I almost want to bash him over the head for it."

"You're just jealous that I was able to beat you in a fight," I teased.

"You're clever, but you're not strong. I hope we can both agree on that," Caspian said. "Don't wander off today. Stick to one of us, and don't fight anyone you aren't sure you can beat. Seriously, Ailith. Soren will be quick to blame—and punish—the closest one of us you're standing next to when you die, if you die."

"You think I'm going to die?" I exclaimed.

He shook his head. "Probably not," he said, his lips curling up before he added, "but there's always a chance."

I reached over to elbow him in the shoulder and then heard Zeus's voice in the distance, beckoning all of the soldiers.

"We have to go," said Caspian, snapping his reins.

I did the same, and off we went.

We ventured down the long fields of grass and wildflowers surrounding the palace, riding adjacent to the looming sea nearby. Fog was beginning to envelop us as it drifted onto land, and it was hard to keep track of where everyone was.

I rode beside Soren, in front of Caspian and behind Lazarus. They had me surrounded, and, as much as I hated it, I would admit that it provided a sense of comfort that, if anything happened to pop out of the fog at any given moment, I would be well backed up.

We soon passed the fields of grass and reached a rocky path with a steep incline. We began traveling at a slower pace, to make sure the horses wouldn't be tired out.

"We're going to be at a higher altitude," Soren told me as we climbed. "If you feel lightheaded, tell me."

I nodded, but didn't say anything.

"Is everything alright, my dear?" he asked.

There it was again. Those bloody words. My dear.

"Everything's perfectly fine," I responded, choking a bit on the words as my face began to flush. However, he didn't seem to notice.

We travelled up and down gray mountains surrounded by swirling fog for the better part of an entire day. The mountains were desolate and covered in snow; twiggy trees surrounding us; bare of any leaves. With the surrounding fog, the atmosphere was bleak and icy.

I shivered as a chilly breeze swept past us.

"Slow down!" I heard Zeus call from ahead.

I could only hear him, but because the fog was so thick, had no idea where he was in front of me. The only person I could see was Soren right beside me, his eyes carefully watching me at all times.

"What's happening?"

I heard Caspian's voice behind me.

I turned, and could barely make out his face in the fog. "I think we've sighted the enemy," I responded.

The rumble of noise was slow but steady, yet perfectly clear. Voices; screaming and yelling as they grew nearer. I could tell these were the retaliators, the ones who had sworn loyalty against Soren.

I gulped.

"They're closer than they appear," Soren murmured, reaching out and taking my hand in his.

I half-smiled. "I'm not used to the cold."

"Isn't it awful?"

I shook my head. "No, I actually quite like it."

"What a strange woman you are, Ailith."

"Hey," I responded, shrugging. "You're the one who agreed to marry me."

"I can't argue against that," he responded.

All of a sudden, I felt the hair on my arms straighten. Goosebumps spread across my flesh as I felt the vibration of foreign footsteps nearby.

Everyone stopped speaking.

There was a moment of silence so quiet that I could have heard the smallest twig snap, before screams broke out, and the sounds of whinnying and swords being unsheathed followed. As soon as we'd gone silent, revolting peasants were visible, and we were all armed, ready to fight.

Nobody bothered to get off their horses, so I followed what they were doing. However, the careful array of warriors seemed to lose its order. Everyone took up fighting on their own, and so I did the same.

A small, goblin-looking man with pointed ears and a nose covered in warts and boils threw himself at me. I thrust forward my sword, letting the blade drive straight through his chest before he fell to the floor. Several more tackled me to the ground.

I flung my sword at them all, slicing each of their throats in the action. They all fell, lifeless, to the snowy ground. I touched my face, and realized it was covered with fresh blood. I wiped my cheeks on my sleeve, and returned to a stance of combat.

This time, an enormous man with milky green-silver eyes stomped my way, a club in his hands. I held out my sword, feeling my knees tremble a bit beneath me. He swung with all his might, but I somersaulted between his legs so quickly that he didn't have time to realize that I was behind him. I drove my sword through his back, and he dropped his club. His body went erect, and he fell to the ground.

I felt a bit sick to my stomach.

"You okay over there, sea girl?"

I heard Soren's voice call me from a few feet away, where he was fighting a pair of small goblin-like creatures.

"I'm fine!" I called out to him, and he quickly finished off the goblins. However, it wasn't a weapon that he used to defend himself.

I had to take a second look.

He was using his bare hands. They seemed to exude an invisible power so strong that even being near it sent his opponent weak at their knees. One swing of his hands, and this force he carried with him sent them sprawling onto the ground, completely lifeless.

I was in awe.

"AILITH, LOOK OUT!"

I heard my name being called, and was suddenly brought out of my lull.

I spun around, and trembled, grabbing my sword, but was too late as I felt a sharp sting at my arm.

My vision blurred at the pain, and my knees collapsed, hitting the snowy ground, before everything went completely black.

AUTHOR'S NOTE:

Dun dun dunnn...what do you guys think is going to happen? IS AILITH GOING TO DIE? :0

Be sure to vote and comment if you liked what you read!

Also: I realized the acronym for this story is HOTS. What. Even. That is amazing (and gives away some...**coughs...critical information about the plot).

Anyway...that's it for now.

Until Monday, my tenacious readers--

Xoxo,

LK

Chapter 17

PRE-CHAPTER ANNOUNCEMENTS:

SURPRISE! Update came a day early. Yay!

WARNING: To the fangirls--this chapter might make you freak out. Be prepared. And don't say I didn't warn you ;)

P.S. Q&A at the end. If you didn't get a chance to ask a question and you want to, you can totally just ask in the comments and I'll be sure to

P.P.S. I am going to be making a characters chapter sometime soon, where I share photos of how I picture all of my characters looking. Be on the lookout :) this week is a good one!

OK, NOW LET'S GET INTO THIS. ARE YOU READY? I AM.

The first thing I felt was the cold.

My body was shivering so relentlessly that I could have been having a spasm for all anyone knew. My bare skin was carefully kissed by the frigid midnight air, as my coat was removed. I felt my body being jolted around, but did could not pry my focus from the sheer pain I felt.

I clenched my jaw, trying to keep my teeth from chattering, but it didn't work.

Slowly, I groaned, and opened my eyes. The face in front of mine was blurry and only slightly recognizable. The gray eyes, and dark hair...but they were not fixed on me. Instead, the eyes seemed to be fixated on the distance ahead.

I felt the familiar rolling of muscles underneath me, and recognized that I was being carried on horseback. I tried to move myself into a more comfortable position, but I gasped at the acute pain in my left arm.

"Ailith, my dear, don't move." His silky, familiar voice caressed my ears, and I closed my eyes again, ignoring how frozen my flesh felt.

I awoke again later, but in a different setting.

This time, I awoke screaming. My face was wet with tears, and my arm was burning. I had never felt anything like it in my lifetime.

"She's losing too much blood," I heard someone growl.

"What's...what's going on?" I gasped.

I looked over to my side, and saw Soren bent over my arm, a needle and thread in hand as he carefully made little piercing stitches.

Next to him were Zeus, Lazarus and Caspian, all looking over me with concern.

However, it wasn't the enormous group of people surrounding me that made me sick to my stomach. It was the sight of my arm. It was completely mauled; pieces of flesh missing from my forearm and blood oozing out of deep gaps. I squeezed my eyes shut, feeling more tears escape.

"You're almost through, Ailith," Lazarus's voice calmed me from afar. I opened my eyes to see him, but my vision was too blurred by tears.

"What happened to me?" I murmured.

However, all Lazarus did was shush me. Caspian, I realized, was holding my right arm, which, thankfully, remained uninjured, as did the rest of me. I turned my head from the left side, clenching my toes. My head was throbbing and I could feel my heartbeat in my throat.

"This next one is going to hurt," I heard Soren muttering.

"More than it already does?" I grumbled.

"I'm afraid so. Don't bite down on your tongue. One more stitch, and I'll be finished," he said. I'd never noticed lovely his voice was; so dark and smooth, like the texture of satin.

I didn't respond, only waited there, toes clenched.

For a few moments, nothing happened. The silence around me was only broken by the occasional sound of someone sighing nervously.

The calming distant breeze was beginning to lull my aching body to sleep, until I suddenly felt an insurmountable surge of pain ripping through my nerves; pounding through my body and shattering me to the core.

I cried out into the night, feeling blood in my mouth and bile rising in my throat, before I collapsed on the bed and felt the lights go out for the second time.

~

There was a soft touch of sunlight on my cheek, which was still faintly glittering, sending little shiny specks onto the side of the white tent. As I awoke, I realized I'd been in a tent all along. I peered to my left, and noticed my arm was carefully bandaged. It was throbbing than that my heart was beating, and as I noticed the pool of blood drying on the floor, I also realized how close I had been to dying.

I peered out of a small opening in the tent, and noticed that the fog had seemingly disappeared. The outdoors were so clear, I could see other mountaintops from where I lay. Their snowy peaks sparkled in the mid-morning light, as did my face.

Slowly, I stood up, feeling my legs a bit wobbly underneath me, and my head throbbing. I groaned, rubbing at my temples, as I made my way to the entrance of the tent. I realized, in that moment, that I barely wore any clothing—simply my pants and an undershirt. My arms and shoulders were completely exposed. Also, my shoes had somehow been removed in the process of the previous night.

I rolled my eyes, guessing Lazarus had done the honor of taking my beloved lace-up leather boots. I bet he'd make me pay him gold if I wanted them back.

All of a sudden, I felt two hands at my waist, pulling me away from the entrance of the tent.

"What do you think you're doing?"

I spun around, and found Soren standing behind me.

"I was just looking at the view," I responded, turning back to the entrance. "Now that the fog is gone, I realize how beautiful this place is. With the mountains, and the snow...it's stunning."

"How does your arm feel?" he asked.

I quirked a brow. "Which one?" I afforded him a smile, trying to show that I was being sarcastic. "It's feeling better," I lied, wincing a little bit at the sharp pain.

"You're lying," he growled, taking me by my uninjured arm. "Go sit down on your cot."

I laughed. "Why?"

"Because you're hurt. You've lost a lot of blood. You need water, and rest," he told me gruffly, leading me over to the bed.

"Well, for starters, can I have my shirt back?"

He narrowed his gaze. "It was ripped apart."

I sighed. "Can I have my coat?"

"We had to leave it behind," he admitted. "We defeated the revolters, luckily."

"That's good," I said.

There was a moment of silence as I looked around, and realized that no one else was inside this tent. We were completely alone.

"Where is everyone?" I asked.

"In their respective tents, around here," he responded. "I hope you're not uncomfortable with this arrangement."

"To be frank, I'm just glad I'm alive," I told him.

He looked at me for a few minutes, bent over a tin bottle, before he unscrewed the cap and brought it over to me.

I eyed the bottle suspiciously. "I can't drink freshwater."

"This," he responded, looking a bit proud of himself. "Is seawater."

I felt my eyebrows shooting up my forehead. "You brought me seawater?"

"I knew you'd probably forget, and didn't want to have a predicament involving you dying of dehydration," he said. "Or...whatever you get from lack of seawater, as I assume the salt content in that does nothing to hydrate you."

"My kind doesn't need to be hydrated," I responded. "We need the salt."

He nodded. "I see."

With that, I pressed the bottle to my mouth, and took big, long sips—the water tasted so good as I realized how thirsty I truly was, and finished the whole bottle, letting out a sigh as I did.

Soren lingered for a few moments, before wandering over to his side of the tent, where he began tidying up.

"Thank you," I said.

He turned, his eyes widening a bit. "For what?"

"For the water... for saving my life," I responded, quietly adding, "for everything."

He afforded me a genuine close-mouthed grin, nodding his head politely, before he went back to doing whatever he was doing.

I swung my legs over the side of the cot, about to go searching for my shoes, when I felt an icy stare from across the room.

I looked over at him, and our gazes met.

"Don't even think about it."

I sighed, and swung my legs back onto the cot, sitting cross-legged and wrapping my bare arms in a soft fur blanket.

I wondered what had happened the previous night. I knew what had happened for the most part, but I was sure that the worst and most painful parts had been blacked out by my memory. I had passed out for different periods of time, and had no idea what had occurred during those hours.

I knew that it was a bad idea to ask, but still, something within me urged me to wonder; telling me I had to know.

"Soren, what happened to me?" I asked.

"I think you know," he responded.

I shook my head. "I really don't."

"I know that you were watching me," he replied matter-of-factly. "You didn't really understand that I am truly not human before then, did you?"

All of a sudden, the memories came flashing back. Being mesmerized and distracted by Soren's godly capabilities, and then the goblin man slicing up my arm up with his dagger, and after that collapsing to the ground and passing out.

I shuddered.

"I'm sorry," I told him.

He chuckled, even though I could tell he wasn't actually amused. "Another uncalled for proclamation this morning."

"It was called for," I muttered. "You predicted that something like this was going to happen, and I didn't believe you. And still, you let me come. And when I got hurt, like you predicted I would, you saved my life."

He stared at me for a few moments, then began shaking his head, laughing in a way that was almost angry. He walked over to me, his footsteps purposeful. His gaze met mine, and he sat at the edge of my cot.

"I wouldn't live with myself," he said. "If I let you die."

I furrowed my brows. "But I acted so...so..."

"Stop berating yourself," he murmured, reaching forward and stroking my cheek with his warm palm. "You've already proven yourself to me, Ailith."

I laughed. "You're much more forgiving than you look."

He leaned closer. "I am a bit biased, don't you think?"

"Biased when it comes to what?"

"You."

I felt my breath go shaky.

"What I said the other night," he told me, his hand at my shoulder. "About my adherence to you—I meant it more than I've meant anything in a long, long time."

I breathed. "How long?"

A slight smile tickled his lips. "Approximately four thousand years."

I bit my lip. "I can't believe you put up with me. I'm just a child, compared to you."

"True," he responded, feigning snideness. "I suppose I could trade you in for an older woman, if I wanted."

"I suppose you could."

Slowly, his gaze seemed to lock into mine, and I felt the nerves squeezing my ribcage against my heart.

With that, a certain ruggedness overcame him, and he gripped my waist, careful not to clutch onto my injured arm. He pulled me towards himself, and for just a moment held me there, his eyes looking into mine, his mouth stifling a low chuckle. He closed his eyes, nestling his forehead against mine. I reached forward, running a hand through his silky dark hair, burying my fingers against his scalp.

His hand caressed my cheek. "You don't know how good that feels," he murmured, fingers tickling my shoulder blades.

The stubble on his face rubbed against my cheeks, and he seemed to bring a warmth to me that I'd never before felt. He was all heat; the atmosphere seemed to create a bubble around us. I'd been shivering minutes before, but now I felt warm...felt safe.

Soren pulled away, opening his eyes and reaching forward to trace lines up and down my cheeks. I felt a gasp catching in my throat.

"Do you want to know something, sea girl?" His voice was dark and smooth; his eyes a sensual tease.

I nodded, eyes closed.

He let out a deep chuckle. "I wanted to mark you from the moment I saw you. It's the first thought I had about you," he murmured, running his hands along my neck. "Putting my mouth to that pale flesh, and making it shine like the sun."

"You do realize you're admitting your pain-in-the-ass tendency to make people glitter against their will, right?" I smirked.

He bent forward and kissed my jaw. I didn't try to stop him as he muttered, "It isn't my only skill, sea girl."

I fake-glared. "Pervert."

"What about you?" he asked.

I took a deep breath. "What do you mean? If you're asking about my skills, I swear"—

"What was the first thing you thought about me?"

I snorted. "Before or after words came out of your mouth?"

His gaze was all taunting now...a dare. "Before."

"I thought," I responded, drawing out the words as I taunted him, my eyes drawn in and glancing through my eyelashes. "That you were the most handsome man I'd ever seen."

A grin. Satisfaction. "I knew it," he drawled, peering at me with taunting gray eyes.

I took the opportunity to smack him.

Q&A TIME!!! (Sorry for how wordy these ended up. But they do sound like me talking in real life, so that's kind of fun. It is for me, at least.)

1. When you write, how do you come up with a story line and what helps you keep writing it?

I commend the very few people who can just come up with a plot as they go--but most of us are not that good! Including me. Especially me, actually. I use a very specific method of plotting. Creating a story, especially a book, takes a lot more detail-oriented planning than just a 'beginning, middle and end' for most of us. Unless you're a writing genius. Which I am not. I usually plan by the chapter, as long as make sure I know

how all of the conflicts I present in the beginning of the story will end, so
that it's all tied up in a nice orderly bow. :)

2. What are your book recommendations plzzz?

Ok. I have 10 million. But I've narrowed it down, even though the process
was painful. The Invention of Wings for those of you who love a historical
tearjerker, We Were Liars for those of you who want your mind to explode,
Sarah Dessen anything for you teen romance freaks, and my most recent
obsession (and this can be for anyone who desires entertainment of the
best sort)--the A Court of Thorns and Roses trilogy by Sarah J. Maas. If
you haven't read it, I don't know what you're doing reading my story when
you still haven't read this series. It's so good. Like so insanely amazing you
will die. And then be reborn as a High Fae. :)

3. What is your most embarrassing story???

Lols. Omg. So many. I have three.

1. Every day of my life.

2. This happened a couple of weeks ago. Back to the Court of Thorns and
Roses series--I made the mistake of reading the second book on the bus on
my way back from class, and I happened to be reading the "inn scene" (for
those of you who don't know, it is definitely an adult-only scene). I think
my face turned so red I probably looked like I had some sort of serious
medical condition. I went into a fit of giggles (because I'm shamelessly
immature about 'R-rated scenes') in front of everyone on the bus. And I
couldn't stop. I was so embarrassed.

3. Another good one was my grandparents getting me tipsy. On purpose.
Because they "thought it would be funny." Half a glass of Rosé later I was
laughing about an empty oatmeal container. The next day, I felt like my
head was going to explode. Thanks, gram and gramps.

4. How old are you?

I get this question a lot. And, while most people think I'm in college, I am actually in high school (but I take some college-level courses, and have taken 2 college Creative Writing courses).

5. How do you describe things so naturally and smoothly in your book? When I attempt it always seems to fall flat in a way...

The answer to this question is simple: practice. I have already finished this first draft of Heiress of the Sea, and when I look back at it, I think, "what the hell is wrong with me? Why would I write it THAT way?" with pretty much every sentence. Now, while my work is for sure flawed (exhibit a: first draft, exhibit b: I'm not a professional, exhibit c: ITS A FREAKING FIRST DRAFT PEOPLE), it is not all terrible. I think that, the more you write, the more your description and narrative will flow together in one nice chain of writing. If you're a beginner at writing (this is the sixth book manuscript I've written, people, so it takes TIME to get anywhere), I recommend reading a LOT. You can't be a good writer without being a mindful and voracious reader. Your spelling, grammar, sentence structure, plot development, character development, relationships and description will ALL get lightyears better if you read quality writing. Also, these things take time. Practice! It's all I can say.

6. What country are you from?

If you haven't realized from the way I write, the good ol' United States of America.

7. Would you survive if thrown on a deserted island by yourself?

That would depend on my mood the day of being deserted. Sometimes I feel like I could embrace the whole island-savage-chique thing and be like "HELLS YES COME AT ME MONKEYS AND COCONUTS AND OCEAN WATER" and sometimes I'm super emotional and high-maintence and feel like I would be so emotional and anxious that I would throw myself off an island cliff and let my body be eaten by dolphins. I don't know. That's kind of dramatic and scary, but who knows?

8. Why do you write?

We artists are generally high-maintence and very emotional about life. Because, if you think about it, there are so many things to do that are better than writing. You could...I don't know...get married, go swimming, maybe make a friend. Or do all three at once. No judgement. But we writers are often stuck in a blob of "life sucks", or at least "life could be better." Because, in all honesty, people who are truly at their peak in life don't have the time or sad/frustrated/ranting/hopeless/meh disposition to write.

9. What do you do other than write?

Tons of stuff. I watch movies...specifically British movies. I love romantic comedies such as Bridget Jones's Diary (don't judge me; Bridget and Mark are the cutest). I also enjoy anything involving Western European history, so I highly recommend the show Reign (it's on Netflix). I am also a competitive cellist and I like to bake. Even though I play a mean game of ping-pong, I am pretty much the least athletic person you could ever meet, unless you count Soul Cycle and chasing my dog everywhere.

AND FINALLY. THE MOST ASKED QUESTION OF THE NIGHT. **DRUM ROLLS...

10. Are you planning to write anything after Heiress of the Sea?

You bet your sparkling skin.

When HOTS (still can't get over that acronym's amazingness) is fully up-loaded, I will be announcing a new story I've been working on. It is super fresh, and something I am SO excited to share with all of you. Before you ask, no--it is not a sequel to HOTS, but I am open to that idea at some point in the future. I can tell you two things: it is a YA fantasy/epic/romance like HOTS, and it is going to be fun. :)

Thank you to everyone who submitted questions! If you want to know anything else, please leave me a comment down below.

Love you all--

Xoxo,

LK

Chapter 18

The sound of footsteps crunching outside in the stiff snow grew closer, the frigid wind howling in the distance.

As I braided my hair, I felt an icy breeze tickling my cheek as the tent's entrance flapped open, and in stepped Lazarus, Caspian and Zeus, their snow-covered boots scuffing against the floor of the tent.

I peered over to the other side of the tent, where Soren was packing up the things strewn around, ready to leave. He'd informed me that we were supposed to journey across the remainder of the area, to make sure Hades wasn't rallying up any other armies of peasants and trolls, before we would descend the mountainous region and return to the safety of the palace.

"When do we depart?" Soren asked the three other men, his voice raspy.

"Not today." Zeus responded. "It looks as if Lazarus's mother is having a bit of a fit. There's one hell of a blizzard headed our way. It's just at the other side of the mountain. We will wait it out here, rather than venture out into the snow."

"I thought a God's tolerance for cold was good enough that any of you could withstand being in a blizzard," I muttered from across the room.

Zeus shot me a look that reminded me of how Goridian had looked at me as a child.

"We could," he responded. "But you're here. And, I'm sorry if you forgot, but you're a mortal."

"You don't know that," I barked in response.

He laughed. "Actually, I do. You may not be twenty years of age, but I'm telling you in advance. And you should feel lucky. If you weren't mortal, then you would obviously not be the one meant to marry Soren. And, correct me if I'm mistaken, you do want to marry Soren."

I didn't reply, only continued tidying up my side of the tent, letting Zeus's words go ignored.

"We need to keep moving," Soren spoke roughly. "I can't be away from my court for this long."

Lazarus rolled his eyes. "You've been gone two days already. What's three?"

"I only have Juniper holding down fort. I thought the journey would be a day and a half, at the most. Something could happen in my absence," Soren growled. "You wouldn't understand, because you're not a king."

Lazarus threw up his hands. "You're right, your majesty. I shouldn't have questioned ye, mighty powerful God."

Soren snarled. "Better watch your tongue, Laz, or I swear"—

"Enough, my sons," Zeus roared.

Surprisingly, they both turned to face him.

"We will leave tomorrow," Zeus commanded. "For now, I want you both to keep an eye on the sea girl. She mustn't be harmed again, or she actually might die this time." He proceeded to leave, but not before turning and winking at me.

I waited until he was gone to roll my eyes.

"Well, this place is much nicer than any of our tents," Lazarus whined, stomping around the pristine white space. Soren reached over to the entrance of the tent and latched it up, to keep the cold draft from getting in.

Lazarus unbuckled his long coat and let it slump onto the ground. He then pulled out a small silver flask, sipping and then cringing, the burn of the alcohol evident.

I waved at him. "Hey, can I have some of that?"

"Sure thing," he responded, sauntering over to me. I took the flask and sipped, coughing as the burn of something stronger than I had tasted before slid down my throat.

"Stop it--both of you. It's barely noon and you're both drinking like old men," Soren growled, snatching the flask from Lazarus. He let a feline grin spread across his face as he tipped his head backwards and drank the remaining contents of the flask.

"Damn," Lazarus muttered, shaking his head.

"I needed that more than you did," Soren replied. "I had to perform surgery on that one last night." He nodded with his head towards me.

"So that's how you're referring to your betrothed now? 'That one?' Nice," Lazarus responded.

"And, if 'this one' might have a say, I was the one who endured your amateur surgical skills, so I should have been the one to finish the flask. My arm is throbbing," I groaned, swinging my legs over to the side of the cot and standing to face the brothers.

Lazarus turned to me, and then to Soren, and then to me again.

"So," he said, half-grinning. "What are we going to do today?"

"You could begin by picking up your coat," Soren responded.

Lazarus ignored his brother's comment, reaching up to scratch his pump-kin-colored head. "I can sense tension. What exactly have you two been up to?"

For just a moment, Soren and I glanced at one another, before we both looked away. I felt my face turning a peachy hue, and Soren seemed to be completely absorbed in continuously cleaning up the same area, which was a good excuse to avert his gaze.

"Oh, so you're not going to tell me? Cool," Lazarus grumbled, sitting down in the middle of the room and toying with his empty flask.

The wind outside howled and wrestled with the tent, warning the three of us not to venture out into the wilderness. I'd never before witnessed a blizzard, but just by the way it sounded, I did not care to. Once in a while, a frigid gust of wind would burst through one of the tent's crevices and I would shiver, thanking the Gods and Goddesses I wasn't completely unprotected.

Soren and Lazarus, however, as Gods, were completely unaffected by the temperature, and just seemed bored out of their minds. They began an absentminded game of poker in the corner of the tent, and I felt myself drifting to sleep, the throbbing in my arm seeming to numb under the effects of alcohol.

~

"Ailith, it's time to wake up, my dear," a familiar voice cooed.

I stirred, groaning lightly and letting a grin tickle my lips, thinking of Soren's chastising grey gaze.

Slowly, I let my eyelids flutter open, and immediately shrieked.

It wasn't Soren.

"Miss me, darling?" he sneered.

I furrowed my brows, feeling a tumbleweed nerve in my stomach. "Hades?"

"You really didn't think we were finished up on that mountain, did you?" he murmured, reaching forward to brush a stray lock of hair from my face.

I shivered, as I realized we were traveling at lightning speed through the white, lifeless forest. A canopy of twigs and branches hung overhead, and all I could see around us was snow. Falling; on the ground...just snow.

"Wait," I said. "Where are we?"

"Oh, a few miles ahead of that tent you were being held captive in," he snickered, his fiery eyes peering into mine, his red hair flicking back and forth as he ran.

"I was not being held captive. Take me back," I ordered.

"Sorry, my sea waif. I caught you just in time," he growled, his hands tensing underneath me.

"In time for what?" I gasped.

His smirk twisted into a wicked grin. "Soren was about to claim you. But he can't claim you if you've already been claimed...luckily."

I felt horror flooding through me. "What? Are you saying"—

"I am going to claim you, my dear Ailith. I knew I'd see your pretty face again, that long hair; those delicate bones, so breakable...," his mind trailed off as he eyed me almost...lovingly, but just for a moment.

I felt my mouth go dry.

"No," I told him. "You can't claim me. Soren is going to claim me."

He roared in laughter as he laughed, panting just a bit. "Oh, so you've actually grown to love that bastard? Really, Ailith, what do you see in him?"

"A whole lot more than I see you," I muttered.

"Is that right?" he growled.

With that, he stopped in his tracks and threw me down with force. My arm throbbed at the impact of the impact with the frosty ground, and I cried out in pain as I sprawled out onto the ice, hearing the cracking of thunder in the distance.

I gulped—it was Soren.

"Oh, don't think he's going to get here in time. You'll be finished off before he has the chance to catch me," he murmured, his gaze dragging from my head to my toes. He licked his lips, running a hand through his scorching red hair. "The underworld really is a nice place. I think you'll enjoy it there."

Bastard.

"I don't think so," I told him, scurrying upwards, feeling myself go a bit dizzy.

"I thought you were going to be weak when I snatched you from that tent, your arm all bound and everything," Hades sneered. "I see you're still as feisty and alert as ever. Whatever. I enjoy a good challenge, especially when I know I can win."

I took a stance of combat, and he did the same.

"You touch me, and I won't hesitate to rip off certain body parts you probably would prefer stay attached," I warned.

He bent backwards, spittle flying from his lips as he coughed and heaved, his body flailing with the laughter. I took the opportunity to scan the area, wondering where the hell we were. We seemed to be completely surrounded by trees and forest, sunlight peeking out through clouds and the remainder of the blizzard overhead. However, the fact that lightning was continuously flashing in the sky told me that Soren was aware I'd been taken at this point. However, the fact that he wasn't already here told me he had no better idea of where I was than I did.

I felt a rush of adrenaline hitting me as Hades lunged, his predatory eyes looming over me as I leapt out of the way, securing myself against a tree. For a moment, he didn't know where I was, so I took the opportunity to dodge in a random direction, my sprint interrupted when he was able to locate me, and run faster, moving quicker than the breeze, and planting his feet in front of me. I skidded to a stop, and secured my feet onto the ground.

So I couldn't outrun him. That wasn't a problem. Right?

"Come here, you little sea waif," Hades murmured teasingly, reaching forward to grip me by the shoulders, but not expecting my bold move as I thrust the bottom of my boot into his stomach, sending him sprawling back.

I knew I couldn't outfight a God, but I needed to buy myself some time.

Hades coughed, but scampered to his feet easily. He ran a tongue over his lips, eyes flickering with fire as he began to chase me, whizzing at my heels. Instead of attempting to run away, which I knew he was expecting, I leapt into the air, as far as I could, and spun my body around in the process, timing the move so that my heel made impact with his jaw as soon as he was close enough.

"Ouch!" he barked, rubbing his jaw and eyeing me again, his gaze now less playful and more angered.

"You should really stop trying to hurt me, little ocean girl," he grumbled, reaching forward and grabbing me by the injured arm. I cried out in pain, completely baffled that he would take advantage of an injury that I received fighting revolters that were loyal to him.

I screamed as he grasped my arm. I could feel some of the stitches Soren had carefully threaded breaking, and then warmth of blood trickling against my arm, staining the bandages red.

Hades sneered. "I wouldn't have had to do that had you just let me perform the Choosing Ceremony when I asked."

"Never," I growled. "Not in a thousand years." Especially when I had no idea what the Choosing Ceremony really was.

I wouldn't let him have his satisfaction. Not after spending so much time recovering from my time suffering from Goridian, and then falling in love with Soren because of his polar-opposite goodness—no way.

"You can make me bleed," I spat, my muscles tense as crimson dripped from my bandages onto the clean, white snow. My torso heaved with my breath; quick and heavy. "You can rip me apart, limb by limb. You can starve me, lock me in a bedroom and drag me down to the underworld by my fingernails, but you cannot—ever—make me do so willingly."

Hades seemed a bit surprised by my remark, his shoulder sagging into a shrug.

"Come on, Ailith," he muttered. "Let me fix that wound. You know, your noble speech and your bleeding arm are making me feel kind of bad about myself. Just...come over here."

"Never," I growled.

"Do you want to bleed to death?"

I bit my lip. "I'd choose bleeding to death over your touch any hour of the day."

"Oh, really?"

Again, he eyed me as his prey, his black eyes flashing sparks of ruby before he lunged a second time.

With all the strength I had left, I brought my arms up in front of me, in a position to defend myself.

All of a sudden, I felt an icy swirl...a spark of magic...and gasped. Just a moment later, a curved wall of transparent ice was stretched out in front of me, acting as a barrier between me and Hades.

He snickered, and ran head-first towards me, expecting the ice-barrier to be easily breakable, but crashed into the ice wall, his body sprawling back onto the ground. He coughed streams of steam into the icy air, his breath thickening.

I couldn't believe what had just happened, but was eternally grateful for it.

I'd known I could control water, but ice...

Suddenly, I recalled that ice was just frozen water. A loophole. I smiled to myself.

I let my hands drop, and the barrier crashed down on Hades. I took the opportunity to start running, as fast as my legs would push me, through the forest. I could feel him struggling underneath the enormous block of ice, and knew I didn't have much time. Hades was a strong God, and would crack the ice in a matter of moments.

I continued sprinting—I had to find the camp where my army had set up, and I needed to find it before Hades caught up to me.

As I looked back, I didn't notice the body in front of me, and as I turned, was unable to stop myself from slamming into this person with a loud thump.

I fell to the ground, peering up at the redhead towering over me.

I gasped.

AUTHOR'S NOTE:

Since I haven't uploaded since Sunday, I feel like I've been MIA since my last update. I am sort of actually sad about it.

Oh well. It's probably just the day-to-day grind of school, bus, etc.

Hello, my lovelies. I hope your week was fantastic and that your weekend is even better. I am definitely excited for the weekend. Like beyond thrilled. I can't deal with early mornings anymore!!!

If you enjoyed this chapter, don't forget to leave me a comment and vote!

Again, thanks to everyone who reads, comments, votes, supports--every-thing! :)

Buenos tardes, mis amigos y amigas! Yo estoy muy feliz para el fín de la semana. Ay Dios mío. Lo siento para mi español mal. Yo trato, chiquititas.

I apologize in advance to everyone for this weird Author's Note where I attempted Spanish because... #highschoolspanishskills.

Ok-- I'll stop speaking now.

Xoxo,

LK

Chapter 19

"Lazarus!" I exclaimed, scampering to my feet and throwing my arms around my friend, gasping for air. I was so relieved I could stop sprinting.

"Dear Gods and Goddesses, Ailith, what happened to your arm?" he gasped, screaming into the wintry air, "Sor, she's over here!"

"Hades took me," I exclaimed. "I fought him...with ice...and then ran for my damned mortal life."

Lazarus shook his head pitifully. "Soren's going to be so pissed."

"You can say that again."

My gaze loomed over Lazarus's shoulder, and I felt tears threatening to bubble up in relief as I saw Soren's familiar gaze from a few feet away. I grew a bit wobbly at the knees, my limbs threatening to collapse to the ground.

I tried to stay still, but was nearly knocked over as Soren skidded in front of me, having run over at his godly speed. Faster than I could breathe, I felt his hands around my shoulders, and then at my trembling, bloodied arm.

"I'm sorry," Soren muttered. "We didn't even realize when he took you...we were in the middle of a heated game of cards, and then I fell asleep. You were so quiet, and I didn't even notice. And look at you—you're hurt again." He grimaced at the sight.

I shook my head. "Don't apologize for something you had no control over."

"But I did," he said through gritted teeth. "I didn't even sense him when he stole you away."

"Let's get going, Sor. Don't you want to go hunt down Hades?" Lazarus exclaimed, the bloodlust apparent in his growl.

"I'd only like one thing more—and that is to make sure Ailith is safe, and far away from here. You go. I'll see you back at the palace."

"The palace?" I whispered.

Soren nodded, "Yes. We're going home...after you've been properly taken care of."

With that, I felt Soren's supportive grip at my waist, leading me in the opposite direction of Lazarus.

"If you find Hades," Soren growled at his brother. "Find a way to lure him to the palace—so that I can kill him."

Lazarus responded with a slight nod of the head, before he took off in the opposite direction.

I peered up at Soren. "Can Laz take Hades one-on-one?"

Soren shrugged, sending me a playful grin. "Let's hope."

It was enough to fester a small grin out of me, which seemed to be satisfactory to Soren. He helped me through the snowy woods, and I began to tell him all about the luck of my power with ice.

"It appears that, just when another man is about to attempt to steal you away from me, you're always able to fight him off yourself," Soren murmured playfully.

I shrugged. "I guess I'm just lucky. Thank the Gods and Goddesses I've always managed to escape in time."

"What—exactly—did Hades say he was trying to do?" Soren asked. I could tell that it was mostly out of concern, even though he tried to mask it by sounding curious.

I sighed, letting out a small laugh. "He said he was trying to perform the claiming ceremony, I think...whatever the hell that means. What does that mean?"

"That's a conversation for another day," Soren grumbled, leaning over and nestling a kiss on my forehead, his lips gently brushing against my temple.

I felt a gasp catching in my throat, but immediately swallowed it down, biting my lip as my cheeks turned a bit darker.

"Seriously," I persisted. "I'm curious. You keep talking about claiming me, and Hades was about to do it today apparently, so I want to know what that means. You know, in the case I run into any other sprightly Gods ready to make me as their forever beloved, or whatever."

"It's a longer, more complex process than Hades probably made it seem," he explained, clearing his throat uncomfortably. "Can we just talk about this later?"

He pulled me forward with a hand pinned between my shoulder blades, grinning for a moment before his hands ventured down to my waist, where he secured his grasp, and mine slid to the nape of his neck, nearly becoming intermingled with his hair. He low out a low, feral growl, before bending forth to create a trail of lingering kisses along the length of my neck. His touch was enough to awaken the festering craving within me...I wanted to feel his lips on mine. I wanted him to kiss me. I groaned as he kissed my jaw.

He snickered at my wordless request. "Ailith," he purred, saying my name as if chastising a small child for being impatient. His fingers traced up my neck.

I gasped at the delicate touch, but was soon disoriented by the sickening drip-drop of liquid from my thumb.

Soren noticed it, too. We peered down to see a steady stream of blood leaking through my bandages and creating a small puddle on the ground. With my clean hand, I covered my mouth in a gasp and Soren immediately pulled away, grunting as he tore away the material of one of his sleeves.

He reached forward, one arm bare and tense, and quickly removed the loose bandages, which were completely soaked with blood.

"You've lost too much blood," he growled. "Did Hades tear your wound open on purpose?"

I nodded. "Long story."

"Not long enough for it to be excusable," he grumbled, carefully wrapping the cloth tightly around my arm. I winced, feeling the pressure against the cuts.

"Soren, please tell me what the claiming ceremony is," I demanded, trying to distract myself from the pain.

"It's a ceremony by which a God devotes his love to a beloved," he murmured, his tone even and level.

I furrowed a brow. "I'm confused."

"Why?" He looped an arm around my waist and we began walking again, slowly but surely. I wondered where we were going, but did not want to change the subject and let Soren out of telling me what I wanted to know.

"Because Hades spoke of it as something he could simply...do, or secure in some way, in a very short amount of time. He threatened that he would be able to claim me before you arrived at my rescue, and you are saying this is a long process. So which one of you is lying?" I exclaimed

He let out a snarl, and then a low chuckle. "I see now why you're perplexed."

"Well then, please, tell me!" I gasped.

"Really, Ailith, it's not important that you know at this moment"—

I fake-glared at him. "Do you really think this will make me more upset than when I found out my body lights up like a Christmas tree—quite literally—every time you kiss me?"

He snorted. "The claiming ceremony is a bit more overwhelming than shimmery skin, Ailith."

"Why?" I exclaimed. "And how did you expect to tell me you're going to claim me for all this time, and not receive a single question about that from me? I won't be submissive to everything."

"My dear, you aren't submissive to anything," Soren muttered. "It's not in your nature."

I growled. "You're stalling. Just tell me, already. My arm is bleeding, and I could die from blood loss at any moment."

He eyed me with slight irritation, his gaze toying with mine.

He breathed in a long, deep sigh.

"Fine," he said, exhaling slowly, "if you must know, in the Choosing Ceremony I would have to seduce you, rip your clothes off and make love to you in front of my entire court, in the throne room, until you scream my name in ecstasy."

He blinked a few times, his stare completely calm.

I felt my eyes widening. "Are you serious?"

What. The actual. Shit.

"I'm just kidding, sea girl." A devilish grin appeared on Soren's face, and I reached forward to smack him with my uninjured arm.

I felt myself taking long, deep breath of relief.

"You really are just...just...," I grumbled.

"Just what? Absolutely spectacular? I know that," he responded.

"I was going to say a completely tedious ass with a tendency towards revolting, shameless flirting, but I'm glad to see your ego got a kick out of that one," I grumbled. "You totally had me convinced."

"So you admit I'm comical?" He grinned.

I shook my head. "No."

"Very well," he muttered. "I apologize, Ailith. I didn't know you were so sensitive to jokes. And, as I can tell by your blushing—you are particularly sensitive to jokes of a sexual nature."

"Who isn't?" I growled.

"Me."

I glared. "Because you're absolutely vulgar."

"I'm so offended," he murmured, grinning to himself.

I was about to retort with a witty comeback, when I immediately felt myself skidding to a halt, as I realized we were standing at the tip of a cliff thousands of feet up, surrounded by swirling clouds and hanging over treacherous trenches below.

"Gods and Goddesses," I gasped, catching myself just in time.

I looked over to Soren, who seemed amused, his brows twisting above his eyes.

"You seem to forget, my dear Ailith, that you stand next to an immortal being who can fly faster than the speed of sound. Yet, you still falter at the sight of a teensy little cliff." He peered down at me, his face smug.

I didn't say anything, only nodded and smiled sweetly, before shoving him, with all my might, off the cliff.

He let himself fall for a few moments, shaking his head nonchalantly, before swooping upwards, his body floating effortlessly back up. A smirk was printed on his face.

"What was that for?" he called from afar.

I placed an uninjured hand on my hip. "For your attitude."

"What attitude?" he responded, before he paused and added, "it's your turn now, sea girl. Ever wanted to fly?"

"No, no, no," I responded. "Soren, don't you dare"—

A wicked grin spread across his face as he swooped forward, securing his arms below my ribcage, and pulling me into midair with him, soaring through the wind, over the enormous, snow-covered caverns below.

Icy wind brushed against my face as we flew. I tried to hide in a shudder, but felt my entire body begin to shake—shivering in the frigid atmosphere. Soren's warm hands wrapped closer around me, turning me around and pressing my face to a warm chest. I breathed in a breath of relief, inhaling a familiar scent of pine and wind and warmth—I sighed.

I was nearly lulled asleep as we floated through the sky, smoothly dipping a few feet lower every second. The journey was less than an hour long, but it felt much shorter with my body wrapped in a bubble of godly heat. It was unfortunate, however, that I could not fall asleep, both due to the rapid pace of my heartbeat, which only quickened as I attempted to slow it back down to normal, and the burning question still residing in the deep trenches of my conscience.

What really was the claiming ceremony?

However, I soon felt soothing fingers trailing my scalp; tracing the ridges of my skull underneath my hair, and my mind seemed to numb, concentrating on the hypnotizing touch. I wondered if he was doing this on purpose; trying to keep me calm, as my mind and heart seemed to race at a matching speed.

We arrived, not much later, at a significantly cooled-down version seaside of the palace's surroundings

It didn't appear to have snowed in this area.

For a moment, my stomach dropped. Snow. I remembered, quickly, that Soren and I were supposed to marry before the first snowfall of winter—or the prophecy would be broken; shattered. Dread seemed to flood through me as I realized that there had been a blizzard in the mountains during our time there.

"Was the snow in the mountains"— I began.

"Doesn't count for the prophecy," Soren finished, reassuring me. I took a deep breath.

"Why not?" I asked.

He shrugged. "The mountains are always snowy. The first snowfall is in regard to this region, where the seasons change. It is always winter in the mountains."

His explanation assured me, and I immediately forgot the absolute dread I'd felt at the idea of not marrying Soren in time.

"So," Soren murmured. "Are you thirsty? Hungry? Exhausted?"

I half-smiled, my mouth closed. "Yes."

"I keep forgetting you're a mortal. A mortal with the powers to control the sea and its direct aquatic relatives. Luckily, ice being one of them," he muttered. He seemed to be mumbling more to himself than to me, to process the information.

"I don't understand it, either," I responded warmly.

His tone was lukewarm as he spoke, "I was surprised when I first realized you were the Sea Heiress from the prophecy."

I quirked a brow. "Why?"

"Because," he drawled, taking me by the uninjured arm and leading me towards the seaside. "I see all this, and I don't picture a funny little thing like you being its grand Heiress." His grin spread wide, and I reached out to smack him on the neck.

"You're not funny," I grumbled.

He cleared his throat, slowly piecing together his ideas like a puzzle.

"Really, Ailith, I didn't expect you to be so...so..."

"So what?" I murmured. In the past, I had been impatient to hear his answer when he'd stopped mid-sentence, but this time, I waited.

And out of the corner of my eye, I spotted something shiny bobbing in the sea.

I turned back to Soren, convincing myself that I was just seeing things.

"You're just so much better than I ever wished for," he whispered, his hand reaching out to graze my cheek.

I smiled gently, my eyes closing at the touch, and then fluttering open again. I viewed him in the light of the sunset, his grey eyes softened by the orange glow around us; his dark hair having been tousled by the wind of the skies, his sharp jaw, as usual, set a bit tensely. I felt the smile growing as I took in the sight.

But there it was, again.

Something bobbing in the water; something shiny...shiny almost like golden hair.

Familiar golden hair.

"Wait a minute...," I muttered, marching over to the seaside, stopping just far enough from the water that I knew it would not merge with my being.

I gasped.

My concerns were confirmed as I stared out into the sea, feeling Soren's looming presence being me, his puzzlement evident without have to see his face. I myself was puzzled by the sight, as well.

Because, floating near the shore, golden locks flickering under the light of the peachy sunset—was my sister.

AUTHOR'S NOTE:

I would like to apologize to all my fangirls. RIP. I would have warned you, but it would've given some important stuff away :)

Happy Monday, people! I honestly cannot believe it's Monday. It was just Friday literally two seconds ago. I quote Ailith (and also myself I guess) directly when I say, what the actual shit?!

I hope you all got a kick out of this one. It's getting to a bit more...*coughs* SCANDALOUS.

So can you tell I'm a nerd yet? And super exhausted from drowning in homework?

If you enjoyed what you read, please don't forget to vote and leave me a comment letting me know what you thought!

In the spirit of my biology teacher who would always say, "Johnson OUT" every time he either exited a room or signed an email--

Lk OUT.

Xoxo, my lovelies--

LK

Chapter 20

"Madalaena," I breathed.

My voice quivered for just a moment. I blinked a few times, pinching my own flesh to be sure I wasn't seeing things out of exhaustion.

No, I wasn't.

My sister was really there, body bobbing in the water.

For a moment, I hesitated. And then I called her name, screaming at the loudest volume my raspy voice could muster.

"I think she's unconscious," I said, my voice barely a whisper.

Soren furrowed a brow. "You know this girl?"

I nodded. "She's my sister."

His brows quickly shot upwards, and he turned towards the shore. "Stay here."

I grabbed his arm. "Is it safe?"

Scoffing, he responded, "I'd be almost a bit disappointed if Goridian didn't try something. Knowing what he did to you, I'd enjoy a meet-and-greet, even if it is a little impromptu." I was afforded a flash of his wicked grin, before calmness spread across his face as he approached the shore, and waded into the water, which seemed to move with his every movement.

The sheer power of his movement guided the tide as he treaded water, and grasped onto my sister's limp body.

I held my breath, and was relieved when Soren returned to shore, Madalaena completely unconscious.

Gasping, I bit my lip. "Please tell me that she...she isn't..."

With that, a gasp protruded from my sister's lips, and seawater began sputtering out of her mouth. I assumed she'd been caught up in a nasty current, but hadn't been as lucky as I had and saved by pirates—her body most likely lost consciousness in her fight with the water, and she washed up on the shore like this.

"Madalaena," I whispered, grabbing her by her slender shoulders. "Laena, it's me."

For just a moment, she shuddered in my grasp. Slowly, her pale eyelids flickered open. Immediately, she viewed me with confusion—and then with happiness.

"It's you," she muttered.

I smiled. "I'm here, Laena. How did you get here?"

A blonde brow curved. "I escaped, with Triton's help. He sent me here to find you."

I felt my stomach turning in one fluid motion.

"What did he say?" I gasped, my breath thickening.

She coughed a bit, spitting up some more water. "He wanted me to warn you that Goridian will be ready for war...soon."

My breath caught in my throat at that word. Soon.

I turned to Soren, who was still standing a few feet away, watching this exchange with silence.

"Thank you for saving her," I murmured.

He didn't even respond; simply nodded in his head and said, "We should get her inside. She needs rest, most of all."

I nodded. "How are you feeling, Laena?"

Squinting, she murmured, "Where am I?"

Smiling, I felt my heart fill with excitement as I realized I would now get to show someone from my kingdom this beautiful place.

"Land," I breathed in response.

~

My sister slept, tucked under a fluffy white comforter, for several hours. I watched her the entire time; her golden eyes closed; her light brown curls spewed across the bed. Laena was the second eldest of my sisters, nearing twenty-five now. She was probably the most beautiful out of all of us, with her cerulean eyes, flowery eyelashes and gold-tinged locks.

Even though she was older than I, Laena had never been particularly mature, so it surprised me she'd been the one Triton had thought to send up, rather than one of the others. While Laena was pretty and docile, she surely wasn't the warrior type...or even the messenger type, for that matter, given her forgetful nature.

She murmured things in her sleep, and I watched as the night lulled on, until finally my sister's eyes blinked open and she peered over at me, her pale face looking a bit more content than when she had washed up.

"Where am I, Ailith?" she whispered.

"You're in the Kingdom of the Land," I reminded her gently.

She looked around, cocking her head like a child. "What is this place?"

"The palace of the King of the Land," I responded, quietly adding, "the man who rescued you."

"The dark-haired one?" she murmured.

I nodded. "Yes. His name is Soren."

Her eyes slowly widened, and a gasp escaped her throat. "You mean...that was the man you're destined to marry?"

I fixated my gaze across the room, away from my sister, as I felt myself blush. "So...you found out about that?"

"Oh, the whole Sea Kingdom found out," she replied.

I groaned, swearing under my breath. Drat. Goridian wasn't going to react well to the fact that his bride was destined to marry someone else (who happened to be more powerful than him) was going around.

"What has happened in the Sea Kingdom since I left?" I enquired.

I was genuinely wondering this, as it'd been over two months since my arrival on Land. Autumn was approaching, and, although I was happily anticipating the sight of leaves changing colors, my heartbeat quickened at the idea of the Sea Kingdom in more peril than it had been the day I left.

"Well," Laena drawled, her voice weak with exhaustion, "Lord Goridian threw a fit the week you left. His armies patrolled the entire Kingdom, searching for you. When he realized that Triton had helped you escape the kingdom, he found Triton, and locked him in the palace dungeons. He then went to the shore to try and find you—but obviously failed, thank the Gods and Goddesses. Recently, he's been strangely quiet. We all know he's training his army, and he's been recruiting everyone strong enough to fight. It won't be long, Ailith, until he declares war."

I gulped. "How many men?"

She shook her head, whispering, "Hundreds. Maybe even thousands. I'm not really sure. Triton sent me—he helped me escape—to warn you that Goridian will declare war, most likely, before the first snowfall of winter."

"Does he expect to fight this war on Land?" I breathed.

Laena nodded her head, filling me with repulse.

"He's found a way to get out of the water, we think," she explained. "Triton believes he has allies in this kingdom, close to you. Close enough to know what you're doing."

My blood seemed to go cold as I realized what this meant.

That someone—one of my allies—was plotting against me.

"Did Triton leave me any sort of personal message; any advice?" I exclaimed.

Slowly, Laena nodded. "He's growing weak, from starvation, and lack of power. But he managed to say that you must find his trident in order to defeat Lord Goridian and his army, and that you have to muster the strength to follow what you know is right."

Vague, as usual. I huffed.

"You should continue resting," I whispered, tucking my sister further under the covers. She did not object, but rather snuggled into the comfort of the bed. My stomach continued to toss with her words, even after she stopped speaking.

I left the room as soon as I was sure my sister was fast asleep, closing the door gently behind me, when I spotted Soren waiting right outside in the dark hallway. His grey eyes shone bright in the light being cast through one of the glassy windows in the hallway, the corners of his mouth turned up just slightly.

"Is she alright?" he asked.

I nodded. "Laena is doing just fine. Thank you, for everything you've done for her...saving her life, letting her stay here..."

"I wouldn't have it any other way," Soren responded, reaching forward and brushing a hand against my cheek. I felt a flutter of nerves in my stomach.

"Soren, I"—

Quietly, he shushed me, and leaned forward to press his mouth to the top of my head. I took a deep breath, letting the silence flood my eyes, calming me down a bit.

However, even with his delicate, soothing touches, I couldn't seem to get what my sister had said about my kingdom—about Goridian building his army—out of my head.

"Sor," I murmured. "I need to tell you what she said."

"Hm?" He looked down at me, his eyes full squinted ever so slightly, a grin toying with his mouth.

I sighed. "Goridian is growing in power. It is rumored that he has found a way to get onto Land, and that he expects to fight this battle here."

Soren shook his head. "That's simply an advantage to us. We'll fight better on Land."

Shaking my head, I sighed. He'd forgotten one very important piece of the puzzle.

"Everyone else will...but I won't."

After all, my powers resided with the sea and with water. Without those powers, all I had were my skills in combat, which were virtually useless with someone like Lord Goridian, especially compared to the powers of those like Soren.

He looked down at me, his gaze retracting a bit.

"I have to go," he simply said, brushing a stray piece of hair from my eyes, before stepping back. "I'll speak to you later."

"Soren, where are you going?" I asked in exasperation.

"I have things to do, Ailith. I am a King, you know," he snapped.

I took a step back, now aware that he truly wasn't interested in hearing what I had to say. It surprised me, seeing him go from being so gentle and delicate to completely locking himself up. He wouldn't even tell me what he was leaving for.

I left in a huff, in search of someone I knew would actually talk to me.

~

Knocking on the door, I called his name.

I knew he'd returned home later than us that evening with Caspian, Zeus and the rest of the army—and if Soren wouldn't talk to me, I knew that he would.

"Lazarus!" I called.

I heard fumbling around in the room, before footsteps led up to the door. However, it did not open.

"What do you want, Ailith?" he called through the wood.

"I need to talk," I responded, my voice a bit squeaky as I placed my hands on my hips impatiently, adding, "Now."

"Sorry, seaweed. No-can-do right now. I'm going to sleep," he responded.

I rolled my eyes. "Lazarus, come out here and talk to me right now, you big horse's ass."

Slowly, a deep rumble escaped the room from the other side of the door. He was chuckling—laughing at me.

"Alright," he murmured, before I heard the doorknob clicking and the big door swinging open. Lazarus slipped through the narrow space he had opened, and into the hallway, facing me with one brow curved.

"I need your help," I murmured.

He crossed his arms in front of his chest. "Why? With what?"

"Soren."

A big grimace took over his expression, and he backed up a bit.

"Yeah, that topic's off limits, kelp hair."

I felt my eyes rolling for me. "Come on, Laz, it's nothing weird."

He eyed me suspiciously. "Promise?"

I nodded. "I just need help because...he won't talk to me."

Lazarus gazed at me for a few minutes, his stare running up and down my face.

"Why won't he talk to you?" he asked.

I shrugged. "That's why I'm asking you, dipshit."

"You think that I would know why Soren is disinterested in hearing you whine?" he asked, smirking. His tone was drenched in sarcasm.

I clapped him on the arm. "I was trying to ask him for some help, and talk to him, but he just...walked away. Said he has 'stuff to do.' What does that even mean? Does he actually have work to do, or is he just bored of hearing me talk? Was he going off to do something secretive? Do you think he's pretending to love me, for the sake of the prophecy, and is secretly running off to another lover in the middle of the night?"

At this point, I was panting.

Lazarus blinked a few times, his eyes wide.

"Ailith, if Sor said he had something to do, then he probably had something pretty damn important to do. I can't think of anything he'd prefer to do for pleasure than doodling around with you." His smirk intensified.

I sighed. "How do I get him to pay attention to me?"

Lazarus shook his head. "I can't believe I'm giving a woman advice on how to interest my brother."

I glared. "Just tell me something helpful."

Shaking his head, he let out a low chuckle. "Look," he said, his tone calm and his voice matter-of-fact. "If you want to get Soren's attention, you could always go about it the old-fashioned way."

I quirked a brow. "What?"

"You know," he said, looking up and down the hallway to make sure no one was there, whispering the next sentence. "Put on something tight and short...waltz around tomorrow at the Autumn's Feast like you don't even know him. Knowing how Sor feels about you, I'd guess that would do the trick."

I could tell, by the way he spoke, that he was being completely serious.

"Fine," I responded, sighing in satisfaction. "Maybe I will."

I could just feel the wicked grin building under my flesh.

AUTHOR'S NOTE:

Heyyyy my lovely readers! Happy Friday!

What do you guys think is going to happen at the Autumn's Feast? How do you guys think Laena is going to fit into this whole dynamic? Anyone who can guess correctly gets the next chapter dedicated to them! ;)

If you enjoyed what you read, don't forget to click that vote button, and leave me a comment down below telling me your thoughts!

As always, thank you to everyone who supports HOTS. *giggles

LK OUT.

Xoxo,

LK

Chapter 21

(And no I don't mean icky stuff. We keep it PG-13 here, people).

The Autumn's Feast was a gathering held at the palace for the God's sons, where seasonal game was enjoyed, along with conversation and drink. Soren stopped by my chambers that morning to officially invite me as his fianceé, and of course, I was quick to accept—not too eagerly, of course.

He would be there, Lazarus would be there, and all of the sons of the Gods would be there. As Lazarus had pointed out the previous night, it was the perfect opportunity to catch attention.

I spent the morning with my sister, bringing her things to eat and asking servants to gather seawater for her. She was making a quick recovery from her near-death experience escaping the Sea Kingdom, and was able to speak enthusiastically with me for the majority of the morning.

Unfortunately, she was aware of the prophecy I was meant to fulfill—and she wanted to know all the details.

"So," she coughed, choking down gulps of seawater in between laughs. "You and King Soren...?"

I nodded, rolling my eyes. "You can say it."

"You're sleeping together?"

I shook my head feverishly. "What? No."

"You mean not yet."

"Don't be a pervert, Laena," I growled, shooting her a glare.

All she did was click her tongue. "I wish I could see the two of you toget her...the way you look at each other. Then I'd know for sure if you're just denying it...which I think you are."

"I can promise you it hasn't gone farther than...," I muttered, stopping mid-sentence as my mind trailed off to the kisses in the forest the previous day, and the ones before that in the tent. I blushed just at the flashback.

"I can tell you love him," Laena murmured, reaching out to take my hand. "Triton knew you would."

"Why?" I asked.

She shrugged. "He just knows those things."

"Yeah," I grumbled, internally admitting that Triton was able to predict and pick up on different likelihoods. "He does."

~

Nela and Cleo were ecstatic this time when I confessed that I was over my days of wearing my precious leather boots to formal gatherings and would, this time around, succumb to the societal pressure on females to wear pokey, horribly painful shoes.

I did need the height, unfortunately.

I curled my locks into big, soft curls, lined my eyes and darkened my eyelashes—begrudgingly—because I knew that I needed to do something to earn attention, even if I was taking the more scandalous route.

As for my gown...well, it was bright red, and mostly lace, with a hem that stopped a few inches above my knees and a plunging neckline that led to a tightly cinched waist. With the dress, I wore a pair of black high heels that made me want to snap my own neck when I attempted to walk in them, but had to say, as I examined myself in the mirror, did a good job of making me look a bit like an adult woman.

Still, I absolutely abhorred high heels.

As per usual, I heard a familiar knock on the door of my chambers and recognized it as Lazarus.

Swinging open the door, I faced him with confidence. He stepped back, trailing me with his gaze and letting himself grin. I could sense the rumbling chuckle building up in his diaphragm, but he managed to cough most of it down.

"Wow, seashells," he said, clearing his throat. "You seem to be riding a wave of gumption right now."

"Why?" I gasped. "Is it too much?"

Quickly, he shook his head no.

"It's perfect," he responded, "I'm just surprised you took my advice."

I shrugged. "I had no reason not to."

"Eh...I guess that's true," he replied, before looping his arm around mine. Slowly and steadily, we floated down the spiral staircase, all the way down to the main corridor.

Lazarus seemed to be holding in a monumental smirk as we strolled down the hallway and through several passageways to the dining hall. As we walked, I remembered my first encounter with Soren there—how we'd fought each other; quite literally--and how that had been the first night he'd ever marked me.

The idea would have repulsed me just months ago, but it was actually quite sentimental now.

Now that Soren mattered.

Lazarus opened the door to the dining hall for me, and I felt nerves fluttering around in my stomach as I stepped in. The room was adorned in orange and red decorations, with little leaves hanging off the crystal chandeliers and pumpkins and squashes stacked up in the corners of the room. The dining table was covered in a rusty orange tablecloth, and silver platters piled high with heaps of seasonal food.

I spotted Soren at the opposite end of the dining hall, crown placed carefully on his head. One seat was open at his left, and another at his right, obviously meant for Lazarus and me. Other men were lined up at the table, all bearing crowns of some sort, as they were the sons of Gods and Goddesses. I wondered how many of them were Zeus's sons.

There was a variety of handsome men at that table, and they all turned to look at me and went silent as I walked in. I couldn't tell if it was because I actually looked good, or because I looked absolutely ridiculous. It was impossible to tell, so I walked in numbing my mind to the effects of their stares.

Lazarus swallowed yet another chuckle at my side as we both walked down different sides of the dining table, taking our seats next to Soren. Even though I so wanted to look over at him, I didn't. Instead, I kept my eyes on the beautifully set table, the food...anything but him.

I was both surprised and disappointed when he seemed to refuse to look at me as well. I bit my lip, feeling my brows furrow.

Maybe I really did look ridiculous.

The silence lasted for a few more moments, before Lazarus broke it—yelling into the atmosphere, "I don't know about all of you, but I'm starving. Let's eat."

Forks hit plates and goblets of ale flavored with autumn spices clinked together as the men began speaking amongst themselves. Luckily, this gathering was hardly political, but rather just an opportunity for the sons of the Gods and Goddesses to keep in touch and maintain friendships.

Music began playing from a corner in the room. Fiddles and lutes, playing to the beat of soft drums. I kept to myself, making sure I didn't spill anything on my painfully thin dress and lowering my gaze away from Soren.

"So," one of the men barked, laughter threatening to spill from his throat. "What is that spectacular thing sitting next to you, King Soren?"

The music stopped, the other men quit talking, and I immediately felt my blood run cold.

Soren's mouth went a bit crooked, in a bit of a pained smile. "She's my fianceé, Mathias, why?"

"Well, if you haven't claimed her yet, I'd be happy to take her off your hands," the man responded, cackling to himself, the men surrounding him laughing as well.

The laughter made me sick to my stomach. I felt my grip tightening on my fork.

"You're so desperate for female attention that you're asking to borrow my fianceé?" Soren asked, sipping from his goblet.

"If she wouldn't mind, of course," the man named Mathias responded, a grin spreading across his face as he winked at me from across the room. "It's a well-known fact that women simply can't resist me."

My stomach flipped.

Soren cleared his throat. "Please, Mathias. Everyone knows that the only way you'd ever get laid is if you somehow managed to crawl up a chicken's ass," he responded matter-of-factly, chewing his food casually. His face remained completely serious.

The men in the room roared with laughter, and I felt myself gasp with relief when the man named Mathias dropped the topic entirely.

The rest of the night was virtually uneventful, which I was grateful for. After practically being referred to as an object, I was happy to simply eat my food, take a few sips of ale and listen to the dull conversation of the boarish misanthropes surrounding me. Most of them either talked about fighting or sex, or fighting and sex. Soren seemed to be listening more than participating as well. However, we didn't speak to each other. I was determined to let him talk to me first, rather than initiating the conversation myself. It would tell me whether or not he was truly interested in speaking to me.

After a few hours, the men seemed to be spreading out amongst the room, taking seats on more comfortable, cushioned sofas as they piled their plates with pumpkin-flavored desserts and crystal glasses of whiskey. As the group was dispersed, I was desperate to find Lazarus and tell him that my plan—his suggestion—wasn't working. The night had passed by and Soren hadn't spoken a single word to me.

I peered around the room, knowing it wouldn't be difficult for his bright auburn head to catch my eye, when I realized that Lazarus wasn't there.

I grumbled to myself, and realized he must have left. I decided that, as long as my efforts weren't making a difference at the dinner, I might as well seek out Lazarus to speak with him, as it seemed like the only option that wouldn't land me in some form of disarray.

Before anyone could notice, I slipped out of the dining hall's entrance and into the main corridor of the palace.

I walked down the hall, feeling my legs growing tired underneath me, stuffed into the uncomfortable high-heeled shoes. I yawned, flipping my stiff curled hair behind me and sighed.

Where the hell was Lazarus?

I was about halfway down the main corridor when I stepped out of my heels, holding them in my hand and swearing under my breath. No matter how many times I made my feet uncomfortable, I'd always be short, and that's just something I would have to accept.

I laughed at myself. I'd known this plan of my version of seduction couldn't work. I just wasn't the type of girl who wore low-cut lace dresses and high heels.

I took dainty steps on my pained, blistered feet, quietly cursing underneath my breath, when I heard a familiar dark chuckle behind me.

"Were those shoes worth it?"

I spun around, and had to bite my lip to keep myself from smiling when I noticed Soren just feet away from me.

He'd been following me?

I shrugged. "Yeah, I kind of gave up on the shoes."

He laughed, sauntering in my direction. "You're something else, Ailith."

"What do you mean?"

He walked over so quickly, that I didn't notice when he was right in front of me. I could hear his breath, husky and raw, as he grabbed onto my arms.

Before I could protest, he pushed me up against the wall of the corridor. He leaned forward, his breath tickling my cheek.

"How dare you," he growled, "show up at my dinner looking like that, and not utter a single word to me, or even look at me once?"

I shook my head, peering down at the floor. "I was waiting for you to talk to me."

He pushed himself closer. "I couldn't. I couldn't even look at you."

I furrowed a brow. "Why not?"

He breathed for a few moments, his breath becoming jagged.

"You were driving me insane back there, looking like this," he growled into my ear.

"I was?" I murmured.

His breath was warm, his mouth parted.

"Do you know how difficult it was seeing you like this, and not being able to rip that dress to shreds?" he grumbled, his arms pinning mine to the wall. "Because that's all I could think about back there, Ailith," he growled, breathing into my ear, "If I had things my way, I would have taken you. Right there."

I gasped, feeling his hands at my waist, pulling me to him before his mouth crashed into mine. His lips were warm and inviting, and I felt my arms wrapping around his neck as his mouth pulled against mine, a dark chuckle escaping him as he gripped me tighter, as his hands slid higher.

He broke the kiss to bend forward, dragging his lips along my jawbone. I bit my lip to keep myself from reacting, to keep myself from gasping aloud.

His next words made my stomach tingle.

"Come to my chambers tonight," he whispered.

I shook my head. "I can't."

"Why not?" he grumbled, leaning forward to kiss the base of my throat. I shuddered from the touch, a breeze drifting in from the open windows, making me shiver.

"Not yet," I told him, taking a few steps back, readjusting my dress. He snickered.

"That's not a good enough reason," he snarled, his eyes alertly primal. "I want you, Ailith."

I smirked. "Haven't you ever heard about the dangers of instant gratification? You're very impatient, you know."

"Your days are numbered. I don't want to waste another moment," he responded, tracing his fingers along my neckline. I glared, daring him to trace lower.

"My days may be numbered," I responded. "But yours most certainly aren't. You have all the time in the world to wait, and that's just what you're going to have to do."

A growl escaped his throat. "You're horribly frustrating. You know that, right, sea girl?" he murmured.

I nodded. "If I weren't, that'd take the fun out of all this."

"Are you sure?" he muttered, kissing me again. "You won't regret it, my dear."

I nodded, biting my lip to keep myself from smiling too big, shaking my head. "I'm sure. Wow. Lazarus was right."

With that, I pulled away, taking a few steps back and walking away from him, my heart still racing from his touch, which seemed to linger upon my flesh.

"Right about what?" Soren called after me in confusion.

But I was already gone.

AUTHOR'S NOTE:

Rip fan girls. Shall we commemorate with a ship name? ;)

Happy Monday everyone! Even though 'happy Monday' is kind of an oxymoron. Ok--a definite oxymoron.

Sorry for the slightly-later-than-usual update. I have a huge chemistry assignment I procrastinated about and am supposed to be doing right now, actually. It's due tomorrow and I had all weekend to do it and I still decided Monday evening would be the best time to get it done. Whatevs. Moral of the story (which I will never follow): do your homework when you're supposed to, kids (me).

Honestly,-the problem with homework is that it exists. (Yes, you can quote me for your senior quotes/gravestones).

If you enjoyed this chapter, don't forget to vote and leave me a comment down below.

As always--thank you to everyone who reads and supports HOTS.

Thank the Gods and Goddesses Monday is finally over.

Xoxo,

LK

PS: Should I make a chapter of character pictures? Like a pinterest board only...here? **(in voice of Gru from Despicable me) LIGHTBULB

Sorry y'all my brain is all over the place today.

Ok byeeeee!

Chapter 22

Training resumed bright and early the next morning.

In fact, I was out of the palace and teaching a class in feigning surrender to my army with Caspian so early, that I didn't even have the chance to talk to Soren or Lazarus. The idea hadn't even passed my mind as I wandered outside, dressed in brand-new leather slacks and freshly polished boots. I knew, since Lazarus had taken my boots on the mountain, that he was the one who had gifted me with these clothes.

I wondered if this was his way of apologizing for his most scandalous advice—after all, neither of us were expecting such an abrupt and intense reaction from Soren.

"Now," I instructed, pacing around with a brand-new sword sheathed at my side (given to me by Lazarus as well), "I want you all to remember that the secret to being two-faced is making sure that at least one of those faces is pretty. You need to express through your facial expression what you want people to think you feel, rather than what you actually feel. Sounds easy, but it's really not. For example, you—Jerin," I said, pointing to one of the soldiers. "You've got a serious look on your face, even though I know for a fact that you don't really respect me. How do I know this? Well, I have the benefit of having overheard you refer to me as the King's bed-thing the other day."

At this point, I was directly targeting this soldier. But I didn't care. He deserved to be targeted for what he'd said. I wished I could rip him to shreds, but I knew that would take significant effort—and I preferred verbal torment, anyhow.

"I'll have you know," I told him through my teeth. "That what Soren and I do in our free time is a thousand times better than anything you're going to ever get on the off-chance you get to screw some unlucky girl." I was inches away from his face; my tone more of a feral growl than a human murmur.

The soldier's face twisted into a scowl.

"Ailith?"

I spun around, immediately feeling the heat rising to my cheeks as I realized Soren had been standing behind me that entire time.

So he'd heard me telling the lie about he things we did...or rather, the things we didn't do, that I had turned down the previous evening.

Soren's amused smirk made me want to die inside. His hands were clasped behind this back as he spoke softly to me.

I lowered my gaze.

"Could you possibly take a break to talk to me for a while?" Soren murmured, bending forward as to keep any of the nearby soldiers from overhearing our conversation.

I nodded. "That's probably a good idea."

He looped an arm around mine, and we began walking away from the lineups of soldiers. I spotted Soren turning his head over our shoulders to glare at the one soldier I'd been chastising, and took a shaky breath as I realized he'd probably heard me say what he'd said about me.

That's what people really thought? That I was Soren's bed-thing?

Ew.

S oren, surprisingly, was the first one to speak.

"I wanted to apologize, Ailith," he told me, as we walked through the fields, along the shoreline. "How I behaved last night was terribly uncouth. I don't know what came over me."

I think I do, I wanted to utter.

I sneered. "No need to apologize. You don't scare me, Sor," I told him.

With that, I felt him grabbing onto my arms and jerking me towards him, a grin toying at his mouth.

"Fine," he responded, his brows crossing smugly. "Because you don't scare me either. And I knew exactly what I was saying and doing last night."

"Way to go. A half-assed apology that you didn't even mean," I snarled, letting him pull me closer.

He grinned. "I heard what you had to say to that soldier," he growled, "and I want to let you know, Ms. Ailith, that when I am finished with you...," he paused, to let out a frustrated laugh. "You will be able to say—with truth—what you said today."

I turned my gaze into a dare. "And what is that?"

His lips were suddenly at my ear, whispering, "that what we do—that what I do to you, is better than anything anyone has ever experienced."

I felt myself gasping at the tickle of his breath at my ear, before he released me from his grip, his face all smugness.

How I wanted to chastise him—until I realized all my energy had been spent on processing his unholy words.

Soren's smugness seemed to mold into curiosity.

"You're silent," he noted.

I nodded, shooting him a fake glare. "Yes, and?"

"Nothing," he responded, bowing his head to laugh to himself, before looking back up at me and saying, "a rare occurrence indeed."

I shook my head. "What did you need to talk to me about?"

"You mean other than to recapitulate my intense emotional and physical need for your...closeness?"

I rolled my eyes at the discretion of his choice of words. "Yes."

"Then there wasn't anything." He smirked. "That was it."

"Well, as long as we're here," I told him, turning my face serious, and he did the same. "I wanted to ask you something."

He took a long, deep sigh. "Fine, I will comply to taking you in my arms right now and bringing you to my chambers this instant, but I hope you know that this cannot become a frequent thing. I do have things to attend to."

I rolled my eyes, sending him a sneer. I didn't give him the satisfaction of a witty remark, and I continued with what I actually wanted to know.

"I was wondering," I said, "why Hades is so threatened by Zeus."

He curved a brow. "What makes you think he is threatened by my father?"

"I don't know," I responded, feeling my taut muscles loosen now that he was finally speaking like a normal person again. "His vengeance and threat seem to have come from out of nowhere. I feel my presence at your court seems responsible for this untimely feud with Hades. You never seemed to have such an up-close issue with him in the past."

Soren sighed, trying to hide in a chuckle. "Ailith, Hades has been around for millions of years. There have been thousands of instances where he has tried to overpower my father, and failed. He tries every few centuries, even if he knows he will lose. He just likes making trouble."

"Then why am I in the middle of it?" I whined.

A grin toyed at Soren's lips. "Because you're my bed-thing."

I still took the opportunity to shove him.

"Oh, so does the idea disgust you that much?" he joked.

I glared at him. "I'm not going to dignify that question with an answer."

"I think Hades is interested in you," Soren murmured, adding, "but as I've said, I am a bit biased. However, as was demonstrated yesterday at the Autumn's Feast, it's hard for any male not to admit that you're the most stunning creature on Land."

Damn that bastard. I felt my cheeks heat up.

He seemed proud of himself as he added, "But I think he mostly is trying to get to me. Because he knows how in love with you I am."

Hotter cheeks. Burning hot. Crimson, blood-colored rosy monstrosities.

I tried to distract myself with another question. "So is Hades scared of you, or your father?"

Soren did not seem to notice my blushing. Thank the Gods and Goddesses.

"Well," he replied, "I think Hades is done tormenting my father. He's moved onto me. He is threatened by my power, which only grows as I continue to be with you."

"What?" I said.

He nodded, his grin fading and his face unfamiliarly serious.

"Something strange about Gods is that we feed off of love. Every time I touch you, every time I make you blush—as I have just done—every kiss we share, every single caress...powers me in a way you won't ever know," he explained. "The claiming ceremony will be the final step in releasing all of my capabilities."

"Have you grown more powerful since I've entered your life?" I whispered.

He nodded. "Everything I feel for you seems to amplify my abilities. You make me...you make me whole."

I felt my breath catch in my throat.

"So," he said. "Not only is Hades afraid of me, but he's afraid of what I will become with you; with your love and affection and attention, as it grows. He doesn't know what I will become, and that scares him to his very core. It is commonly accepted amongst Gods and Goddesses at this point that, when I claim someone, I will most likely become even more powerful than Zeus."

I felt myself going a bit dizzy.

"You're that important?" I exclaimed.

He shrugged. "Not important. Just...made by the two most powerful beings ever to grace the galaxy. It shouldn't be as surprising as it is to everyone."

"And you actually want...me?" I whispered.

He went quiet for a few moments, before he laughed.

"Well," he responded. "I thought I'd been a bit too zealous with expressing my feelings and wants, Ailith, but if you somehow want me to be even more direct"—

"No, no, that's perfectly fine," I said, holding out a hand. "I just don't understand why...me."

"Because that's just what the Gods and Goddesses decided," he responded. "And you have to admit, we work well together."

I nodded in admittance. "You're right. You antagonize me, yet I manage to rein you in when necessary. I'm practically your governess."

Suddenly, I felt protective stone arms wrapping around my shoulders, pulling me to a familiar warmth, where I buried my face in the scent of pine and wind. For the first time in a few days, this wasn't lust-driven Soren, and just how it had been at first.

His hands stroked through my hair as he bent forward to press a kiss to the top of my head. I dared look up, and was met with a slight grin before he kissed me on the cheek, his breath tickling my face.

"I have to go," he told me. "But I'll see you later, my bed-thing."

I would have slapped him, but his silky voice used the term so endearingly that I couldn't help but stay silent, and savor the sound of his voice lingering in the air like ocean spray before he turned and walked away.

~

Laena was insistent that I give her a tour of the palace.

Strangely enough, I was excited to show my sister where I'd been living these past months; everything that made this palace the wondrous Land Kingdom monstrosity that it was. Plus, I finally had someone from the Sea Kingdom who understood what it was like to be on Land as a person from the Sea.

"So," I told her as we strolled across the main corridor of the palace. "This is the main hallway. In there is the dining room, where the Land Court hosts banquets, feasts...the occasional jousting tournament between King Soren and whomever he's tormenting." My tone was casual, even though I was referring to a past occurrence.

Laena gave me a suspicious hiss. "Did that have to do with you?"

"Oh, come on," I responded, rolling my eyes and smiling at her. "Of course it did."

"And what's over there?" she asked, pointing to the throne room.

"Oh," I gasped. "That's the throne room. They hold balls and parties in there, and you'll never guess what they use to decorate."

"What?"

"Dead flowers!" I exclaimed. "Can you believe it? Snipped right from the roots, and put in vases, or strapped to the walls!"

In the Sea Kingdom, we were accustomed to our balls and parties being decorated with shells, fish scales, seaweed...but nothing dead.

"Gosh, that's bizarre," Laena agreed, shaking her head. "But I have to say, I received some flowers in a vase in my chambers yesterday and they smelled absolutely divine. Like the outdoors, only sweeter."

I cocked my head. "You were sent flowers?"

She nodded. "Yes, were they not from you?"

"No," I responded, my tone concerned. "They weren't."

I shrugged it off, assuming that the flowers had been delivered as a gift by the Court. Soren, I thought, would do something like that—order flowers for my sister. I smiled to myself, thinking about it.

"The funny thing is," Laena said, her tone a bit confused. "That the flowers were delivered in the middle of the night."

My blood curdled.

Now that did not sound like something Soren would do.

"Delivered? By who?" I gasped.

Laena shrugged. "I don't know, some guy."

Damn Triton and his choice in my sisters. Laena wasn't ready for the Land; she wasn't perceptive enough to determine threat, the poor thing.

"What did he look like?" I asked.

She smiled. "He had a kind smile. Red hair."

I took a long, deep breath. "Oh, that's Lazarus. He's the king's consort, and the king's brother."

She laughed absentmindedly as we sauntered into another passageway. "Really?"

All of a sudden, a wave of a breeze passed by, and in a split second, Lazarus was standing in front of us.

"Hello, sea girl and sea girl's sister," he said, "I heard my name being thought in your minds and thought I'd stop by." He shot a particularly broad grin towards Laena. I stepped in front of her protectively.

"Why did you deliver flowers to my sister in the middle of the night?" I asked, raising a brow suspiciously.

All of a sudden, Lazarus's face scrunched up. "I didn't."

I felt the air being knocked out of my lungs.

"Laena," I breathed, turning to my sister and feeling my face turn pale. "What did the man who delivered the flowers wear?"

She shrugged nonchalantly. "A fur cape, why?"

I clasped a hand to my mouth. No. No. This couldn't be. I didn't want to say his name, but it simply slipped out.

"Hades."

AUTHOR'S NOTE:

Heyyy lovely people!

THANK GOODNESS it's Friday. Quick chemistry homework update: it took me all week to figure out. Luckily, my teacher gave me an extension. But still. It was SO stressful. Moral of the story: homework sucks.

Now I have something more sentimental to say.

Today, I was at lunch when I nonchalantly decided to check Wattpad (because mis amigos were asking about it), and I saw that Heiress of the Sea now has 10,000 reads. That's INSANE. When I first began uploading this story, I was hoping for a few people to look at my story! The fact that I have so many if you is incredible, and I want to say a huge THANK YOU to everyone. Writing is my favorite thing in the world, and I am so happy that this story has gained this kind of following.

Now, some fun stuff--

As a thank you to everyone who has been supporting me, I decided that I'm going to do what I do best and begin a new story! (HOTS will still be updated regularly and everything...no change with that).

I recently began writing a contemporary criminal romance called Devil's Advocate. I will be uploading the first chapter tomorrow (Saturday). Go check it out! I know this isn't the genre of HOTS, and I will be writing another YA fantasy in the near future--I'm just taking a break for a little while and writing what has become inspired within me.

Here's a little tease:

Devil's Advocate

Nineteen-year-old Jenna has spent most of her life running from those more powerful than her.

However, when becomes the victim of a crime of passion, she finds her life twisted upside-down when she wakes up having been saved by the mercy of the charming, handsome cold-blooded New York mafia leader Rafael Devillo. Trapped in a mansion bigger than a museum and forced under the protection of a group of men she sees as criminals, Jenna will have to figure out a way out...even if that means playing devil's advocate.

Chapter 23

Lazarus's beaming face twisted into a grim frown.

"Wait," he murmured. "Madalaena, you saw Hades in the middle of the night and didn't think to alert any of the palace guards?"

My sister gasped. "I—I didn't realize he was actually Hades. And is that bad? I mean, he is just another God, is he not?"

"No, Laena," I murmured. "He poses a threat to me, and to King Soren. I thought I told you that."

"I must have forgotten," she whimpered. "I'm sorry, Ailith. But I don't think he meant any harm. He was in and out of my chambers in a flash."

"Which means he's found a quick way in and out of the castle," Lazarus growled, his tone menaced. "I must go tell Soren about this immediately. Ailith, take your sister back to her chambers, make sure there are guards there with her, and then meet me and Soren in his study. Do you know where that is?"

I blinked. "I have no idea."

Soren's study? How come I hadn't been there before?

"Fine. I will come with you to drop her off, but we must hurry," he said, his eyes lowered and his tone grim.

"Come on, Laena," I whispered, taking my sister's hand and squeezing it to reassure her.

The three of us dashed towards the staircase at the end of the corridor. We scampered up the stairs (unfortunately, there wasn't a floating spell on every single flight of stairs in the palace), and across the passageway, which led to Laena's chambers.

"Go inside," I directed my sister, concern making my voice a bit squeaky. "I'll come for you when I know it's safe."

My beautiful sister followed my command silently, stepping into her chambers with light feet, and I wished to comfort her in that moment, even though I knew I was needed elsewhere.

Two guards stood outside the doors, and as Lazarus instructed them to keep a close eye on her, and make sure her windows were locked, I kept running through the idea that Hades had invaded my sister's space—my space, essentially.

I felt a low, feral growl burrowing inside my throat. I coughed it down, and turned to face Lazarus.

"Let's go," I told him, any hint of emotion curdled in my boiling voice.

He took me by the arm and we rushed down the stairs, through the main corridor of the palace, and into another passageway I'd never been in before.

It was narrow, and lined with beautiful, colorful stain-glass windows interpreting the stories of the birth of Zeus, and other Gods, sending flickering jewel tones across the hall. However, I did not have time to further admire them as Lazarus yanked me down the passageway and into a room, shutting the door behind us.

I wanted to be able to focus on the problem at hand, but I couldn't as I stepped into the room, immediately in awe.

It was surprisingly bright, with clean marble floors, a large wooden desk and bookshelves, with velvet furniture surrounding an enormous fireplace. However, it wasn't the furniture or floor that was particularly astounding, but the enormous, dome-like ceiling that was made out of clear glass, filtering in warm sunlight.

I felt a gasp escaping my mouth as familiar eyes settled on my jaw, glittering in the sunlight from where I'd been kissed earlier that day.

"Lazarus," Soren murmured. "What are you doing here? Why have you brought Ailith?"

"I wouldn't have brought her, were it not an emergency," Lazarus quickly told his brother, adding, "and even if it weren't an emergency, she is quite adamant on being of help, as you know."

"But being safe and of help are two entirely separate priorities, one being more important by far," Soren muttered under his breath, calling out to me, "Ailith, my dear, what are you doing here?"

Quickly, I turned, setting my jaw. "Hades brought my sister flowers last night."

As soon as I'd spoken the words, Soren was right in front of me, toying with my folded hands. "Are you positive it was Hades?"

I nodded, blinking back worried tears. "She said a redheaded man came into her chambers last night, and it wasn't Lazarus. The clothes she described him wearing...the fur cape. That's what he wears...it's what he wore when he abducted me on top of the mountains." I took a long deep breath, my diaphragm shaking with the memory.

A broad, familiar hand lazily stroked the waves of hair draped across my shoulder blades.

"Is there a possibility she could have been dreaming?" Soren whispered.

I shook my head, shuddering. "I don't think so. She spoke of his appearance as if the image was still vivid in her head. I don't know anyone to ever dream so clearly and remember the details the way she did."

A tug of my arm, and he had me pressed up against him, an arm wrapped around my waist securely.

"Let's go investigate," he breathed.

The speed at which Soren flew, Lazarus close behind, was enough to make me dizzy-headed. We landed in front of Laena's chambers not a moment later. Soren set me down with a bit of a chuckle as I stumbled to regain my balance, before we knocked on the door.

Guards let us into the room, and I immediately spotted my sister sitting in a large white armchair, arms folded in front of her chest. She almost looked...guilty.

I rushed over to her, taking her hands in mine and whispering, "It's okay, Laena."

However, it was not I that seemed to bring her out of her worried daze, but a grey gaze from across the room.

Immediately, my sister's demeanor morphed from one of worry to one of pure curiosity. I felt a groan festering within me, knowing that when Laena wanted to humiliate me, she very well could.

"So you're King Soren," Laena said, her full lips parting as she sauntered over to Soren and lightly shook his hand, probably just to instigate touch. "I wanted to thank you for saving my life."

"Of course," Soren responded, a grin taunting his lips as he gently stepped back. "I appreciate your willingness to cooperating in this investigation."

"Oh, of course. Anything for my sister's...whatever you are," she murmured, her big eyes peering up at him in keen interest.

Soren took her words as a challenge. "Well, I could tell you what I enjoy inflicting upon your sister, but I feel like that wouldn't be as fun as letting you guess for yourself. I mean, look at her." He sent a teasing glance in my direction.

I nearly choked on my own tongue.

"Excuse me?" I exclaimed.

Before I could smack him, Laena nodded towards a vase on her bedside table. "Those are the flowers Hades brought to my chambers the other night."

I peered over at them, feeling my stomach jolt as I spotted the little yellow flowers, tied up in a pretty ribbon and everything, so close to where my sister had slept at night; so innocent...so helpless.

"We should remove them from the room to check that they aren't poisoned," Lazarus said, taking the vase and moving out of the chambers, but barely getting a few steps into the hall before Soren called him back in.

"I would have smelled if they were poisoned," Soren muttered, taking the vase and examining the flowers. "Madalaena, you're sure this wasn't delivered by castle staff? You're positive it wasn't a dream?"

She nodded her head. "Yes."

I stopped in front of my sister. "Why do you keep asking that?"

Soren eyed me for a moment, his gaze completely calm as he said, "Because these are flowers that grow very close to the palace."

I could feel Lazarus's muscles tensing from across the room. He seemed to be studying me closely; probably trying to make sense of what he could feel of my thoughts and feelings. I knew he had good intuition with that sort of thing, but even I was confused about what I was feeling that day.

I couldn't decide which emotion was taking over. My concern for Laena, my annoyance for provoking Soren, my annoyance at Soren for being provoked, my worry that Hades had found a way into the castle, the confusion of why he would leave my sister flowers...

It was all highly overwhelming.

"Why flowers?" I murmured.

Soren's gaze jerked up from the bouquet and then to me, when he said, "He's trying to send us a message."

"But what message?" Lazarus asked from behind him, hands placed on his hips as he, too, gazed at the seemingly normal vase of yellow flowers.

"I'm not sure," Soren muttered, speeding across the room and setting the flowers back down on the bedside table. "But thank you, both, for alerting me. This is an issue. If anything, Hades is telling us that he knows how to get in and out of the palace. And that's concerning enough."

Soren turned to leave, but not before Laz could ask, "Where are you going?"

"I have to do some investigating of my own. To see if anyone else saw Hades last night. I need to figure out how he wasn't spotted by the guards. They do watch the palace at all times, so I assume—unfortunately—that he used magic. I will see you later, Ailith."

His gaze pulled at mine for just a moment before he walked out of the room, his footsteps only audible for a few moments after he left.

Lazarus turned to Laena and me and said, "This isn't good."

With that, he took off after Soren, and we were left alone in Laena's chambers.

~

I found Caspian outside in the fields, dripping with sweat from just having finished his own training session, but grinning nonetheless.

Approaching him casually, I was surprised to find a smirk trying to peak its way onto my face. I wasn't truly sure why.

"Hey there, sea girl. Funny not seeing you around training today," he remarked, running a hand over his sweaty head.

I grimaced. "Yeah. I'm sorry for what I said to Jerin. I don't know what got into me. I kind of just...exploded."

He shrugged, poking me in the rib with his elbow. "Hey—at least the rest of the army got a laugh out of it. A lot of them still won't stop laughing about it."

I eyed him carefully. "What about you?"

"Laughing my ass off. Really."

My eyebrows shot up to my forehead. "Seriously?"

"Of course. Jerin was pissed. It was hilarious." I couldn't tell whether or not he was being facetious, so I decided to simply brush off his response.

As we walked through the fields, back towards the palace, I told him about what had happened that afternoon with the flowers, and Hades. I told him how worried I was about my sister; how helpless and naïve she truly was.

As I told him this, he furrowed a brow and asked, "Don't you come from a family of warriors?"

I half-smiled. "I was the only one really trained after our parents were taken away."

Caspian slowly shook his head. "I don't know how we're going to win this war against Goridian, Ailith."

The words rumbled in my core.

"Do we need a bigger army?" I whispered.

Slowly, he nodded his head. "We need a bigger army, more power...the trident. You're going to have to find everyone you can to fight."

I cringed. So much to do, and so little time to do it.

"So you've heard about Goridian's advances too, then?" I asked.

Again, he nodded. No words sputtered from his lips.

"That's why Triton sent my sister. That's why Laena is here, and that's why she's in danger now," I responded, speaking more to myself than to Caspian.

"How is Soren dealing with all of this?" Caspian asked.

I shook my head. "Honestly? I'm not really sure. He just disappeared after we found the flowers on Laena's bedside table."

"He loves you, you know," he murmured.

A small smile flashed across my face. "I know that," I whispered. "I just wish we had more time. More time to get to know each other, to think about this wedding, to talk about everything going on. But we're going to have to manage it all sooner than we think."

"He's a multi-tasking bastard, is what he is," Caspian whispered. I nudged him gently, and we both chuckled.

Caspian eyed me for a moment. "Do you love him?"

A small autumn breeze grazed my cheek for a moment, and I paused, sighing.

"Yes," I said. "In spite of everything—he's one of the only people I've ever met with whom I feel truly comfortable."

Caspian laughed as we stopped for a moment, staring at the vast sea, just feet away from the gently swaying shore. The afternoon sun flickered against the calm green-blue waves, and we watched, stopping to sit down on rocks at the seaside.

"Are you still going to fight?" he asked.

I turned to him. "Fight Goridian?"

He nodded persistently.

I sneered. "With every ounce of will in my goddamned body."

For a moment we sat there, just looking. Just feeling each other's presence. ..the tension of my last words, as they dissolved into the air. I tried to focus my breathing; focus my gaze on the water, the fluffy sand, the grass and weeds near the ocean, the blue and purple wildflowers, the sunny yellow wildflowers...

Wait. Yellow wildflowers.

Slowly, I felt myself standing. I rushed over to grass, and plucked one of the yellow flowers, turning it around in my hand and glaring at the sea. That Gods and Goddesses damned sea.

And all of a sudden, it came to me.

AUTHOR'S NOTE:

Heyyy lovely people! Early update today, since I am low-key really sick and at home and should probably go to the doctor. Blah.

Anyway...

Mondays are the worst. Seriously. But at least next Monday is a holiday.

What do you think Ailith's epitome about the flowers means about Hades? I want to know your theories.

If you liked what you read, don't forget to vote and leave me a comment down below!

Also, go check out my new story, Devil's Advocate. I will be updating that soon as well.

Thanks everyone, and have a great week!

Xoxo,

LK

Chapter 24

"The sea," I breathed.

I felt Caspian's perplexed gaze peering over my shoulder, before his deep voice enquired"What about the sea?"

Turning to him, I responded, "I have to go talk to Soren. I'll come find you and explain later."

He threw his arms up, shaking his head as the corners of his mouth tugged upwards ever so slightly. "You know where to find me."

"Thanks, Caspian," I told him quickly, beginning to take off in the direction of the palace, before turning back to him, and saying, "Really. Thank you."

All he did was nod, before I took off sprinting, the tiny yellow flower getting smushed in my clenched fist.

~

The doors to Soren's study were locked, but with the adrenaline pumping through my body, I had no problem prying them open and stalking into the room. It turned out he was all alone—thank the Gods and Goddesses.

He looked surprised when he saw me, but luckily not upset.

"Ailith," he breathed, muttering under his breath, "thrice in one day."

I glared. "That's right. You actually have to talk to me."

"What a lucky man I am," he responded, a faint grin flickering on his face, letting me know he meant it. "What is it?"

"I know the meaning of the yellow flowers," I planted, bending over and clasping my hands to my knees, trying to catch my breath.

"Ailith, where were you?" his silky voice purred, helping me up by my arms, his grey gaze boring into mine.

"I was outside with Caspian"—

"Caspian?"

I nodded. "Yes. Anyway, he and I were sitting near the seaside, and I noticed all these wildflowers growing near the shore, and then spotted these yellow ones. Don't you recognize this?" I gasped, unclenching my fist and showing him the crumpled flower.

His face seemed to scrunch up, mimicking the flower's current state. "The ones from your sister's room," he whispered.

I nodded. "And I realized that these wildflowers only grow beside the sea," I explained. "And I know that getting into the palace was supposedly a message from Hades, but I think that everything he did was a message; to both frighten and inform us of what's to come. In his own wicked, strange way. And these flowers definitely mean something."

"What are you thinking?" Soren asked.

I took a deep breath. "Because they only grow by the sea, I think this is Hades's way of telling us that he and Lord Goridian are working together. Merging their armies to fight us. This is an act of intimidation."

Soren's eyes widened as he considered my hypothesis, taking a few steps towards me and pushing the flower into the right pocket of his pants.

"Why would Hades have offered you allegiance before, if he was already working with Goridian?" he murmured.

"Why would Hades have tried to claim me a few weeks after that? Who knows," I responded. "As you said, he enjoys making trouble."

"I cannot argue with that," he admitted, "but Hades hates Goridian. He considers him a traitor, not an ally."

"Or he wants us to think that," I said.

Soren seemed to consider my point, nodding his head slightly.

"It's very possible," he responded. "I think you are correct." However, there was something other than conclusion on his face...something a bit more unsettling.

"What is it?" I muttered.

He stepped close, his nose grazing the top of my head. "I don't want you to be correct. Because...if Hades and Goridian are planning to fight us together..."

I looked up, meeting his gaze with mine. "Then we fight."

Slowly, he nodded in agreement. "You do realize why I am so hesitant, don't you?"

"You mean to let me fight?"

His face seemed to grimace at the idea. "You especially. But to let any-one—even my most experienced and skilled soldiers—fight an army formed by Hades and Goridian...our chances of victory..."

"Don't say it," I begged him, feeling my eyes turning liquidy. I pressed my face to his chest.

"We can win," he whispered, kissing the top of my head. "But it's unlikely."

For a moment, I felt my heartbeat quickening. I had a flash of an idea. My mouth let out a slight gasp.

"What, my dear?"

I looked up at Soren. "I just had this narcissistic, lovely idea. About us."

He quirked a brow in interest, a slight grin on his pained face. "Enlighten me."

"I just want...I just want this," I whispered, reaching forward to stroke my hands against the sides of his face; his neck. "And I had the thought of disappearing—of leaving everything and everyone behind, and going into hiding. Just us," I said, before letting my face fall and pausing. "But that wouldn't be very heroic of us at all, would it?"

"It wouldn't be close to decent," he responded, before leaning forward to whisper in my ear, "Ailith, I have that fantasy every time I think of anything happening to you. Anything at all that might harm you. I wish more than anything that I could simply sweep you away; take you somewhere serene and peaceful. But then I remember that both of us are so God-and-God-dess-damned with responsibilities."

I clutched him, letting my fingers curl around his shoulders. I squeezed my eyes shut, pinning my face to his chest, but felt him reached forward, his touch against my chin light as he pulled my face up, securing his other hand at the tip of my spine, between my shoulder blades, before he yanked me close and met my lips with his.

His fingers dug into my back and gently pulled at my hair, his mouth pushing closer against mine; wanting more. His arms swung around me as he bent forward and lay me down against the floor. The cold of the marble was shocking, and I winced as he leaned me backward to trail kisses down my neck; my shoulder; his hands trailing up my ribcage...

All of a sudden, there was a knock at the door.

"I swear to the Gods and Goddesses," Soren growled, standing, and I did the same. "If that is Lazarus, I'm going to kick his ass."

He sauntered over to the doors and swung them open, placing his hands on his hips as, indeed, we were met by the familiar redhead. I myself was a bit annoyed at Lazarus, as he had interrupted such a seemingly important moment, but my irritation was quick to harden as I noticed the ghastly look on Lazarus's face.

"What are you doing here?" Soren growled. Apparently, he wasn't notching the horror in his brother's face.

"Laz," I breathed. "What is it?"

To my surprise, Lazarus turned to me, rather than Soren.

"It's Laena," he murmured, his voice quivering as he spoke the next words. "She's gone."

Before I could even have a reaction, I felt arms wrapping around me and whizzing out of the study, all the way down the corridor, up the stairwell, and to Laena's chambers in a matter of seconds.

Soren stood behind me as I tore open the door, and found no one inside.

Laena was gone. The guards were gone. The room looked completely undisturbed since the last time we'd seen it, except...

I gulped. The vase of yellow flowers were missing.

"This was Hades," I snarled, turning towards Soren. "How didn't you know that he was going to come back?"

"Ailith, I had her protected," he responded. "I don't know how Hades managed to take three of my best guards and your sister."

"But he did," I gasped, a sob catching my throat. "She's gone."

I was about to buckle over, my knees feeling a bit wobbly, when I felt a certain fire envelop me, and, barely knowing what I was doing, I threw myself at Soren.

He was shocked as we toppled to the floor. I secured my hands at his neck and began to press.

"How could you?" I shook, squeezing harder as tears began to blur my eyes. He began gasping; sputtering under my squeeze.

My body was overpowering my sense of logic as my hands clutched his throat, shaking feverishly.

"She's gone," I sobbed, before I felt two hands pry apart my grasp, as it was also weakened by my current stare of distress, and flip me over, onto the floor.

Soren gasped for air, taking a few deep breaths before securing two arms over mine, and leaning over my body.

"I'm sorry," I breathed, my sob beginning to choke me. I expected him to begin yelling at me, to be angry that I would react in such a way, but was surprised when he reached forward and began wiping away the tears.

He shushed me as I kept whimpering, "She's gone."

He grasped my wrists, shaking them in front of my face, and saying, "No, she's not. We're going to get her back." His voice was seething with rage. I couldn't tell if it was at me, or Hades...or a combination.

He couldn't have been that angry at me. I knew that, as he took me in his arms; held my body there, limp like a corpse in his warm hands.

~

Lazarus ate silently, shifting food around on his plate; not really moving in the direction of his mouth as he absentmindedly sipped his ale.

I was silent, too.

We were eating dinner alone that evening. Soren had said he couldn't join us because he had "things to attend to."

I didn't believe him.

Lazarus shot me a look of irritation. "Of course he has things to attend to." His auburn head flickered bright red in the candlelight.

"I think I scared him back there," I murmured, shrugging. "If he is angry with me, he is rightfully so."

Lazarus let out a deep chuckle. "Come on, kelp hair."

Eyeing him, I hissed, "What?"

"If Soren had gotten really mad—or even mildly hurt—today from your little episode, he could have totally taken you down. You do realize that he's a God, right?"

"I think I really upset him," I murmured, feeling my blood run cold at the realization. I'd been feeling guilty all afternoon.

"You?" Lazarus scoffed. "Never."

"Why not? I've angered him before," I seethed, standing up from my seat.

He glared. "Why do you think? He's an immortal God, and every bloody time you touch him he becomes more and more powerful. Plus, the bastard loves it."

I was shocked. I mean, I knew Lazarus knew about Soren's growing powers. However, the way he spat the words told me that he was angry about it...almost resentful.

Was Lazarus...jealous?

"Why are you so angry?" I enquired, sitting back down in my seat. "Is it because Soren is the one inheriting all the power, and not you?"

He glared. "Well, you seem angry that he hasn't told you he loves you yet."

I rolled my eyes at his weak retort. "Come on, Laz. Can't you just talk to me like a normal person?"

"Fine. Do you want me to tell you something about Soren?"

"Well, I was actually hoping to drop the subject for a little while. I need to get my mind off of him," I responded, my voice cracking a little.

Lazarus seemed to be ignoring everything I was saying. "He's with Juniper right now."

I shrugged. "What of it?"

"I mean he's with Juniper right now."

I felt my jaw dropping to the floor. "WHAT?"

A faint, wicked smile flickered at his lips. A smile that was almost familia r...almost different, but that I couldn't place.

It was a smile that made me realize he was kidding.

I groaned, slouching in my seat. "You're so full of shit, Lazarus. What's going on with you tonight?"

"Just feeling a little spunky," he responded. "But seriously, Juniper wants him. She told me. You did see her dress at your engagement ball, right?"

I rolled my eyes. "I'm not falling for this again."

"Why would I kid about her wanting him?" he mused, taking another sip of his ale.

I sneered, before I stood up again and threw my cloth napkin at the table, hissing a two-faced, aggressively saccharine, "Good night."

He looked at me with feigned surprise. "You're not going to stay and finish this delicious meal with me?"

"I'm not hungry anymore," I hissed.

With that, I stomped out of the dining room, through the stony hallway and out of the door, my breath thickening as I felt an eery chill creeping up my spine.

Because that man in there hadn't been the Lazarus I was used to. The joking, kind-hearted Lazarus.

He was someone else entirely.

All of a sudden, I heard panting from the end of the hall.

The hair on my body seemed to stand up straight as I peered across the shadowy corridor, and saw a familiar, muscled figure collapsing to his knees as he spotted me, calling out my name like a specter.

AUTHOR'S NOTE:

I would like to apologize for this chapter. I wrote it six weeks ago at 2am, and now that I'm reading it again all I can think is "literally wtf."

LITERALLY, THOUGH. WHAT THE ACTUAL--

you get it.

Happy Friday, everyone! I hope you've had an amazing week. I'm happy to report that my week hasn't been that awful, but it hasn't been the best week of my life either. I've had some tests, switched to an easier chemistry class (didn't we all see that one coming), and tonight I think I'm going to watch Bridget Jones's Diary and cry about being forever single before the three day weekend. COME AT ME COLUMBUS DAY. Seriously.

Now I am going to apologize for whatever that was. I'm at school as I write this (in a free period, y'all, not in the middle of class) and I'm just really excited to go home in three hours. Except for the fact that it might rain and I take the bus home. Ugh. Nothing worse than the rain-soaked people on a crowded bus in rush hour traffic.

Have a spectacular weekend, and I'll see you all here for another chapter on Monday.

And--I just realized. HOTS is over halfway uploaded. Whaaaaaat?!!! We're gon be wrapping this up into a nice bow pretty soon people. It's happening!!!

If you enjoyed what you read, be sure to vote and leave me a comment down below!

What do you think is going to happen next?! Since this is apparently "wtf" week, wtf do you think is going on with Lazarus? Or with Ailith attempting murder...? What...the...

I don't know. I honestly couldn't tell you.

Peace out, my lovelies!

Xoxo,

LK

Chapter 25

Caspian's body collapsed on the stone floors of the corridor, and I immediately sprinted towards him, forgetting all of the nonsense in my head from before. I bent over him, my eyes sharply scouring his body for any sign of injury.

"Come on, buddy. Let me help you up," I murmured, securing an arm around one of Caspian's cantaloupe-sized biceps and pulling with all my might. After a few moments, he grunted, sending me a smirk, and scampered to this feet.

"Thanks," he grumbled; still panting.

"What's going on?" I gasped, eyeing the sweat rolling down his face and neck. "And did you just run across the entire Land Kingdom, or something?"

He half-smiled. "Sort of. I was over in the East, fighting against some revolters, when I caught word from one of my spies that Goridian...."

He continued breathing heavily, his breath slowly catching up to him.

"That Goridian," he continued, "is going to strike today. Tonight. I didn't believe him, but then I realized that it was true. The sea is in a state of complete disarray. Storms, just miles away from the shores, waves the size of mountains...he means to come to Land soon. In fact, he already has soldiers beginning to invade. It will be no time before he's here."

I gulped. "Gods and Goddesses."

"I know. I ran all the way here, since my horse was injured in the battle. It was forty miles."

I ran my gaze up and down him once more. "You ran forty miles?"

He sneered. "I'm half-god, Ailith. It was a light jog."

Rolling my eyes, I responded, "Well, you should probably lie down. Let's go to Soren's study."

Caspian curved a brow. "Is that were he is?"

I shrugged. "That's where he's been spending a lot of his time lately."

"Why don't you ask Lazarus where he is?" he mused.

Slowly, I shook my head. "Let's not. Laz is in a mood tonight. He's all pissy about life and whatnot."

I could have sworn I heard Caspian growling in irritation under his breath as we headed down the corridor, in the direction of Soren's study.

We arrived not minutes later, and were shocked to find the doors closed.

"Closed?" I whispered.

Caspian nudged me. "Someone's nervous."

I shot him a glare. "What are you talking about?"
"You're worried that he's not alone."

"And you should be worried that you're about to go into your boss's study, all sweaty and panting, with his fianceé," I retorted.

Caspian held back a snort as we heard footsteps approaching the wooden doors. Murmurs escaped the room, and we took a few steps back, having no idea what to expect. I felt my stomach turning in one fluid motion as I realized that the murmurs were not only Soren's, but Juniper's as well.

I swear, to the Gods and Goddesses—

All of a sudden, the doors were opened. Soren was standing there, fully clothed and hair still perfectly in place (to my great relief), and Juniper was slung over one of the velvet divans in front of the fireplace.

I felt bile simmering at the bottom of my throat as I eyed her; the short, low-cut pink silk gown, the way she lay on her side, head propped up by a willing elbow, the curve of her hips fully displayed in the flicker of the fire.

However, as I looked, I felt comforting arms wrapping around my waist from behind; his arms, and I immediately felt my tense muscles loosen.

Soren snickered into my left ear and murmured, "Someone jealous?"

I ignored his comment and instead looked over to where Caspian was standing a few feet away, surveying the awkward situation. Juniper seemed ensconced in her own daze of sorts, and Soren and I were simply waiting to see which one of us exploded first.

"I hope you'll forgive my fiancée's highly noticeable anger," Soren said to Caspian, his back straightened as he ran a finger down the length of my collarbone and let his eyes trail over his army general; sweaty and messy-haired, before he snarled, "Neither of us are exactly the...sharing type."

I felt myself instinctively elbow Soren in the ribs, and he coughed back what I could tell was another riposte.

"Goridian is attacking Land," Caspian simply said.

Damn that ethical man; not about to stall by responding to any of our bullshit.

Soren's eyebrows flicked upwards. "He is attacking...now?"

Caspian nodded grimly, taking a seat in a velvet armchair across from Juniper and removing his mesh gloves, warming his hands by the fire. "Indeed. He isn't here yet, but we believe he will be in a few days' time."

I shuddered. Just the though of Goridian...

"Don't worry," I felt Soren whisper against my earlobe. My breath thickened.

"When do we need to be on the battlefield?" Soren asked bluntly, gesturing his head towards the two of us.

I felt my heart swelling when he said us. Not him, not them—us.

"I should have the army collected and armored by the end of the night. I recommend you both rest, if you anticipate joining us tomorrow, outside the palace."

Soren nodded. "Find Lazarus."

I turned to Soren, resting a hand softly on his chest. "I wouldn't pursue Lazarus tonight, if I were you."

He quirked a brow. "Why?"

"I'll tell you later. Caspian, maybe...send him a message?" I suggested, to which Caspian nodded.

Soren added, "Juniper, go with him."

I was relieved when Juniper put up no fight, and slinked off the soft divan, sighing as she smoothed her tight dress and sent Soren a close-mouthed smile, before strutting off with Caspian. The two shut the door behind us, and finally, it was quiet.

Soren turned to me. "What was going on with Lazarus?"

He looked genuinely confused, as if an ill-tempered Lazarus was as shocking to him as it had been to me.

"He seemed angry that...that you are Zeus's more powerful heir, or something," I explained. "He was spitting his words all through dinner. I ended up just having to leave him. He was beyond irritating."

"What did he say?" Soren asked, toying with my fingers.

I sighed. "He provoked me...argued about everything, complained about you having the more power out of the two of you, and tried to convince me that you were in here with Juniper. And he was very clear when he said with her."

He shook his head slowly, saying, "Dammit. He must be in a really bad mood, then, because I've never known Laz to behave in such a way. When he's angry, he usually keeps to himself. I'm sorry he lashed out at you; it's so unlike him."

I shook my head. "Maybe he has a right to be upset."

Soren looked a bit taken aback, his brows raised. "What do you mean?"

"Well, you've always been referred to as Zeus's most powerful heir, the King of Kings, the one to be feared the most. At some point, your brother—or brothers; I'm not sure how many you have—are probably going to be jealous. Even Juniper might be jealous."

He smirked. "Juniper comes from an entirely different family tree than I do. She is not a descendant of either of my parents. Lazarus and I are both spawn of Zeus, but Juniper only shares a mother with Laz. Her father, I believe, was some demigod. I don't really remember the story."

I furrowed my brows. "Are you really that surprised that Laz could be at least a little jealous of you?"

He nodded. "I can believe it—any logical man would believe it. I just don't understand. It's not in Laz's nature to be so purely envious. And he really likes you; considers you a best friend, Ailith. I don't know why he would be so snappy towards you."

"I don't know, either," I muttered. "But we shouldn't dwell on it."

Soren nodded, reaching forward to tug on a loose piece of hair that was sticking to my shoulder, reining it back in. "You're so right," he purred. "Let's focus on something else for a while. Something like...us."

I did not object.

He took my hand and led me over to the sitting area, where he sat in one armchair, and I sat on an ottoman across from him, trying to avert my eyes from looking at the imprint Juniper had made on the velvety fabric of the divan. It was so noticeable, though, in the orange-red firelight.

Soren chuckled, and I immediately realized how my thoughts had trailed.

"I promise," he murmured, choking back bigger laughs. "Juniper and I had—and have—nothing to do with each other."

I blinked, deciding to keep my face serious. "Good. And, I guess I knew that."

He leaned forward in his chair, grabbing the ottoman I was sitting on and pulling it towards him, scooting me closer so that he could peer into my eyes from just inches away. His grey gaze melted into mine.

"Were you really all that worried that I was cheating on you with my half-brother's half-sister?" he smirked.

I shook my head. "Not really."

"Serves you right for spending the majority of your time training with Caspian, and one hundred male soldiers," Soren remarked, a hand venturing across the curve of my shoulder. He pulled me closer, and I studied his face.

"Now who's the jealous one?" I grinned, feeling my gaze daring him.

"Oh, don't worry, my dear," he responded, running a hand along my cheek. "I've always been the jealous one."

"I knew that," I confessed, leaning into the touch. "But now you've had a little taste of you own medicine. You have to admit, it is a bit of a pain to deal with jealousy."

His eyebrows crossed, and a grin grew. "I don't know, sea girl. I kind of liked seeing you growl at Juniper today like you were defending your property."

"She has to be in love with you," I said, rolling my eyes. "To dress like that..."

He shrugged. "Whether she loves me or not is irrelevant. I have no interest in her. You, however...I cannot even begin to describe my level of intrigue in you."

I shivered. "You've made that perfectly clear."

He laughed. "Fair enough. But, there is one thing I'm unclear on."

I raised a brow. "Oh?"

"I'm wondering, sea girl," he said, speaking softly, trying to keep the corners of his lips from curving upwards. "What your level of interest is in me."

I parted my lips, barely breathing the next word. "High."

He leaned forward, about to kiss me, when I stood, letting out a long, deep sigh, and walking over the fireplace, standing in front of it to warm myself; my tired legs.

"Cruel but beautiful," Soren murmured, shaking his head and stretching out on the armchair, studying me with calculating eyes.

I shrugged. "I can't believe this is what everything has come to."

"What do you mean?" He propped his head up behind hands, elbows pointed away from either side of his head.

I shook my head. "I can't believe Goridian is actually trying to fight on Land. And with Hades, and his army..."

My mind seemed to trail off, trying to calculate the amount of men, ammunition—power—we would need.

I didn't notice when Soren was standing right in front of me, a hand ready to graze my cheek, a body ready for me to mold into; to wrap my arms around and warm myself with.

"War is never easy," he told me. "But it is necessary, in this type of situation. When power gets into the wrong hands. It happens more often that you'd think, and isn't easily taken away once misplaced."

I nodded. "I wish Goridian had been stopped before he had the chance to take Triton's power."

"I know you do. And I do, as well," Soren murmured against the top of my head. "Not only for what he does to your people, but mostly for what he did to you. It was a personal offense against you, which now makes it a personal offense against me."

The last few words, he growled.

I looked up at him and took his face in my hands. "Just promise me," I said, feeling a wicked smile tugging at the corners of my lips, and his. "That when you find him, that you'll hold him down for me so that I can pummel him to death."

A dark chuckle rumbled in his diaphragm as he responded, "It would be my absolute pleasure. Really."

I took a deep breath. "I need to find my sister."

"We will," he responded.

I took a long, deep breath, whispering, "How are we going to survive this war?"

He bent forward, tickling my nose with his.

"We will," he said once more.

And then he gathered me in his arms, hesitating for just a moment before he pressed his lips to mine.

AUTHOR'S NOTE:

Well...happy Columbus Day, people! I hope all of you are in a good mood, since we get the day of off school/work. That's always good. Even though Columbus pretty much got credit for discovering America, even when the Vikings discovered it like waaaay before him. (My ancestors were Norwegian emigrants, what can I say...)

I don't know about y'all, but I'm just chilling today, celebrating the mostly pointless holiday by doing the AP US History homework I promised myself I wouldn't procrastinate on.

I hope you guys liked this chapter. It's personally one of my favorites.

If you enjoyed what you read, please don't forget to vote and leave me a comment down below. Thank you so much for reading!

Xoxo,

LK

Chapter 26

B right light tickled my face. However, it wasn't what woke me.

My eyes fluttered open, and I immediately remembered the previous night's encounter; falling asleep talking to Soren in his study, before he awoke and flew me back to my chambers in the middle of the night.

The memory was mirthful, but the sounds that had brought me out of my state of slumber were enough to make me gag. Screams, shrieks and sounds of blades hitting one another were audible from my chambers.

The sun had already risen in the sky, and I realized it was hours past dawn. Evidently, there was war going on outside...how had the palace—my chambers—remained so peaceful for my night sleep?

As I wondered, I eyed a sheet of paper across the room, taped to my door, which had a note lazily scribbled onto it.

Sea girl,

I sealed this room off of the rest of the palace with a spell. It cannot be opened from the outside, because the door is now invisible (and locked, just in case any enemies can see invisible doors). Leave if you'd like, but please bear arms. I write this at dawn, as I am about to join my army in avenging the overthrower of your kingdom. I'll holler if I actually see the bastard. He might be too cowardly to face me...I suppose we'll see.

Stay safe, and I'll see you later, my love—

Soren

I blinked. Read the letter twice.

My love. He'd never written that before. Actually, he'd never actually written me a letter before, but the fact that he'd said that for the first time on paper...made me realize he'd been thinking it. The idea was in his head; the words touched his lips before he wrote it down for me to see.

I smiled.

Dressing in my slacks and tunic, I laced up my leather boots. I'd put on some of the armor Caspian had given me to practice with during training (I couldn't manage to stand up straight with all of it on), and sheathed a lithe sword across my back, keeping it tightly strapped to my being.

And with that, I left.

I could tell the palace was in somewhat of an uproar. It was funny, to me, how Soren had secured my bedroom, but not the entirety of his palace. I snickered internally, thinking how Soren might tell me, "Well, I suppose our enemies might grow a little suspicious if, all of a sudden, my palace disappeared into thin air."

I surveyed my surroundings, noting the fact that the majority of the battle was happening outside in the fields, near the seashore. I could see warriors I'd known from the orphanage fighting out there; warriors I'd seen in the Sea Kingdom all my life. Never had I known that we would end up forced against each other in a war.

I gritted my teeth and took a deep breath. It was time.

~

Stalking out onto the green fields, I stayed hidden in the meadows, moving swiftly and quietly through the tall grasses. I wanted to fight at Soren's side, and Caspian's. I wanted to be at the front line, so that when and if Goridian came to Land, I would be waiting for him.

The corner of my lips seemed to want to tug upwards at the idea of slaying him, even as I breathed slowly, combatting the nerves tumbling around in my stomach.

I scurried past a few more tall clumps of grass, before eyeing the seashore, and feeling my mouth bursting open as I gaped.

Monsters and warriors emerged from the water, clad in blue-green armor made from the scales of fish, bearing weapons made of coral and sheathes made of dolphin skin.

And there, at the very front of it all, was Soren.

He bore no weapons, simply fought with his bare hands, and, to my dismay, wore no armor. He did not even stand on the shore, but hovered rather above it, in the air, with a hawk's view of the action. With the mere thrust of his arm in a given individual's direction, they could be blasted into a million pieces.

I tried not to look, but my eyes felt glued to the sight.

Nearby was Caspian, but Lazarus seemed to be missing. I chewed on my lip, thrusting the concern into the depths of mind as I ventured out to the shore, unsheathing my sword and keeping it pointed in front of me.

My legs shook as they pushed me forward, marching across the sandy ground, before I felt a presence behind me.

From the flicker of blue-green onto the ground, I could tell it was a Sea Kingdom warrior. I spun around, sword flinging with the movement of my wrist, slitting the monster's throat in one smooth sweep before I could even get a good luck at what it was. It was enormous, with a large, serpentine face, a forked tongue and covered in black scales.

As soon as it fell to the ground, three more identical to the first were all facing me.

Monsters of the Sea Kingdom. I couldn't believe Goridian had summoned them. They were highly dangerous.

I did not hesitate as I swung my sword from one direction to the rest, slicing their throats before they had the chance to attack. Blue-black blood sputtered from their bodies, onto my face, as I thrust my sword into the body of the closest one. It was too preoccupied to do anything but clutch its bleeding throat as its eyes misted over. I did not hesitate as I drove the sword right through its scaly flesh.

I did the same with the next two, shoving my sword through their armor; through their leathery skin—right into the dirt and sand below them.

Each monster lay dead before me, and I ventured on, now sprinting towards the shore, wiping dirt and blood from my hands.

I made it with not so much as a wave to or from one of them, before I felt my body being throttled to the ground, my face buried in the shore. Sand coated the inside of my mouth as I rolled over, scampering to my feet, and found a mortal warrior opposing me, gills flapping as he grinned, his bloodthirsty eyes grabbing out before he lunged.

I somersaulted between his legs before he knew what to do, and then stabbed him straight through the back.

Blood pooled from his wound, and from his mouth, as he fell to the ground. I spat the sand out of my mouth, and kicked his body to the side.

I wish I could have shown the warrior, who hailed from my home, more mercy. But I didn't.

I beheaded a few more monsters and warriors before I felt a hand on my armor, plucking me from the action and, in one fluid motion, dragging me into the air, above the battling, with him.

"Ailith," Soren breathed, scouring my body for any injuries, holding me out in front of him midair. "I didn't see you arrive. I'm sorry."

I took deep, panting breaths. "I have to get back down there."

"Don't push yourself too hard," he murmured, securing one arm around my waist and wiping blood from my cheeks with the other. A low chuckle escaped him as he said, "How are you doing, sea warrior?"

I shrugged. "I'm fine. Now, we need to get back. This is not the time for romantics, as much as I appreciate your conern."

"Fine," he said, sighing. "I feel horrible putting you back into the frontline of combat. But...if it's what you want..."

I nodded my head feverishly. "It is. I want to be here when he comes. So that you can hold him down, and I can kill him." Fire laced my breath.

"Very well," Soren said. "When and if you need my help, or need me to take you back, you know where to find me."

I nodded my head. "Noted."

And with that, he accepted my priorities, and placed me right back down into the angry jaws of war, as I had asked.

The hours lagged on as I fought monster after monster; with their dark, scaly skin, claws and snakelike faces. The mortal warriors, who looked almost human as I did, were harder to slaughter. It was more difficult seeing the light leaving their eyes as I drove my blade through them; as I felt their blood, still warm, spraying my face.

Their blood...nearly human, like mine.

But I couldn't leave. I needed to wait for him. And I needed to provide proper contribution, as I had been the one to start this war, technically.

Thoughts were seeming to run through my head like a river as I looked behind me, and noticed the Sea warriors sauntering through the fields. Our warriors were well-trained, but we so outnumbered. With the monsters and mortal warriors, Goridian easily had each of our soldiers outnumbered by at least twenty to one.

I gulped.

Morning turned into afternoon. That was the most difficult part, as the hot autumn sun bore down on us, threatening to burn uncovered pale skin.

My immediate bloodlust and power was drained by afternoon, but I had to continue as I had, no matter how badly I ached; how much my muscles told me to stop. The drive to kill Goridian was the sole thing powering me forward, through every kill...every ruthless slaughter against my own people.

Afternoon soon flickered away, and things were slowing down as the sun began to set. Several of Goridian's warriors were returning to the Sea for the night, from which they would emerge again the next morning. Some were stalking across the Land Kingdom, scouring places to hide and camp out for the night.

Our army members were still fighting well. So far, I could tell we had at least twenty fallen; out of approximately one hundred and fifty. Considering how overpowered we were, I found this to be good for the first day.

As the sun set, I felt silent arms wrapping around my waist. I cried out in exhaustion as I was lifted from my feet, into the open air, and turned around. Pressed against a warm chest. Flown back to the palace, but through a window, rather than through the barricaded entrance.

I didn't look behind Soren's shoulder as he travelled fast as lightning. Through the main corridor, into the one filled with stain glass, then through his study, and through another door—one I had not noticed before—into a quiet, warm room.

"What is this place?" I asked, my face frowning at the sight of only one bed.

"A haven I created for us, when I knew the war had commenced," he responded. "And, before you ask; no, I will not take you to your chambers. You mustn't be alone in the night. And I don't trust anyone with you."

"Fine," I sighed. I knew I needed to pick my battles.

He dropped me off as soon as he landed, and immediately my body crumpled to the floor. I gasped, feeling my knees buckling underneath me.

Soren smirked. "You're completely limp after one day of battle? Pfft, it must not take much to be considered a warrior in the Sea Kingdom."

I shot him a glare. "I slaughtered one hundred and eighty four of our enemies today."

His brows shot up his forehead. "You...you counted?"

Slowly, I nodded, propping myself up on shaking forearms. I muttered, "I always do," and then fell back to the floor, letting my limbs sprawl out against the soft carpeting.

The room we were in consisted of smooth wooden walls, a soft rug lining the hardwood floor, a burning fireplace, and a large, four-poster bed covered in blankets and furs. Another door to my left led into a clean, brightly lit bathroom. There were no windows.

I heard Soren's footsteps leading into the restroom, before a clunking of leather boots hitting the floor, and then the rush of water.

"Water," I breathed. My throat dried. I needed seawater. I would have to go back.

Soren clicked his tongue in a reprimanding manner. "You always seem to forget that you need seawater. How fortunate for you that I have a few bottles in this room, having predicted your chronic forgetfulness. Must be a genetic thing with you sea people."

I didn't even have the energy to respond to his witticisms. I gasped as he opened up a wooden cabinet near the fireplace, taking out a glass bottle, and handed it to me.

Taking the bottle in my shaking hands, I lay on the ground and pressed the tip to my mouth, gulping down its contents faster than I thought I'd ever drank water before in my lifetime. I let out a sigh as I let the bottle clank to the floor, feeling Soren's chuckles vibrating through the room.

"Why this place?" I whispered.

"Because no one will ever find us here," he responded absentmindedly. "I sealed the door off to the rest of the world. You're safe as a kitten, between the spell I put on the door—and me."

"That's nice," I mumbled. "Thank you, Soren." I tugged at the metal helmet constricting my throbbing skull, but it wouldn't budge.

Soren's footsteps approached me.

He leaned over my lame body, and purred, "Having some trouble getting out of your armor, sea girl?"

I nodded. "Urgh."

"Urgh, huh? I will consider that a challenge," he murmured, before he leaned over me and tugged the metal helmet from my head, letting my black curls, damp with sweat, spring free. He then gently removed the sword sheathed around me, and then the metal chest armor. Finally, he unlaced my combat boots, his light touch tickling my feet, before he leaned forward, sliding his hands underneath my limp body, and floated upright in a single sweep, placing me gently onto the bed.

I stared at him, stared at his eyes, at his dark, messy hair, at his ripped clothes; at the pure exhaustion in his grey eyes.

I reached behind his neck and pulled his face to mine, pressing my mouth against his. I closed my eyes and blocked out all of the memories of that day. I was hungry...hungry as I clutched his shoulders; felt his hands venturing down my ribcage, then venturing higher, stopping at a spot where I gasped. He slipped hands behind my back and pulled me up, brushing hair from my shoulders onto my back; warm lips exploring mine.

Pulling away for a moment, I said, "We need a bigger army." I felt a sob now catching in my throat, and wondered why.

He seemed to notice, and laid me back down, crawling onto the bed beside me, where he pressed his head into the curve of my neck and shoulder.

"I know," he murmured, his breath tickling my skin.

Taking a deep breath, I said, "And I need to find that damned Trident."

AUTHOR'S NOTE:

LOLlll you guys thought something scandalous was about to go down for a moment there. Whoops. Must have forgotten to write that part ;)))

What do y'all think is going to happen next?

Let me know.

I'm so glad it's Friday. You guys have no idea.

Since I've kind of begun updating my life in these author's notes, I guess I'll say a few things. First of all, my easier chemistry class kicks ass. I'm loving life in the chemistry world, because it actually feels like being in preschool again, and I am not ashamed of that. Also, I'm really salty because I have to be at my school on Sunday for a series of performances that will last SIX HOURS. Like I DID NOT SIGN UP FOR SUNDAY SCHOOL. This is literally why I am a closeted atheist people (closeted meaning everyone but my old relatives and parents know). Also, I think I'm going to make some cookies tonight. Cause why not?

And I looked at my manuscript, and HOTS has 15 more updates until it's done! (Not including an epilogue, or any other additional chapters I may decide to throw in). Whaaaat. That's insane. Not really. That means approximately two more months of updating.

Wait. That's actually kind of a long time.

Well my sense of time sucks.

If you enjoyed what you read, don't forget to vote and leave me a comment down below telling me your thoughts!

See you guys on Monday!

Xoxo,

LK

Chapter 27

W ARNING TO FAN GIRLS: You are forewarned bout any emotional outbursts and/or hysterical ugly-crying during this chapter.
;)

I was nearly asleep when Soren snapped his fingers and, out of nowhere, two plates of food appeared on the small wooden table that sat in front of the fireplace. He furrowed his brows as I groaned, and brought one over to me.

His murmur was a gentle command. "Eat."

I picked up the fork and began shoveling food into my mouth, too quickly to actually taste it. Within thirty seconds, the food had disappeared, and I placed the clean plate on a nearby bedside table and crawled between the blankets of the bed, my body begging for the peaceful release of slumber. I yawned, letting my eyes go droopy.

"It's been a long day," Soren noted from where he sat at the other side of the bed, taking more time to actually chew and taste his food, as a normal person might.

I nodded. "I'm spent."

"You don't have to fight tomorrow, if you don't want to," he said gently. "No one would judge you. You were so successful today..."

I shook my head. "Don't even try to convince me. I'd love nothing more than to sit around all day, but this war isn't going to end itself."

He nodded. "Then I shall not object. I trust you."

The words sent warm flickers through my chest.

"I wonder where the hell Hades put that Trident," I muttered to myself, shaking my head in frustration.

"How do you know Hades has it?" Soren asked.

I sighed. "Lazarus told me. And then Hades confirmed it, when we first met. He didn't say he wouldn't give it to me, though. He just told me he wouldn't tell me where it is. He said...he said I had to 'find it within myself.' He's so full of shit."

"He was probably just messing with you. To try and get you to trust him," Soren reminded me. "Don't believe a word he says, Ailith. Because all he wants is to get his hands on you. Why do you think he's fighting a war sided with his sworn enemy?"

"Goridian also is his son," I pointed out. "They could have been feigning this rivalry for all these years."

Soren eyed me. "That's possible...but unlikely. I assume they forged this alliance out of necessity, as soon as they realized you would have the protection of my armies in this war. And me and Lazarus fighting on your side, as well."

"Hey—speaking of Lazarus—where is he?" I enquired.

"Last I checked, he locked himself in his chambers," Soren snorted. "I guess he really is in a mood."

"We don't need in him a mood right now. His kingdom is at war. How can't he see that he needs to help us?" I exclaimed.

Soren slowly shook his head. "I have absolutely no idea. But this has always been the problem with Lazarus."

"Laziness?"

"Well, yes. But also his sense of urgency is...what is the word? Delayed," Soren explained. "If one compared our histories, it would be discovered that my brother, quite evidently, does not have my sense of responding to issues in a timely matter."

I nodded. "I understand what you're saying."

"Do you think I'm being too easy on him?" Soren murmured, shaking his head. "We really could use his help. I'm trying to give him space, but this is a dipshit move to be pulling in the middle of war."

I nodded. "Why don't you try talking to him?"

Soren let out a long, deep sigh. "I did. Today. He refused to speak to me; barricaded the door to his chamber."

I felt my eyes widening. "Did you actually hear him speak? I mean, what if Hades got to him?"

Soren laughed. "He called me some vulgar things and then demanded I leave him alone when I went and checked on him this morning. I'm pretty sure he's in there and perfectly safe, Ailith."

I let out a sharp exhale. "We're so outnumbered in this war."

"I know...," he responded, shaking his head. "I know."

"We need to find more warriors," I told Soren. "You need to find more warriors. You should go first thing tomorrow morning. Caspian and I can hold up fort at the frontline until you come back."

Soren's eyes widened. "Ailith, no."

"Why not?" I exclaimed. "The only person who will actually be listened to by potential warriors is you, Soren. Their king. You have to go."

He bent over, taking my hands. "I will not leave you to fight all alone."

I raised a brow. "Oh, really? What was I doing out there today? I didn't realize you were holding my hand while I killed all those people."

Quickly, Soren shook his head. "No, I didn't mean"—

"I know," I mumbled quietly. I didn't have the energy to argue with him, so I simply stopped.

"Good," he responded. "And, you're right. If I only go for a few hours, I can get a good idea of how many mortal warriors I can summon. We're going to need more, especially if Goridian's army keeps growing at the rate it is now."

The two of us laid there, utterly silent for a few moments.

Sighing, I asked, "What happens now? At night?"

He breathed deeply. "We rest. We reflect."

"I can't bring myself to think about what we did today. To all of those people simply fighting for their kingdom," I admitted.

Soren nodded in agreement. "Me neither."

"I feel awful," I whispered.

He peered over at me and, without speaking, pulled himself close to me, so that we both were laying on our sides, facing one another. Almost out of instinct, I reached forward and brushed my fingers against his face.

His eyes closed with the touch.

"I haven't felt something like that in four thousand years," he breathed as my hand trickled up to his hair, smooth as satin, even after a day in battle; in wind. I ran a hand along his scalp, and he let out a low growl that almost sounded like a purr.

"I love you, Soren," I whispered, my breath tickling his face.

All of a sudden, his eyes blinked open. His brows crossed against one another, almost in a frustrated fashion.

I felt my heart dropping into my stomach as he uttered one single word.

"Shit."

I felt my blood run cold. I wanted to apologize for making things awkward, for saying the words in the first place, but felt my tongue struggling to utter a single word.

He rested a hand on my face. "Dammit, Ailith, I was going to say that first."

I took a deep breath. "Not funny. Seriously."

"You really make things so difficult for me, sea girl," he murmured, his smirk returning. "I was about to make a big soliloquy and everything."

My own grin began to grow. "You were, were you?"

He nodded, lifting himself up from the spot next to me and leaning over my body with his, tracing his hands down the sides of my torso; over my legs.

Leaning forward, he pressed his mouth to my neck.

"You...," he breathed into my flesh, growling the words in pretend-anger. "You ruined my plan."

I couldn't help but laugh. "Why don't you just pretend like I didn't beat your ass to the finish line and say what you were going to say?"

He gently pinched my hip as he kissed me, chuckling against my lips. "I would, my dear, but my mouth seems to be quite occupied at the moment," he murmured in between kisses.

When I smacked him on the head, we both laughed.

And then he said, "I love you more than anything, sea girl."

~

The next morning, I awoke at dawn, beside Soren.

The first thing he said as he kissed my temple to awaken me was, "Are you ready for today?"

Yawning, I nodded my head. There weren't any windows in the sealed room, so I couldn't actually tell that it was morning already. I had no idea how Soren had somehow known it.

Four thousand years of experience, I guessed.

"I will venture out East, towards some of the more...agreeable villages," Soren explained. "Since we both know what happens when I go to the mountains." He shot me a wink. "I should be back before midday, either with soldiers or with soldiers on the way. I want them to be protected with armor and weapons before they are summoned to battle."

I gulped. "What do you mean by 'summoned?' You're not going to...to force them, are you?"

He sucked in a sharp breath. "It's complicated. Young men, with no families to take care of—whom are healthy and strong, yet unwilling—I might have to force."

I shook my head. "I'm sorry. For them, but also for you."

"I'm glad you understand," he murmured. "Because war is all about the greater good."

Slowly, I furrowed my brows. "No, it's not."

"Hm?" He looked puzzled.

"It's about the future...about protecting the future. What happens now doesn't matter, as long as we protect whomever comes after us—the future generations—from the evil on the other side," I whispered, wrapping my arms around him as we pulled ourselves out of bed.

My legs were still sore, but perfectly functional, thank the Gods and Goddesses.

He sighed. "You are so, so right."

We left the room quickly. Kept it invisible and locked to the outside. Our own personal haven to return to after our responsibilities were fulfilled for the day. We wrapped our arms around one another in a farewell for the day, both of us made invisible by a spell Soren cast on us. Just for a few moments.

"If only we could just stay, tucked away, in a place sealed off from the rest of the world," I mumbled.

Soren's fingers tickled my shoulder blades in agreement. "I was thinking the same thing."

"Too bad we're the most sought after couple in the galaxy," I muttered, sending him a smirk. "Everyone wants to separate us, kill us...et cetera."

"Exactly," he said, tugging at his leather jacket. "I'm going to have to leave before my judgement goes to hell and I pull you far away from here, somewhere secluded where we can spend the days away in bed; somewhere where I can have you all to myself, sea girl." He sent me a twisted grin.

I glared. "Do you have to make absolutely everything dirty?"

He blinked. "Of course I do."

And with that, he kissed me, murmured, "I love you", and was gone.

I turned, facing the battlefield. I was ready. After having spent the previous night in such comfort and warmth, my energy was regenerated...refocused.

Which was a damn good thing—because as I turned towards the seashore, where the battle was beginning to heat up between the opposing sides, I noticed something enormous emerging from the water...something near God-like. It made my palms sweat, my head spin, and my stomach turn.

Because, emerging from the water on a throne of water, surrounded by fellow sea warriors, was Lord Goridian.

AUTHOR'S NOTE:

Hey people! Happy Monday!

So...that was another chapter just dripping with scandal, am I right?

Can we make #Sailith a thing por favor???

Small life update/story time: experienced some serious bus drama today. A woman began to give birth on the bus on my way home from school. It was crazy. And do you know what the bus driver said?? The pregnant lady was all like, "OH MY GOODNESS MY WATER JUST BROKE" and the bus driver said, "Oh, hell no. Not THIS again."

Like...__(00)__/

What??!

Needless to say, I'm safely at my home now and GLAD.

If you enjoyed this chapter, please don't forget to vote and leave me a comment down below telling me your thoughts!

Xoxo,

LK

Chapter 28

Wind swept the loose hairs that frayed from the edges of my metal helmet and grazed my cheeks as I stepped forward, away from the palace and into the open jaws of battle.

The sun was just beginning to rise over the choppy blue tourmaline sea that day; a little orb of light against the horizon as my shaking legs kept me walking forward, sword held out in front of me by nervous arms. Now that he was here, and now that Soren was gone, I knew this wasn't going to turn out well unless I had the courage to take Goridian on myself, or flee.

And the latter simply wasn't an option.

He rose from the depths of the sea, seated on a throne of swirling waves. My jaw gasped at the sheer monstrosity of it; the slight grin printed on his evil face; his frigid gaze drawing me in from across the battle field.

He was gliding towards the sandy shore, golden blade in hand; an iron crown sitting atop his head. Goridian was surrounded by hundreds of the scaled monsters I'd fought off the previous day. I gulped. If Soren didn't return with hundreds of skilled warriors soon, then our army would be doomed.

We only had about eighty left of the original army I'd trained with Caspian. It appeared as if Caspian had shared my fears of being overpowered and managed to find a few more warriors overnight, but the increase wasn't nearly enough to make a big impact on who won—and who lost.

I couldn't even fathom the idea of losing this war.

Trident...I needed to find the trident.

My mind's focus was swaying relentlessly as I fought my way to the front-line, ready to take on the man who had terrorized me since I was a child. The man who had murdered my parents and friends, taken over my kingdom and assaulted me.

I was ready to avenge my entire existence by killing him.

Blood sprayed onto my face as I whipped my blade around in different directions, my hazy sight overwhelmed by the groups of serpentine monsters and gilled warriors surrounding me. I was making my way straight through the battlefield, but was forced to fight my way there. I spotted some of the warriors I'd trained with as a child around me, fighting as hard as I; blood sprayed on their pale flesh as well.

I moved swiftly, keeping my gaze everywhere. I remembered to survey my surroundings before I continued moving, and to always keep my senses alerted to anyone who might think to attack me from behind.

Such senses were particularly helpful when I felt a blade being unsheathed over my shoulder. In the split second I had, I spun around and blocked the opponent's swing with my own blade. I let the tension between our two blades slip, and rammed my sword into the warrior's stomach, swiftly pulling out.

She fell to the group, choking on the blood pooling out of her mouth and gasping at the wound that cut straight through her abdomen. Her eyes glossed over as soon as she hit the grass.

I turned away, and didn't look back.

Soon, I made it to the shore. In fact, I arrived perfectly on time.

To my ultimate dismay, Gordian effortlessly slipped from his water throne as easily as he had overthrown my kingdom. He wasn't supposed to be able to leave the water...to come onto Land. But alas, here he was.

My stomach twisted.

I gritted my teeth as he approached. I was the first thing he saw as he walked on sand...on Land, for the first time. A wicked grin spread across his face, flashing his white teeth. I spread my feet apart, ready to lunge at any moment, when I felt an enormous figure hauling itself in front of me.

Caspian, covered in blood that was both his own and that of others, stood between me and Goridian, his own blade held out in front of him; arm muscles flexed.

I could see the veins sticking out of his skull as he snarled at Goridian. A warning.

Goridian simply laughed, sauntering over to where we were standing, and spread out his arms in a peaceful gesture.

"My dear Ailith," he beamed, his eyebrows barely even crossing. He actually looked happy to see me.

With the flick of his hands, Caspian was thrown out of the way by some unknown force of power, and Goridian stepped right in front of me.

"What do you want, Goridian?" I seethed.

He looked a bit taken aback. "You need me to tell you what I want?"

I looked to my right, then to my left. The soldiers around me were all occupied fighting the monsters and warriors continuously emerging from the water, just as Goridian had. They barely even saw the exchange happening up at the very front; on the seashore.

Caspian coughed, trying to scamper to his feet, but another flick of Goridian's wrist kept him pinned to the ground, gasping for air.

"Let him be," I snarled.

Goridian feigned a pout. "Oh, do you care for him?"

"He's my friend," I responded.

Goridian ignored my comment, and simply reached forward, taking my head in his hands. In one swift motion, he pulled the metal helmet from my hair, allowing the black waves to spring loose. He seemed liberated by the action, taking in a deep breath.

"You look radiant," he growled, reaching out to take my hand.

No.

"Not this time, you bastard," I growled, before I swung forth my sword, stabbing him straight through the stomach.

The injury wouldn't be fatal to someone who was as powerful as Goridian (which was highly unfortunate, as I was so swift and skilled with my blade), but it did temporarily disable him, at least for a few minutes—giving me the chance to run.

I took my sword, which was covered in fresh blood, and dashed back into the battlefield.

Soren wouldn't be back with his troops of warriors for some time. I knew he was the only one who could help me defeat Lord Goridian, so I needed to stay on Land until he arrived; I needed to stall. If Goridian took me back to the Sea Kingdom with him, then all bets were off. However, if I managed to stay in the Land Kingdom, I perhaps had a chance...

"Run, Ailith. Go ahead and run. See what happens when I catch you." Goridian barked after me, choking through the pain of his wound.

So I did. I ran.

I ran through the battlefield, my exhausted legs discovering a second wind; a new bounce of energy as adrenaline shot through my veins. My heart seemed to ricochet of the sides of my ribcage as I sprinted for my life.

No one dared impale me as I struck with my sword; the one that had injured the Lord all my enemies and opponents were fighting for. I was running so fast that anyone in my way would most definitely be fatally ended by my sword.

When I reached the palace, I knew I couldn't go inside. It was barricaded, but if I could just somehow find my way into my chambers or the room I'd been in with Soren the previous night; somewhere safe where only he could find me...

I looked around, but found nowhere else to run.

"I've found you, Ailith."

Goridian's voice sent chills down my spine. He was so close...damn those Gods and their faster-than-sound speed.

I felt tears forming in my eyes. I had nowhere to run. The meadows were unprotected and my scent could easily be tracked there, the battlefield was blocked by Goridian... and the palace was blocked to all outsiders.

A whimper formed in my throat, but I guzzled it down.

Goridian's arms wrapped around my shoulders. I felt a sob escaping my mouth.

"Hmmm," he rumbled. "How good it is to feel you in my arms. How good it is to hear your quiet cries."

I quivered as he bent down and sniffed my hair.

I wanted so badly to fight, but my muscles seemed to turn to jelly at Goridian's presence. I was able to fight off Hades; I had been able to combat Caspian and many of the other soldiers in training. But this...this was different.

My mind tried to block the memories. I could feel something bubbling in my stomach; in my chest as I remembered.

Gordian ran his cold, white fingers along my arms, then hooked them onto my waist as he bent forward, pressing his cold lips to my neck.

He let out a deep, guttural growl.

"Leave me alone," I begged.

He chuckled. "Oh, I don't think so." More cold, moist lips. The visions swirled around in my mind.

My stomach tightened.

"Please," I pleaded.

"Oh, I promise you'll be begging a lot more than that later on," he responded. His latch on me tightened, and I felt whatever was festering within me begin to grow.

My gumption seemed to seep back in. "I swear to the Gods and Goddesses, Goridian, I will destroy you."

He barked in laughter. "You're really cute today, Ailith...absolutely hysterical. Now come home with me, my bride. We've wasted too much time here on Land."

His hands slid down my arms, and for a moment, my vision went stark white. A flash of a memory invaded my eyes, and all I could feel for a moment was the pain from when he'd bitten my arm; left that marker upon my skin.

"No," I seethed.

And then it happened.

I let out a deafening shriek. A pulse of golden power erupted from within me, sending Goridian sprawling back, limbs shattering against the ground. He roared in protest as I approached him. Somehow, my muscles had begun working again. However, this time, I felt the energy; the power.. .simply hovering above my flesh.

I felt another wave of rage driving its way through my mind as another memory snuck its way past the gate between my subconscious and conscious.

I snarled, and let the golden power leak out from me; swirling around me like a tornado before I thrusted it forward, in Goridian's direction.

He was sent flying back, all the way into the battlefield. I could see familiar faces—soldiers I'd trained—taking the opportunity to attack him. I took a deep breath, realizing that I had some time now.

And so, again, I ran.

My mind began to race through the different possibilities. How in the world of Mother Gaea had that just happened happened?

I knew I had control over water and ice, but now this? I didn't even know what this was...it just seemed to be some nonspecific form of power, from what I could tell. I felt tears of both relief and terror blinding me as I ran past the palace.

East, Soren had said said.

He was going East, and so I would go East, too.

~

I ventured through the Eastern villages for several hours. They all seemed to be in some order of disarray, but I didn't find a trace of Soren anywhere there. Nothing particularly abnormal-looking that would have suggested a visit from the king.

At some point, I simply began to walk. And think.

Where had this power come from? I was racking my brain, trying to find some memory that would provide a clue, or some inkling of an explanation. I'd never felt such rage and terror before in my life. I'd never felt my muscles turn to jelly as I had there; never felt power building up so internally.

And then the release when I unleashed that power...

It had been mind-boggling. As if every single concern and angry thought I'd ever had was somehow being let go of.

All of a sudden, a familiar sound—now one that I considered lucky—sounded in the sky. Thunder.

I looked upwards, and grinned, waving my hand. "I'm here, Soren," I called with all my might, with every ounce of breath I had in me.

Not a moment later, he was standing in front of me. He appeared untouched; thank the Gods and Goddesses.

"Are you okay?" he enquired.

I nodded. "Just fine. You?"

"I'm fine, but...but—Ailith you're...," he murmured, the concern within him seeming to loosen a bit as he gasped, "you're glowing."

I felt my brows flicking upwards. "I am?"

I held up an arm, and realized that my slightly-tanned skin was emitting a golden glow, similar to the power it had recently expelled.

I gasped.

There was only one thing I'd ever beheld in my past that had glowed with power like that.

"Hades was right," I exclaimed.

Soren looked confused. "About what, my dear?"

He began scouring my being for any sign of injury, wiping the blood from my cheeks and checking my hands and arms for little cuts. Normally I would have noticed the careful touches, but as I went over everything in my head, I was finally able to piece together what I hadn't before.

"When he said to find the Trident within me."

"What do you mean?" Soren asked absentmindedly. His fingers traced lines across my shoulders.

I took his face in my hands to focus him, and peered into his eyes as I told him in a hoarse whisper, "I am the Trident."

AUTHOR'S NOTE:

Whaaaaaat? Do y'all believe this? I don't. Really. I forgot about this plot twist and just re-shocked myself.

Just kidding.

Anyway, I hope you guys have had an awesome week. It's Friday, which is a good thing. I love me a Friday. Just a little warning: next chapter is another personal favorite of mine. ALL THE FEELS. Be ready on Monday!!!

Small life update: casually sort of wrote a second book. Not sure what I'm gonna do with it. It just happened. Also: did no one read my bus story from last week? I'm surprised not many people saw that; it was CRAZY. If you haven't read it, go see my author's note from last week. Going to go to sleep at 8:30 tonight because I had to perform in TWO concerts this week (meaning being at school for an extra 6+ hours each time. No joke. It sucked). That's about it for this week.

As always, don't forget to vote and leave me a comment down below if you enjoyed what you read!

TGIF, my lovelies!

Xoxo,

LK

Chapter 29

WARNING: FAN GIRLS. JUST...YOU KNOW WHAT TO DO. YOU HAVE BEEN WARNED.

I explained what happened with Goridian. I explained how he'd brought up memories of my time in captivity. How the power had somehow grown within me, and hadn't stopped until I unleashed it upon him.

"Hades was trying to tell you that you are the trident all along," Soren grumbled. "That's so like him. To know such a critical piece of information, and dangle it in front of us. I should have been more alert to what he was saying to you." Soren's muscles went taut as we both processed the idea...I was the embodiment of the trident.

How—I had no idea. I assumed it had been molded into my soul at some point when I was too young to remember, but I did not know when or by whom.

I truly was the perfect hiding place, as well. I wondered, thinking back to all the time Triton spent with me, if he'd known.

I laid a hand on Soren's arm, trying to calm him down. "It's okay that you didn't recognize that he meant it on a literal level. I didn't either," I said to him. "And I'm glad I found out when I did. It was so meaningful; the ability to overpower the man who tyrannized me for so long."

He shook his head, taking me in his arms, holding me close to his warm body. "I continuously feel like I'm failing you, Ailith. Every time I try to help you, I feel as if it backfires. I don't want to hurt you anymore, as long as I live."

I reached up and slowly ran my hand through his soft, soft hair.

"You have to stop blaming yourself," I told him. "This is war. Things will go wrong, things will be discovered, and we'll have regrets...lots and lots of regrets. But we can share the burden together."

The corners of his mouth tugged upwards. "Marry me."

I blinked for a few moments as he bent forward to kiss me, saying it again, the words brushing my lips. "Marry me, Ailith."

I felt a small laugh escaping my mouth. "I thought I already agreed"—

"You agreed before...," he said, securing his arm around my waist. "You agreed before you ever actually loved me. You agreed because you thought you had to, for the prophecy. But now I'm asking, as a man who loves a woman, if she loves him back, and if she will agree to be his."

Slowly, I nodded my head. "Of course I will marry you."

I could see sparks in his eye as he brushed his lips against mine, speaking the words into my mouth. "Let's go now."

I felt my eyebrows raising. "To—to get married?"

He nodded. "Let's forget this damned war for a few minutes. One hour of our absence will distract Goridian; keep him from controlling his army so closely. Plus, I want to marry you before I have the chance to create another regret," he explained.

I smiled. "One hour?"

He nodded. "You don't even have to put on high-heeled shoes."

I eyed him. "Or a dress?"

"Or a dress." His smirk was more of a playful expression than a means by which to tease me.

I shrugged my shoulders, letting out a pleasant little sigh. "Well then I suppose there's no reason I cannot marry you right now. But, Soren, you do remember your statement about your judgement going to hell a few hours ago?"

He grinned. "It's getting there. But, I promise. We'll only be gone long enough to become husband and wife. Not a minute more."

~

There was a small stone church on a cliff above the sea, right off the main road of the little village we were in.

Soren flew us there in a matter of moments. The sound of the sea nearby and the breeze in our ears was the most clarifying noise I'd heard before in my life. After days surrounded by the sounds of war—of suffering; of death—hearing the elements in their barest forms was nothing short of mesmerizing.

It seemed to affect both of us. Soren stood in front of the church for a few moments, peering into the distance for a long while before he turned to me and smiled. His grin was much less cheeky than usual. It was regal; it was...loving.

He was telling me he loved me in that moment, and he didn't even have to say it.

"Let's get hitched," he murmured, tickling the top of my head with his mouth in a light whisper of a kiss.

I looped an arm around his, and we hauled open the doors of the tiny church, and stepped inside.

"This is how Land people get married," Soren whispered.

The church was dark, and smelled of must—but danced with the light of a hundred different colors; the walls all covered in enormous, elaborately detailed stain glass windows, similar to the ones in the corridor in the palace that led to Soren's study. I looked around, and found that there were no people inside. It was silent, other than the sound of the breeze slowly creaking the wooden doors back and forth.

"It's not the wedding I wanted to give you...," Soren muttered.

I laughed. "Do you really see me as the type to have a big wedding?"

His eyes widened. "Ailith, I'm a king. And I love a good party." He shot me a wink. "We are going to have a big wedding no matter what. In fact, I will probably still make you attend a big ceremony after the war."

Rolling my eyes, I responded, "I can't catch a break with you."

"No," he responded, pulling my body to his. "You can't."

He was just about to kiss me when I spotted a presence at the other end of the chapel. Standing as quiet as a mouse, dressed in long, worn blue robes tied with silver string, a man in his late sixties strolled towards us, a genuine grin beginning to tug at his mouth. His teeth were yellow and crooked, and his eyes surrounded by little spidery wrinkles.

"My king," the man said, before he kneeled in front of us.

Soren clutched my hand in his. "Father," he murmured, bowing his head respectively.

"I am the village marriage officiator. What are you doing here, my Lord?" asked the man.

Soren nodded his head towards me, a slight smile parting his lips before he purred, "I want to make this breathtaking creature my wife."

The man then bowed towards me, whispering, "Greetings, my Queen."

I laughed nervously. "Oh, you don't have to do that. I'm just"—

"The Heiress of the Sea," gasped the officiator, spreading his arms across the floor, his head facing downward in a most dramatic bow. "My Queen; my future ruler. Wife of Zeus's most powerful heir, King Soren."

I felt myself blushing. "Well if you say it like that..."

"Yes, you do sound rather important, don't you?" Soren said, turning towards me and furrowing a brow. His tone was drenched in sarcasm. "Hmph. Well, let's get this marriage officiated, shall we?"

The man's eyes grew wider. "You want...you want me to officiate?"

"Yes," Soren responded.

The officiator's eyes gleamed with pride. "Why, of course, my Lord. Allow me a few moments to head into them back room of the chapel and find my book."

"Of course," Soren responded.

With that, the old man dashed off, and we were left there, holding back laughs.

We could hear the man scrambling around in the back of the chapel, before he emerged with an old, tattered tome bound in black leather.

He opened the pages, quickly flapping through to find the right sections. Thick, yellowing paper filled the book, covered in fancily-written text.

"Well, let's not waste any time, then," the officiator told us, beckoning for us to follow him. Three thick steps led onto a platform at the front of the chapel, where a built-in wooden altar was already waiting. It was somewhat dilapidated, but served its purpose perfectly fine.

"Well...l-let's see," the officiator stuttered nervously, flipping through the book to the right pages. He lifted a pair of spectacles to his eyes, letting them sit at the tip of his nose as he read aloud. "My Lord, King Soren, do you agree to the terms of being a husband; of caring for your wife as long as she shall live, of loving her unconditionally, of forgiving her mistakes, accepting her flaws?"

Soren smiled. "I already have."

"Do you vow to take care of her as long as you shall live?"

Soren paused, his fingers gently running up and down mine before he said, "Of course I do." His eyes bored straight into mine, and I felt my knees go a bit wobbly.

"Very good," the officiator commented, before turning to me. "Ms. Ailith, do you agree to the terms of being a wife, and a Queen? Of caring for your husband as long as he shall live, of loving him unconditionally, of forgiving his mistakes, and accepting his flaws?"

I felt a grin spread across my face as I repeated Soren's answer. "I already have."

Soren bowed and shook his head, trying to keep his grin from growing.

The officiator cleared his throat. "Do you vow to take care of him for as long as you shall live?"

In that moment, I saw Soren. I really saw him. Different colored lights shone through the church window, highlighting the softness and contrast of his dark hair; his slightly tan skin illuminated by the color. His grey eyes pulled at mine; his beautifully symmetrical face was carved out against the hues of rainbow behind him. I saw him, in all of his glory, and felt myself choking down tears. Dammit, I thought. This is so cheesy.

Even then, I let the tears roll down my cheeks as I whispered one word.

"Yes."

The officiator closed the book with a loud clap. "Are there any words either of you would like to add, before I pronounce you husband and wife?"

Slowly, I shook my head, but Soren proceeded to whisper something to the officiator. I was a bit surprised that he had something to add; knowing this elopement had been completely impromptu.

However, Soren wasn't shy to wipe away my tears, take my hands, and begin speaking to me like he'd had everything planned out.

"Ailith," he murmured. "Before I marry you, I want to tell you something. I want you to know that...for the longest time, I've been searching for something—for anything—to live for, for the past four thousand years. I was nearly hopeless for a while, but over the past months, my answer seems to have made itself evident. And that answer, undeniably, is you. You have become my sole purpose for existing; my one reason for living, and for being noble and good. You are my love...your very flesh and blood defines me. I'd give anything for you, and I'll love you until I die. Whenever that is." He looked up, and grinned at me.

I wasn't sure I was breathing.

"I don't know what to say," I whispered.

"Don't say anything," he murmured, before he leaned forward and pressed his lips to mine.

The officiator chuckled under his breath. "By the power invested in me by"—

Suddenly, there was a deafening crack at the front of the chapel. We all looked to the doors, and found they were blasted open.

And, standing in the doorway, was a familiar face that made my blood run cold.

"Hmm...it appears that someone is trying to steal my bride. This will not do."

AUTHOR'S NOTE:

As I reread this chapter, I screaming "WEDDING CRASHER" really loudly and all of the people in my house came downstairs and glared at me for a solid two minutes. So yeah...that just happened. NO SHAME.

What do y'all think is gonna go down now that Soren and Goridian are in the same room? What is Ailith going to do about this? I'll give you a hint: they ain't gon be having a tea party.

I hope you all have a great week! Be sure to vote and leave me a comment down below if you enjoyed the chapter.

EW I JUST REALIZED IT'S MONDAY. WHYYYYYY?!

See you in four days :)

Xoxo,

LK

Chapter 30

S oren's breath thickened as he took two gliding steps: one step forward, and another to center himself right in front of me.

"What," he growled, "are you doing here, Goridian?"

As if he didn't already know.

Goridian prowled forward. With one sweep of his hands, the musty old pews lining either side of the chapel were blasted into a million pieces. I felt my heartbeat quickening. My knees began to wobble. Every single piece of my being was telling me to turn and run.

My feet began to pivot—more out of instinct than judgement—when I felt Soren's hand gripping me by the wrist, keeping me pinned there. I stared at him with wide eyes, but only found one thing in his gaze.

Boredom.

It was a mask, to cover up the rage I knew was boiling underneath his skin. The rage for what Goridian had done, and was now doing.

"I hope this won't take too much effort on my part," Goridian grumbled, sighing. He stepped towards us, but Soren held up a hand.

"One step closer, and I'll rip your head off," he told him.

Goridian crossed his arms in front of his chest, curving a brow. "And why should I be afraid of you?"

Soren sighed, and snapped his fingers. In just that tiny motion, Goridian was sent flying across the chapel, his body slamming against the wall before he hit the ground with a loud thump. I watched my almost-husband; gaping.

Soren turned to me and whispered, "It's alright. I will protect you." His words were nothing short of a promise.

Goridian stood, his feet heavy against the floor as he stalked up to us once more. His icy blue eyes burned with fury as he reached for me.

"I want my bride back," Goridian growled.

"Ah...not so fast," Soren murmured. He squeezed my wrist, and turned to Goridian. "What are you willing to give for her?"

I felt my knees going weak.

"So you're telling me you're willing to make a bargain?" Goridian's eyes suddenly danced with ideas.

I felt a whimper escaping my lips.

I clamped my free hand over my mouth.

"What are you willing to give to get her back?" Soren restated, his tone growing with anger and impatience.

I took a deep, shaky breath. I felt as if my heart was being ripped away from my being. I couldn't speak...I couldn't even think.

"I'll give you the seashore territory. Everything between my kingdom and your land, you can have," Goridian offered. "It could be a completely protected, safe space for you to dock ships carrying cargo and goods. It would be highly beneficial to your majesty, if I do say so myself. From a ruler, to a ruler."

Goridian's eyes flickered over to me. I felt the golden burn beginning to grow in my chest once more. Soren's grasp tightened.

He sighed again. "Hmm...an intriguing offer. But you're going to have to do better than that. I don't need more space to dock ships. And, frankly, I wouldn't ever trust your advice as a ruler."

Goridian furrowed his brows. "I could offer you...gold. Yes, gold! More gold than you could imagine. Silver, too. And coral, from the Sea Kingdom. All perfectly valuable. You could buy another palace, or more servants. Anything you desire."

Soren shook his head, clicking his tongue. "Oh, I have plenty of gold, and no need for yours. Try again."

Goridian seemed to be growing impatient, too. "How about slaves? I can strip all of the strong youths from my kingdom and hand them over to you. Use them as you may; I don't care. I just want Ailith."

Slowly, Soren shook his head once again. "I don't need slaves, either. Although, your offers are finally becoming interesting, if barely considerable. You've finally come up with an offer that has to do with one thing I am interested in...life. Human life."

Goridian eyed Soren. "Life?"

"Yes," Soren responded, his eyes trailing over Goridian a few times before he spoke once more. "I want to hear another offer. Bigger...bigger sacrifice.

Of life. On your part. Think, and then try once more. Maybe you'll finally get it."

Goridian shook his head. "You want me to kill someone for you?"

"If you could inflict death upon a certain individual...yes, that's what I had in mind," Soren responded.

He the proceeded to wrap an arm around my waist and pull my body to his. His warmth seemed to shield me.

"Who, Son of Zeus?" Goridian enquired. "Whom must I kill to get my bride back from you?"

Soren took a long, deep breath. "This isn't going to be easy for you, Goridian. You're not going to enjoy the idea of this person dying. In fact, you're going to be pretty Gods and Goddess-damned pissed about it."

Goridian rolled his eyes. "Just say the name of the person you want dead, and I'll be happy to comply. Believe me."

He spoke through gritted teeth.

A purely wicked smile, laced with wrath, overtook Soren's face as he spoke one final word.

"You."

With that, he thrust himself forward, and grabbed Goridian by the arms. He pinned his arms being his back, and then jerked him so hard, I heard a sickening crack of bone.

Goridian hollered in pain, swearing under his breath.

I'd known Soren was powerful...but not so powerful that he could so easily overpower someone like Lord Goridian.

He then left him on the floor, pinned there by some form of invisible magic.

"Let's see," Soren growled. "This is going to be fun. Ailith, you may stay or leave, my dear, depending on how eager you are to see this wretched excuse for a being with a soul suffer...considerably."

"Please," Goridian pleaded. I was shocked to see, for once, real fear in his eyes. Terror, even.

He didn't know what Soren was really capable of...and to be fair, I didn't either.

"There are many things I wish to thank you for, Lord Goridian," Soren told the man pinned to the floor, his tone both casual and even a bit cordial, as if he was addressing an acquaintance in a purely respectable manner. "The first thing...I would like to thank you for tricking and overpowering the most honorable and peaceful leader the Sea Kingdom has ever seen; King Triton. It was possibly the most foolish thing a young, traitorous demigod could do."

With that, Goridian cried out pain. A large snap in one of his left legs, and I felt bile burning the back of my throat.

I coughed it down, and watched as the golden glow within my flesh began to simmer.

"The second thing," Soren said to him. "Is...I would like to thank you for killing the mothers and fathers of the children who serve you; who now fight on my battlefield. Most of them are giving up their lives for you unwillingly, and have grown up orphans. Ailith was one such child. So, I thank you for killing a numerous amount of beloved parents...mothers, fathers, aunts, uncles. You get the picture."

With that, I could hear cartilage and muscle being ripped within Goridian. His eyes were blank with horror; his face unable to do anything but shriek as he endured what I could see was immeasurable pain. I wanted to cover my eyes, but somehow, I couldn't.

"Right. We can continue," Soren murmured. "The third thing I'd like to thank you for is for orphaning and brainwashing many children into becoming your loyal warriors. Those are children now fighting out there as we speak; children who cannot do anything but give their lives for you because they have no other choice. And even if they do, they don't know that. They are dying—willingly—for your cause, which is, by the way, to retrieve a girl. And that brings me to my last point."

"Please," Goridian breathed. His voice was sickeningly hoarse. "Please—stop. Just...kill me."

"Hm...a compelling idea. But no," Soren responded, clasping his hands behind his back as Goridian writhed on the floor beneath him. "Because I have one more thing to thank you for, Lord Goridian. And that is how you took my dear Ailith under your wing. Trained her, taught her...served as a makeshift family member after you removed her actual parents from her life. And then you left her. You abandoned her; threw her to the wolves—and then took her away, once again, from the one person who actually made a difference in her adolescence."

"If you're talking about Triton," gasped Goridian. "He can go...to h-hell."

Soren shot him a glare, which somehow turned out to be a bought of power. A simple snap, and Goridian's lips were closed shut by some invisible glue. Not glue, I had to remind myself, but magic.

"And, after you ripped her away from the one person who had a good influence on her," Soren snarled, "you forced her to work. You starved her; took control of her entire life. You took advantage of your power, and you hurt her. Trust me, I know how you hurt her. You ruined her; you bit her...you committed a very personal offense. And, in the moment, you probably felt good about it. I can just imagine how proud you felt as you hurt this young girl, and took the control you never had when you lived with your wretched father."

Soren took a few deep breaths. At this point, my stare had become blank. Unfeeling.

"You hurt a person I now love more than anything else," Soren growled. "I could have possibly forgotten—not forgiven, but at least forgotten—your other crimes. Mass genocide, overthrowing a good king in a peaceful kingdom. Many before you have committed similar offenses. However, you hurt Ailith. You've caused her nightmares, fear...terror. And that...I will surely never forget."

I felt like I was watching myself watch this exchange. I felt as if I wasn't inside my own body, but rather outside of it.

Nothing but a specter.

Soren turned to me. "I made you a promise," he whispered, gesturing to Goridian's quivering body—whose eyes were rolling into the back of his head.

I knew he meant what I'd said earlier—about how I wanted him to hold Goridian down and let me kill him myself.

However, now I didn't feel the anger I'd felt at first. I somehow felt numb to it all...just numb.

"I don't want to do it anymore," I responded weakly. "You do it."

He nodded grimly, and I turned my face.

There was a quick, easy snap—and that was it.

So quickly afterwards, Soren had his arms wrapped around me. His hands hooked around my back, and he rested his face on my shoulder, his breath tickling my gills.

"I didn't have a choice," he muttered, shaking his head against the crook of my neck. "I'm sorry if I made you uncomfortable."

"It needed to be done," I murmured in response. "I wanted it to be done. I'm sorry...I don't know what came over me. For so long, I've been wanting to kill him myself. And, when the opportunity actually arose, I thought it was going to be easy. But, I just...froze. It was so surreal, that moment. I felt like I was finally free, yet I didn't want to be the one to unlock my own cage."

"That's perfectly fine." He kissed my neck, right below my gills. I let out a long exhale, and begin crying.

He shushed me gently, breathing into my hair.

"It's all over now," he kept murmuring, "I love you."

We stood there for a few moments in silence. The wedding officiator had fled as soon as Lord Goridian had exploded his pews, meaning we were in there alone. And so we stayed for several minutes in each other's warm embrace. I let my hands wander to his hair; tracing lines over and over.

All of a sudden, we both turned as we heard the wooden doors being opened at the other side of the chapel.

"What the hell is going on here?"

Soren wrapped his hand around mine, keeping me close.

"What are you doing here?" Soren asked the man who now stood at the either side of the chapel.

"Well, I thought I'd come to find you. It's been three days."

I gasped. It had been so long since the last time I'd seen him. For the millionth time that day, I was purely shocked.

Because standing at the other end of the church was Lazarus.